The Adventures of Brotherhood

James Ray II

two75game
publishing

Copyright 2021. James Ray II

TXu002264204 / 2021-06-08

ISBN: 978-0-578-95272-7

Editor: Stephanie Pragel

Lettering artist: Kristen De Palma @kdpletters on Instagram

Cover art: Jerry Padilla @jerry.ilustrador on Instagram

Cover design and interior formatting: M Borgnaes of The Electric Scroll services.electric-scroll.com

Published world-wide by two75game publishing, all rights reserved.

Thanks

I'm grateful to God and my family.

Chapter One

It was the summer of 1985 when everything seemed mysterious, and the world was innocent through the eyes of a child. Johnny was only eight years old that year and little did he know that a birthday party would change the rest of his life, not only his life but the life of his elder brother as well.

It was a hot summer's day on a small little retreat outside of Savannah, where you can go back in time to when the first settlers came to Georgia. Johnny's parents rented a day down at the Ebenezer Retreat to celebrate his older brother, Tomas' birthday. The place had a courtyard to play tennis beside a graveyard that was overlooked by old oak trees with hanging moss. Across the street was a brick house that had stood for a few hundred years.

It sat off on a hill side that ran down into the Savannah River. There were rumors that even George Washington stayed there in the early days of Georgia. Big ships used to travel up and down that river mainly to carry loads of cotton and silk made by the Salzbergers.

Ebenezer was rich in history, rich in memories that built that small town of Rincon, and for those who lived in that town, held close some sense of pride, proud to be part of the richness of history.

It was not only the history that made them proud Georgians, but the kindness they shared for one another. Kindness was the fabric that built their little town, along with hopes and dreams and the unwavering belief to love their neighbor as themselves.

Now that little house that stood over across the street was built a few hundred years ago, but for some reason it always caught Johnny's eye every summer he visited Ebenezer and he couldn't help himself but to always wander off to admire it.

"You should be where your parents can keep an eye on you!" Grandpa Harold said.

"Grandpa!" Johnny said as he took off running to his grandfather's open embrace.

"What are you doing out here? You're going to worry your parents to death!"

"Grandpa, what was it like growing up in the old days?" Johnny asked as he took his grandfather's hand as they begin to walk back across the street.

"Not like you have today little one. In our time things were bad."

"How bad Grandpa?" Johnny asked as he looked up to his grandfather's towering figure.

"Let's just say life is better now than it was in my day. Let's hurry. We're going to be late!"

"Oh, you found him. I was starting to worry where he was," Johnny's mother, Carolyn said.

"He was looking at that old brick house over across the street again," Grandpa Harold replied.

"Thanks for bringing him back. Could I interest you is some sweet tea?"

"Will there be ice involved?"

"Of course, on a hot summer day like today, ice will always be involved."

"That's the best thing about being southern, a glass of sweet tea with some ice and maybe a good ole shade tree and a nice book to take you on some adventure," Grandpa Harold replied.

Harold pointed over to an old oak tree a little distance from the party and said, "That's where I'll be if you come looking for me. I'll be waiting on that ice tea."

"I will have Johnny send it right over once I get it poured," Carolyn replied.

"Thank you, very kindly," Grandpa Harold said with a tip of his hat.

"Kids, come gather around. It's time to open the birthday gifts," William said out loud.

Johnny's older brother Tomas was eager to see the all the gifts he would get for his birthday, but he had been waiting for a football all summer long.

Tomas and all his friends would play and every Saturday in the summertime, Tomas' mom would drop him off at his friend's house and they would play a game of tackle football. He was tough so the tackling never bothered him much, but then again, every kid thinks they're somewhat immortal, and that Georgia mud never bothered him much.

Him and his friends would play rain or shine. They didn't have a big field to play in, just some dirt road. An orange phone transponder was one touchdown goal, and an electric pole was the other touchdown goal at the other end.

"Go long!" Derick shouted as Tomas ran as fast as he could. Derick threw the football like a quarterback's last play in the dirt road Super Bowl. The ball hurdled through the air in a perfect spiral making its way to Tomas.

Tomas leaped through the air magically catching it by the tips of his fingers and tucking it quick to his stomach and dashed off to the touchdown goal.

"Yea, you got it!" Derick yelled as Tomas left a trail behind him. Not another kid was to be seen in his sights as he made his way to the touchdown line and rejoiced. Glory had its part on some back Georgia road accompanied with dirty shirts and muddy shoes!

Tomas didn't just want glory, he wanted his own football, something he could have of his own, a dream of his he could actually hold, and today was that day. He just knew his mom and dad bought him a football for his very own.

All the kids and parents had now gathered around to see Tomas' excitement as he opened his gifts.

"Is everyone here?" William asked intriguingly looking around, counting faces.

"Your father, he isn't here," Carolyn replied.

"We can't start without him!" William said looking over to the shade tree where his father sat.

"I'll go get Grandpa," Johnny said as he dashed across the yard.

"I thought you was going to bring me some sweet tea?" Grandpa Harold asked.

"They're about to open the gifts. Come on Grandpa, we're going to miss it if you don't hurry."

Grandpa Harold leaned on his cane pulling himself up as Johnny put his hand under his grandpa's arm to help him up.

"Oh, I got it son. These old bones feel like giving out, but I can still muster up enough strength to mosey on over there."

"We got cake and presents. You do like cake, don't you

Grandpa?" Johnny asked leading his grandpa by the hand to the birthday party.

"Yes sir, I've enjoyed some cake a few times in my day!"

As they made their way to the party Grandpa Harold's son, William, met them both, not with a greeting gesture but more of a malice demeanor, and the look on his son's face could only suggest him and his father had been in a few mishaps.

"Look who decided to show up?" William said with an edgy smirk.

"Shall we begin?" Carolyn asked. Then turning to her husband William, she said, "Behave!"

Now, for the last twenty years Grandpa and his son William had not been as close as they once were when he was a boy. His father used to tell adventures to him when he was a kid, but when he got older and went to law school his whole set of views in life changed. His father never grew out of the story telling and his son, well he just grew out of hearing it.

Tomas scanned over the gifts' shapes and sizes narrowing down to which gift he thought might be his football present. He didn't want to give all his excitement away first, so he chose to open the one he thought was the football last.

He opened his gifts, one was a fishing rod, new socks, a football jersey of the Houston Oilers, and a toy gun.

He loved the gifts, but his heart was set on one thing. So, when his dad handed him the box light in weight and wrapped in wrapping paper, he knew this was it. He closed his eyes and put his fingers to the edges of the paper and ripped away.

There it was, a Wilson pig skinned football like all the pros played. This wasn't like all those footballs he would play with on the weekends with his friends, no sir! This was the real deal. This was a top-notch football. This was his wish come true. When he opened his gift for first time his eyes nearly swelled up with tears and joy overcame him. Tomas got his birthday wish.

"Thanks dad!" Tomas said as he threw his arms around his dad with a grateful hug.

"You have been asking for it, so me and your mom thought you should have it!"

"Thanks! Thanks mom, thanks dad!"

"So, I take it you like it?" William asked.

"I love it! Thanks! Thanks dad!"

Chapter Two

Later that day Grandpa Harold finally got his iced tea and was sitting under the shade tree admiring the excitement and joy of his grandson while he played a game of football with his friends.

"Sorry I was late with that sweet tea," Carolyn said.

"I know you have your hands full. It's easy to get sidetracked in all this commotion," Grandpa Harold replied.

"William and I are planning on taking the boys down to Tybee Island next weekend. If you'd like to come along, we would be more than happy."

"William who?"

"Your son. Oh stop, you know right well who William is!" Carolyn touted.

"Do I? The boy never gives me no mind no how. I used to know him, now I'm not so sure anymore. There was a time I did know him. When he was a boy, he was happier than all those out there playing that there football game. He used to be filled with so much imagination but now his mind is just filled with paperwork, money, and mortgage. Funny how sometimes we all grow out of who we were. If we lose our sense of adventure, we lose the meaning of what life is all about."

"He does his best for us," Carolyn replied.

"Oh yes, I know he does his best. I'm rather proud of him but he has lost his self trying to find himself. He's just forgotten his imagination that's all," Grandpa Harold replied.

"Well, it's up to you. You're more than welcome to come along next weekend if you like," Carolyn added.

Carolyn didn't know quite how to respond. She knew her husband and father in-law's relationship was a little rocky, she felt like a mediator between the two sometimes. But deep down she knew Grandpa was right and sometimes it seemed like his work just drowned out any ounce of passion he had left in him. She's thankful that she at least got him to come to the birthday party much less agreeing to go to Tybee Island the following week. At times, she often thought Grandpa Harold was eccentric with all the tall tales he used to tell her husband when he was a boy, even though she was quite intrigued to hear one herself.

"William said you have had a few adventures in your day. I'd love to hear them if you don't mind?"

"My stories ain't just storying, they're more than that!" Grandpa Harold replied.

"Well, I would love to hear one sometime if you wouldn't mind."

Grandpa Harold knew this would be a great opportunity for him to share one of his stories with Carolyn, but he knew it wasn't the right time to tell any of them.

"Well, I can't say opportunity has arisen yet, but tell me would you want me to share one of my stories and your kids get left out of hearing it?"

"Certainty not. I'm sure they would love to hear them as well."

"Well, every story needs an opening and I'm just waiting on

the opening. When I see it, I'll let you know."

"Well, you better let me know or no more sweet tea for you," Carolyn said with a smile.

"You got yourself a deal!" Grandpa Harold nodded his head.

"Sounds good, well I need to be getting back to things. I'll come back and check up on you later."

"I'll be here with my sweet tea."

*   *   *

Once Carolyn left, Grandpa Harold turned back his attention to the kids playing football as Johnny sat on the side watching the other kids play. Picking the tops of grass with his legs crossed and a look of loneliness on his face and a pouting lip, he would gaze back up to see the other kids playing, wanting to be part of all the fun. But he was smaller than the rest, so they never gave him much mind, especially his older brother. He never really involved Little Johnny in any of his activities, he would just tell him he isn't old enough or tall enough to play.

"What's the matter?" Grandpa Harold asked.

Johnny didn't respond to his Grandpa Harold but just kept his hanging head low looking at the ground, as he sat picking at the tops of the grass plucking them off one by one immersed in his thoughts.

"Now you ain't going to ignore me now, are you? I got up and walked over all this way. I might be old, but I sure can see something's ailing you!?"

"My brother, I hate him!" Johnny spouted, gasping for air with tearful eyes while shaking his head as if he was plotting some sort of revenge.

"Nah... now come on you don't hate your brother!"

Johnny lifted his voice with stress and anguish and said, "I do Grandpa, I do! He never lets me play with him. He always has an excuse why I can't play with him. He says I'm not old enough or there's not enough people to have me on his team. I even said he can be all time quarter back when teams were uneven, and he still don't ever let me play. He don't even let me play hide and seek with him. You don't need to be older to play hide and seek. He is just mean to me, I hate him!"

"I see. So you really hate him, huh?" Grandpa Harold replied.

"I sure do grandpa, I wish someone would just throw that ball right into his bahooggies."

"Now that's not nice son, you shouldn't wish any hurt on your brother. You're lucky to have him!"

"Well, he doesn't like me, I just wish…" Johnny paused in mid-sentence then said, "I just wish he liked me…"

Johnny's eyes started to fill up with tears. He wiped at them until the red begin to show up on his face. "Grandpa, did you and your brothers ever get into fights when you were kids?"

"Oh no son, we didn't have time to fight growing up, times were tough enough as is. There was a time all we had was each other and there was a time we didn't have each other at all."

"What do you mean Grandpa?" Johnny asked wiping away his tears.

"Well, it was in the early forties when World War II was going on. Me and my brothers just moved to New York to be with our Aunt Louise."

"I see you're telling stories again," William said as he walked up.

"You didn't mind those stories when you were growing up," Grandpa Harold replied.

"Yea, I was a kid and stories were just that stories, not make-believe stories you say happened to you growing up. Which one are you going to tell him? How you were on a stranded island hunting for treasure with fierce pirates chasing you, or the time you made friends with a dragon and fought against evil in the dark ages? Oh yes, and the giant and the list goes on and on doesn't it Dad?" William said.

"They ain't just stories, they really happened." Grandpa Harold replied.

"Sure, they did! Dad, you can't be filling kids heads with a bunch of stories. They are going to have to face life one day."

"Son life is full of imagination. When we stop using it nothing comes to fruition."

"Okay Dad, let's hear one of your amazing adventures. Actually, why not tell your adventures to everyone here?" William said reviling his father.

"Yea Grandpa, tell all of us. Did you really become friends with a dragon?" Johnny asked.

"Best friends, he was my best friend." Grandpa Harold replied.

"See, that's what I mean. You can't be honest about anything. You're always telling some story."

"Fine Son, I won't tell them any story."

"No, Dad by all means tell us."

"Yea Grandpa, tell us," Johnny insisted.

"Matter fact Dad, tell all of us," William said then lifted up his voice and beckoned for everyone to come near saying, "My beloved father is going to tell us all one of his stories. Gather around you don't want to miss this."

Grandpa Harold looks down and begins to walk away hoping a little distance would put away any animosity or enmity that plagued him and his son's relationship.

"William, you didn't have to be so harsh on your father. He just wants to share a little time with his grandkids. That's not too much to ask, is it? Besides, they're not going to have him around forever and neither are you!"

William pauses and looks at his father understanding his father has become frail and this was his way of bonding with others and telling stories meant the world to him!

"Sorry, you're right Hun, I just got carried away." William replied responding to his wife's wisdom.

"Don't apologize to me, apologize to your father." Carolyn said.

"Sorry Dad, I got carried away. I know how much it means to you."

"It's okay Son, the fault is not your own."

"So, are you going to tell us one of your stories? We would like to hear it."

"Well, I don't mind, but you don't expect me to tell you all my stories standing up do you? I'm getting old and these ole bones need some rest?"

"Sure, I'll get a seat for you Dad," William said as he pulled up a chair for his father as a peace offering. As Grandpa Harold took a seat in that ole wooden chair, he leaned upon his cane and looked over to his eldest grandson Tomas hoping he would be intrigued by the story he was about to tell while everyone gathered around to hear.

"Everyone gather around, I got a story to tell you, a story like no other story you ever heard. This is a story about brotherhood, where brothers who were separated by distance had the chance to be by each other's side despite the hand they were so wrongfully dealt, overcoming the obstacles of life and living many adventures."

CHAPTER THREE

It was the early 1940s. Our father joined the Army to go overseas to fight the Germans. It was me and my two brothers, Danny who was the eldest, and Timmy the youngest child, and me the middle child. That summer we were forced to go stay with our closet relative Aunt Louise in New York. Our mother had died during childbirth to our youngest brother Timmy.

Aunt Louise had been living there for the last few years working in a sweat shop making trousers for a sewing factory. She always said life was big in the big city, but the south had bigger skies. I never really understood what she meant until I lived under a city sky.

The streets of New York were filled with lots of people, not like the small town of Reidsville where we grew up on Daddy's cotton farm. Sometimes I think if we had never fell on tough times, he would never have joined the Army, and I never would have had any adventures to be telling the likes of you good folks. But life is strange, and things happen for a reason."

"You're going to be okay. It's only for a little while, then I will come and get you boys," Daddy said as we sat in the back of that Ford Plymouth. Our youngest brother Timmy was trying to hold back his tears as his glasses kept falling off his face.

"But why Daddy? Why can't you stay?" Our youngest brother Timmy cried.

"I need money to keep the farm. You might not understand it now, but you'll understand when you get older. Besides, my country needs me right now."

"But I don't want you to go!"

"I don't want to go either Timmy, but sometimes we got to do things we don't want to do."

"Well, I don't want to go to New York," Timmy said.

"Me either," Danny said agreeing with the youngest.

"Boys, I got to go now. I'll be back soon enough to get you. Now you promise me you won't be giving your Aunt Louise a hard time."

"The three of us gave Daddy our promise and we meant it. As much as we didn't want Dad to go, we meant our promise. We wouldn't give Aunt Louise any trouble. After all, she made the best chocolate cake we ever had, and she always treated us boys particularly good to say the least. Aunt Louise was all right by me."

"Okay boys, you be careful and give your old man a hug," Daddy said as he reached out wrapping us up in his arms as if that hug was saying goodbye and as if that hug was saying he promised he'd be back home soon.

I remember us giving Dad a hug and watching the dust pick up in the wind from the rolling tires on a back Georgia road, putting an old cloud between what was our past and our future.

The image of Dad faded away from my vision through the back glass as we drove away. That was the last we had seen of Dad. Our hearts were heavy as we made our way to New York.

CHAPTER FOUR

My brother took a job as a newspaper boy at one of the local newspaper routes selling newspapers on the street corners.

"Come get your daily news," my brother would shout loudly over the crowd hoping to make a sell. Businessmen in their suits would give their change for the daily news or some soldier dressed in uniform would buy a newspaper hoping to get some information on what was happening with the war. I think Danny was pretty good at it. He always sold out all his papers on his route. I guess that's why he found good grace with Mr. Owensby who owned the newspaper printing company.

The job at the paper gave my brother a feeling of value. At least my brother had some money coming in and a sense of pride, plus it gave him an opportunity to keep up with what was going on in Europe with the war.

We all were hoping for good news, and that by some miracle Dad would be sent home. Good news never came, but I do remember one evening my brother Danny came home sad and distraught. Maybe his work had him weary or he was just tired of waiting for Dad's return and was compelled to do something about it.

"He's never coming back, is he?" my brother Danny murmured.

I really didn't know what to say. I was beginning to think that maybe he was right and maybe Dad wasn't ever coming back.

"You know what Harold, I wish we could go and fight the Germans and save Dad," Danny blurted out not taking into account what he was saying.

"We can't even get into the Army; we are just kids. Besides, how are we supposed to do that?" I replied.

"We can sneak on a boat going to Europe. There is always a Navy ship on the ports," our youngest brother Timmy revealed.

"How do you know that?" Danny asked.

"There's soldiers that come to the theater all the time and they do this," Timmy said.

Timmy puts his lips to his hand and starts kissing his hand making a reference to how the soldiers would go to the theaters and kiss on their girlfriends.

"What, they kiss their hand?" I asked.

"No, they are smooching on their girlfriends," Timmy responded.

"What does that have to do with them getting on Navy ships?" I asked.

"I don't know, but they won't let you into the Navy unless you kiss a girl. It's considered basic training."

"You don't have to kiss a girl to get to get into the Navy," I replied.

"How do you know? Have you ever joined the Navy? Besides, that's what one of the sailors told me anyways," Timmy said.

"They were lying to you. Besides, we can't even sneak onto a

Navy ship anyways."

"Not if you're smart like me. I sneak into the theater all the time and never get caught." Timmy replied.

"You never get caught cause ole man Perkins always turns a blind eye to you every time he sees you. Besides that, what about food and water? How could we survive without food and water?" I replied.

"Well, I guess I never thought about that Har Har."

Har Har was a nick name Timmy use to call me every now and then, but I really didn't mind. Matter fact it kinda stuck. But that's how we were sometimes, we just made-up nicknames for each other. It was our own little way to bond with each other, besides that, the nick names normally stuck with us.

"We got to come up with a plan!" Danny said scratching his chin in deep thought.

"Well, what do you suppose?" I asked.

"Well, it's going to take lots of skills and planning."

"We need someone with skills. Besides, how are we going to find out anything about Germany or even where to go or what's going on? It's not like we can figure it out on our own."

"That's easy, we got all the information we need!" Timmy answered.

"How's that Timmy?" I asked.

"The newspaper, it's got more information than we can think of and will let us know what's happening in Germany and the location of the German armies. It's the best way to devise a plan to save Dad."

"Timmy you're a genius!"

Timmy responds shrugging his shoulders with his modest way and says, "Yeah I know."

We all looked at each other knowing in our hearts this was it.

This was the plan, and this was the answer, and nothing could stop us!

"But...Aunt Louise, if she got wind of this, we would be in so much trouble," I replied.

"We do our planning when she's not here. Besides, sometimes she's too busy to pay attention to us."

"We did promise Dad to not cause her no trouble."

"But Dad didn't tell us we couldn't save him either," Danny replied.

My intelligence had been checkmated; my eldest brother was right. There was no need to argue but only agree with his intellect. The next day the plans of rescuing our father were in motion. Even though we knew we were never going to do anything we just wanted to feel like we could do it and I suppose the thought of saving Dad had high value on what was our imagination.

CHAPTER FIVE

The following day we stood outside the newspaper factory out in the back alley. Here we were the three of us acting like some modern-day Robin Hoods, not trying to steal money, but newspaper articles from the printing press.

"Tell me, why are we doing this again? Why can't you just take a newspaper left over from the newspaper stands without having us to break into the factory?" I asked.

"If we don't practice, how are we going to defeat the Germans? We got to act like spies," Danny replied.

"Yea we got to be spies Har Har," Timmy said agreeing with our eldest brother.

"Did we really need Aunt Louise's stockings to wear as mask?" I asked.

"We don't want to be recognized," Danny responded.

Yea there we were three kids in ladies' stockings, like that's an ordinary sight most people see every day and from the view through Aunt Louise stocking's covering my face all I could see was this was not going to be a good day!

"Yea, but Aunt Louise's stockings?" I couldn't help asking.

"Okay, you don't have to wear it. But if you get caught, I don't know you," Danny said.

"Me either," Timmy said agreeing with our older brother that he didn't know me if we got caught.

"Fine I'll wear it, but I'm not going to like it. So, what's the plan?"

Danny looks up to a pipe going up the wall that leads next to a window about fifteen to twenty feet in the air and points.

"Oh god, I wish I didn't ask," I said regretfully with tug at my gut whispering to myself, "This is a bad idea!"

Now we scaled up trees out on our farm in Reidsville, Georgia, but this was different from a small pine tree or an oak tree. I wasn't afraid of heights or anything but everything about this just didn't set well with me. I felt like I was in one of those old movies were the bad guy dresses in a mask wearing striped clothing, and I'm sure that would be the style of clothing we would be wearing if we got caught. Nevertheless, I didn't want to seem like the odd man out, after all it was for a just cause, so I braved the obstacle of death and sucked in my gut and took on the old saying *no guts no glory.* Oh, why didn't I listen to my gut on this one? Yea, something bad was going to happen! And I was pretty sure there was no glory going to be involved in this little adventure.

"I can do this," I said under my breath grabbing hold of the black rounded pipe that led up the wall of despair. It looked very easy as my older brother Danny who braved the wall like he was a superhero in disguise, which later lead to his infamous nick name Super Fly Danny.

"Come on," he said as he made it to the top of the pipe that stood beside the window to the printing factory. Earlier that day Danny unlocked the window so it would be easy to break into to take some newspaper articles.

Unannounced to Danny and much to his surprise someone had locked the widow at the end of the work shift and our sure-fire plan just went down the drain, not to mention I was hanging halfway up the wall with my eldest brother above me and if he fell, sure I'd break his fall, but it might have broken me in the process.

"Change of plans, the window is locked," Danny spouted in a haste.

"Change of plans? What you mean change of plans?" I asked.

"Nothing, we're going to have to climb back down."

I swear you could hear my sigh of relief a mile away, but I still had a good ten feet to climb back down and Danny a good twenty feet. As I was making my way back down, I heard an awful scream coming from up above me. The likes one would never want to hear a day in his life, a blood curdling scream.

"Rats! There's rats!" Danny screamed.

The ledge that wrapped around the building was a playground for the rats. Actually, that was a mild expression. Let's just say New York itself was their playground, and it just so happened, that day we came in contact of their playground and if there was one thing that could ruin a perfect mission it was a locked window and the company of rats.

If there was one thing me and my brother had in common, it was the unlikeness for rats and I for one did not want to hang out anywhere near them, especially while hanging ten feet up in the air. I was down that pole like a fire fighter hearing the siren bell go off. He didn't have to tell me twice, the word rats meant get the heck out of there and fast!

As my feet hit the ground, knowing full well I had made it safely along with my younger brother Timmy and unaware of the danger lingering above me, I heard the wrenching screams of Danny in his boy like voice.

"Move! Move! I'm going for it," Danny yelled.

Yep, you guessed it. He jumped. You could hear a splat aloud with the sound of trash and boxes being impacted and the aftermath sound of bottles rolling onto the concrete. Thankfully, the cardboard boxes softened his fall otherwise it could have been a very messy decision.

"Oh my god, you looked like superhero flying in the air," my younger brother said with excitement.

"Are you okay?" I said in shock as we both ran over to check on him to make sure he was alright.

Danny looked up and right before his eyes rolled in his head he said "Rats, there was rats!"

A door behind us flew open banging against the wall, "What's going on out here?" It was Mr. Owensby, Danny's boss at the paper printing factory.

"You can't be playing out here," Mr. Owensby said as he took off his hat and wiped the sweat from his brow. "What are you boys doing? Why are you wearing stockings on your head?"

"Danny fell from the windowsill and went out like a light bulb," Timmy said.

"Why would you be climbing up to the windowsill?" Mr. Owensby asked.

"We're going to defeat the Germans!"

I couldn't but help but think one thing when Timmy said that standing over my unconscious brother Danny. Yep, you guessed it. Our little brother Timmy ratted us out.

"Tabatha…" Mr. Owensby hollers, "Quick call the police!"

As Tabatha ran to the door to see what happened my heart sank within me. Yep, we were going to jail!

"Quick! Call the police! Danny fell from the window," Mr. Owensby spouted.

"Yes sir," Tabatha responded in haste.

We knew we was in deep trouble. Aunt Louise was going to find out about it. We were going to jail, and my brother was going to lose his job, and we wouldn't be able save our dad from the Germans and stop the war. We failed our mission! Thanks a lot, you pesky New York rats!

CHAPTER SIX

Later that evening Mr. Owensby stood talking to the police officers in the hospital lobby right before our Aunt Louise showed up. I never had been so nervous and worried in all my life. Mr. Owensby would look at us then back to the police officers as we sat sweating bullets, waiting for our life sentence in a New York jail cell. Then he shook their hands and they walked toward us. My heart was pounding in my chest as I made eye contact with the officer as he approached, then walked right past me out of the lobby.

A sigh of relief overcame me as Mr. Owensby stood alone in the hall by himself waiting on the word of our brothers' condition. Could it be Mr. Owensby was a cool guy? Surely if he wanted to press charges he would've. Maybe he was willing to show mercy on a few kids, who like most kids do some stupid things sometimes, considering how unfortunately, my brothers' health was a concern due to our mischievousness, not to mention the punishment we were going to face when Aunt Louise showed up.

Now when Aunt Louise showed up her manner of demeanor was that of anger mixed with worry, more frantic than anger.

"Is he okay?" she asked, tucking her purse to her side as she drew near in haste.

"He suffered a mild concussion, but he should be good in a few days," one of the nurses replied.

"Thank God. I promised their dad I would watch out for them while he is overseas. What happened?" She questioned.

"Apparently they were trying to climb in the window of the paper factory," Mr. Owensby replied.

Aunt Louise's face turned to confusion as she looked upon her two little angels sitting on the bench with their little halos hanging about over their heads while the other brother laid on his hospital bed in the room next door.

"Why would you boys do such a thing?" she asked.

"No telling, boys will be boys at that age," Mr. Owensby answered.

What? Mr. Owensby was not telling her what really happened? I cannot believe it! I thought for sure he would tell her after Timmy spilled the beans to him, and surely he would be upset! I couldn't believe that Mr. Owensby was a cool guy. Why would he not tell her? I thought for sure he would tell her our plans to defeat the Germans. Could it be that maybe he was an ally and could be trusted on our mission? If so, maybe this was something to look further into once our brother Danny got better.

"I will keep a better eye on them," Mr. Owensby continued.

"And you are?"

"Oh, where's my manners? I'm Mr. Owensby, owner of Owensby Printing Press. Your son Danny works for me selling newspapers."

"Oh no sir, you're quite mistaken. They're not my children. I'm merely their Aunt Louise. Their father, my brother, is off in Europe fighting the Germans. I'm only taking care of them until he comes back from the war."

"So, your Misses not Mrs.?" Mr. Owensby asked.

What? Did a light bulb just go off in my head? Can it be Mr. Owensby is interested in my aunt and what if she's interested in him?

"Yes, Misses," my aunt replied extending her hand as Mr. Owensby gracefully shook it in a formal greeting.

"Sorry to meet you under such circumstances. but life has and odd way of introducing us to the ones it wants us to meet. Who are we to disappoint destiny's opinion?"

What? Really, am I hearing this correct? Did he just say it was destiny they met? Is he trying to flirt with my aunt? This was disgusting and more than likely going to work in our favor!

"Well, yes I guess I can agree with that. We never know who we might meet under such grievous circumstances," Aunt Louise responded gracefully.

Really? She's eating this up? I can't believe it! We were trying to break into the factory window, my brother falls, suffers a concussion, our plans get ruined, he doesn't rat us out to Aunt Louise, and when he meets her, he starts talking about destiny. Man does my brother have a lot to hear once he is feeling better. Surely if Mr. Owensby was a bad man, he would get us in trouble. Strangely, I was quite taken aback and strangely impressed myself with him, to tell you the truth. And by all means I oddly approved.

But did my aunt and Mr. Owensby see the sparks flying as I did between them? Surely, they can't be so blind as to not see it? I guess I was just going to have to swallow my pride and become match maker if they didn't notice it. Well, it was just up to me to make them notice it. Besides, if she took up with him it would give us more time to plan our tactics of defeating the Germans. New mission, the match maker!

Chapter Seven

The air was filled with smoke from the bombs that fell from overhead. The loud sounds of bombs echoed through the air and the sound of small rounds fire could be heard. This wasn't make believe, this was the real thing.

"Get down, get down!" one of the sergeants yelled.

"Give me supporting fire!" a soldier shouted making his way through a barbed wire jungle.

No man was immune to the fear of war knowing today could be his last. But there was a form of bravery knowing you live beside your fellow soldiers, you fight with them, you eat with them, you laugh with them, you cry with them and sadly some unfortunately die with them. This was the truth and the truth spoke no louder than the sound of bullets flying across the top of their head. Fear may have accompanied their side but bravely fought well with them.

And there my dad was in the trenches, the guns blazing as he fought back along the side of his men. Our dad was our hero, but today he was the worlds hero, him, and the men along with him. To this day I cannot say enough of how proud I was of my father to be part of something so heroic. Without him and others we don't know where we all would be without their sacrifice.

Those young men charged the hill to victory, from the beach through the barbed wire jungle, through the trenches with casualty of life, they fought and won. That day would be forever called D-Day.

Now the news of the battle had reached the local papers, but we had not heard from Dad and did not know if he made it out alive or not. At least we had the newspaper to let us know what was happening in Europe, but still it wasn't the same. We needed to hear Dad was okay.

I suppose a good week had passed since the whole window/rat /-superman flying maneuver had happened.

"Look at this," my brother Danny said as he handed us the daily paper showing the allied forces had invaded Normandy.

We knew this wasn't just news but the real reality that war was really happening. We knew it was real but now it struck to the heart of things, Dad is there, and this is really happening. Even though we were happy for our country's victory, our hearts still feared for Dad's safety.

"Do you think dad is okay?" our brother Timmy asked with concern.

"Yes, I'm sure he is!" our big brother Danny said as he put his hand on our little brother's head to assure our brother Timmy that things were okay.

"But he hasn't wrote us yet. It's been two weeks since we've heard from him."

"I'm sure it's in the mail, you know how it takes forever to get anything. I'm sure he is okay. You are worrying over nothing."

I wished my brother Danny was right, but our brother Timmy had the right to worry. This was war after all and it's not like people did not get hurt or lose their lives. I hoped Dad was okay as well, but I wasn't about to spill out my doom and gloom rhetoric for the sake of my little brother Timmy. But me and Danny we knew anything was possible even though we didn't publicly admit it.

"Yes, I'm sure Dad is okay," I said to my brother Timmy, then looking to my older brother Danny.

"I hope you're right I just want to go home."

"Me too Timmy!"

But we just couldn't leave even though we all wanted to, it was just impossible. Besides, Dad wasn't home, and we were stuck in New York.

Later that week our mission to save Dad from the Germans became increasingly more desired than ever before. Even though we might have failed our first mission, we were getting ready to try again and this time our plans had changed a little.

"You should've seen them! They were hitting it off."

"What, you can't be serious? You want to try setting them up?"

"Yea, if we can get them to fall for each other that means she won't be paying close attention to us. Plus, she will be more worried about how she can impress Mr. Owensby and it will give us more time to plan our mission to defeat the Germans."

He knew I was right, not only right, but onto something! After all Mr. Owensby was a good gentleman and was a hard worker just like Aunt Louise. And after I told him how Mr. Owensby did not press charges knowing we were trying to break into the printing press and did not tell our Aunt Louise to get us in trouble, it meant that he could be trusted.

"Okay so what if you're right and they like each other? So, what's the plan?"

"That I haven't really figured out yet."

"Why not invite Mr. Owensby over for dinner one night? Tell him you want to learn more about the newspaper business. Plus, our aunt would like to see him, and she makes the best chocolate cake in all of New York!?" Timmy said.

Our Little brother Timmy's suggestion almost made him look like a genius and he was right. Aunt Louise did make the best chocolate cake in all of New York, if not all the world. And besides, what man could disagree to powers of persuasion of chocolate cake? A man does have his weaknesses.

"Timmy, you know you just might be a genius!"

"Really?"

"Yea, but how did you come up with that idea?" Danny asked.

"I watch a lot of movies. Guys are always eating food with girls outside of the theater," Timmy replied.

"Well, what do you think Super Fly Danny?" I asked.

"Sounds like a good plan to me. It just might work!"

"Okay, now what about Aunt Louise? How do we get her to agree to it?"

"She doesn't have to know anything. All Mr. Owensby has to do is show up thinking he's teaching Danny something. And you know Aunt Louise is southern, so she pretty much has to show her hospitality."

I couldn't believe it. My little brother Timmy was right again and not only was he right, but he was using big words like hospitality. Clearly, he's been watching way too many movies!

"You're a genius! I love it! Let's do it!"

"I know," Timmy replied as he put his hand under his chin tapping his fingers as if he was mentally envisioning patting himself on the back.

"How in the world are you coming up with all this?" I asked.

Timmy looked and smiled and said, "Cause, I'm a genius!"

CHAPTER EIGHT

The following day Danny, being slightly nervous, knocked on Mr. Owensby's door after his shift had ended selling newspapers.

"Mr. Owensby, do you mind if I can have your attention for a moment?"

Mr. Owensby took off his glasses and placed them on his table and said, "Sure, how can I help you?"

"Well, I was wondering if you could teach me a little more about how the newspaper business works."

"Is this what you had in mind when you tried to climb through the window with women's stockings on your face?"

"I can explain that," Danny nervously replied.

"Well, I'm waiting."

"Well, you see my dad is in Germany fighting the Germans, and we wanted to get all the information on Germany we could get and the best way we could get it was the newspaper articles. I was well.... We were thinking there was some old newspapers lying around talking about the war and they could help us find out what's going on over there. We didn't mean no harm"

"Germany? What are you planning an invasion on Germany or something?" Mr. Owensby chuckles under his breath.

Why was Mr. Owensby asking this? Maybe Mr. Owensby knows everything Danny thought to himself as he pondered and searched for the right answer. Luckily, Danny didn't have to answer Mr. Owensby's rhetorical question because it could have jeopardized everything.

"How long have you been working for me Danny?" Mr. Owensby asked.

"A few months now. I'm not fired, am I?" Danny sheepishly asked.

"If I were going to fire you, I would have when you tried to break into the building not so long ago," Mr. Owensby replied.

"So, I'm not in trouble?"

"No, but did it ever occur to you that you could've just asked me?"

Stumped at Mr. Owensby's answer Danny shook his head and said, "I didn't think of that. I guess I didn't think that through."

Mr. Owensby made a small chuckle and responded by saying, "Well it sounds like it, but the women's stockings?"

"Um yes, you see we were practicing a mission. If we got the newspapers, it would've been a successful mission. It was only for disguise."

"Oh, I see, that explains why the window was left unlocked that evening. Well, I can't say I haven't ever done any silly things when I was a kid."

"So, does this mean you might teach me some things about the newspaper business?"

"I tell you what, if you really want me to teach you I will, but it will have to be on Saturdays. That's when I'll have some free time."

"Well sir, I was hoping."

"You can take it or leave it. The weekend is all that I got open."

"Well Mr. Owensby, I was thinking that maybe you could teach me at my place. And besides, my aunt makes the best chocolate cake, and she might be interested in seeing you."

"She asked about me?"

"No sir, but I'm sure she would be delighted that I'm learning something besides math and science."

"Let me give it some thought," Mr. Owensby said, but knowing he was feeling all giddy inside at the thought of seeing my Aunt Louise once again.

"Chocolate cake, huh?" Mr. Owensby said.

"Yes sir, and it's the best in New York, maybe the best in all the state of Georgia!"

"Maybe in all of the world?" Mr. Owensby chimed in.

"Yes sir Mr. Owensby, maybe in all the world!"

"Well, I can't pass up on some chocolate cake. And besides, if it helps to learn something, well I guess my stomach is going to have to make the sacrifice."

"So that's a yes Mr. Owensby?"

"That's a yes."

"Thanks Mr. Owensby. You won't be disappointed."

"I'm sure I won't be. Oh yes, and next time you want a newspaper article just ask. There's no reason to be visiting the hospital each time you want to read a newspaper."

Danny broke a smile and said, "Yes sir!"

"Now get out of here before I change my mind."

"Yes sir, and thanks again."

"Don't mention it."

Danny left the room, closed the door, and took off running. He slid to the door entrance to the stairs, ran down a flight of stairs, and burst open the door to the outside where me and Timmy were waiting out in the back alley.

"It's a yes. He's going to help me. Everything is going to plan."

Danny hugged our brother Timmy and said, "you're a genius!"

Timmy straightened his glasses and responded, "Yeah, I know!"

Back in the office Mr. Owensby was doing a little celebration dance of his own knowing he was going to see Aunt Louise again as Tabatha knocked opening the door.

"Sir, I'm done," Tabatha said as Mr. Owensby was startled a little and slightly embarrassed at her surprising presence.

"Great, see you tomorrow."

"Okay. Anything else before I go?" Tabatha asked.

"No, I think we are good for the day," Mr. Owensby answered.

"Okay, well I'm going to go."

"Well, this little dance thing, can we not tell anyone?"

"Your secret is safe with me Mr. Owensby!"

"Good!"

"Great moves by the way!" Tabatha snickered.

"No one, absolutely no one!" Mr. Owensby said.

"My lips are sealed!" Tabatha said again.

Chapter Nine

That evening greeted us with a local radio station and Aunt Louise's chicken dinner with cornbread, mashed potatoes, and green peas.

"Are you going to eat your green peas?" Aunt Louise inquired as Timmy looked down at his green peas contemplating if he was going to eat them or not.

"If you don't want to eat them you can give them to one of your brothers. There's no need to waste any food," Aunt Louise continued.

"Nah, I'll eat them. I was just wondering Aunt Louise, have you ever thought of going back to Reidsville? We used to grow green peas on Daddy's farm. Sorry it just got me to thinking that's all!" Timmy asked.

"I made New York my home. It's not much but a woman has to grow her wings and fly and see what the world has to offer. Sometimes she just finds a job and works and that's all she has but she grew wings to get there."

"Aunt Louise it don't look like you have any wings. If you did, you'd look really funny!" Timmy inquisitively responded in his boyish childlike humor.

"You know what?" Aunt Louise leaned forward to whisper,

motioning for all of us to lean in forward to hear the secret she's about to give away. As we leaned in with itching ears, she put her hand to her lips and whispered, "You're eating my wings," pointing to the freshly fried chicken she had baked earlier.

Timmy jolted his head back with a look of shock, pushed his plate back from the table looked down at the chicken wings and wiped his mouth and said "Gross. I don't want to eat your wings!" as Aunt Louise busted out laughing.

"What? You're not going to eat my wings? What are you chicken?"

"Yea, Timmy," she went through all that trouble to cook it!" Danny said playing along with Aunt Louise's joke.

"Yea, she literally broke her back just to cook it," I said joining in on the little joke.

"Yuck, no wings for me!" Timmy said.

"I guess you better eat those green peas then," Aunt Louise said.

Aunt Louise had that charm about her, we never knew when she was going to brighten our day up. It was one of her greatest qualities, she made us smile. Sometimes we felt so at home we forgot about Georgia and when we did remember, she went out of her way to make us feel at home. She was special that way. God knows we loved her!

CHAPTER TEN

The next several days seemed like they were the longest days for Mr. Owensby, not only for him but for me as well. His normal routine of the day was mostly sitting at his office doing paperwork and answering calls or giving out orders to the head of the production staff to see the papers get made. But today his normal routine was traded for his oddly new behavior of pacing the floor. The glass doorway gave evidence of him walking back and forth rehearsing his next encounter with Aunt Louise.

"Hey, I'm Mr. Owensby, we met at the hospital. That's a lovely necktie you're wearing." Mr. Owensby shook his head, "What if she's not wearing a necktie?" A light bulb went off in his head. "Lovely scarf your wearing! Ahhh...I sound like a babbling idiot! Just introduce yourself and that's it. But she was a striking young lady," he said to himself as he played out their next encounter in his head.

As Mr. Owensby paced the floor Danny knocked to inquire if he was still interested in coming over for a visit to teach him a little about the newspaper business.

"Come in," Mr. Owensby said at the sound of the knock on the door.

"Ah, just who I wanted to see," Mr. Owensby prompted his

attention to Danny as he entered the room.

Oh no, Danny thought to himself. Mr. Owensby had changed his mind, maybe he is upset over the whole break in thing. But surely not, he seemed okay with it all the other day. Thoughts ran through Danny's mind wondering if Mr. Owensby was upset or still forgiving. Danny hoped for the best as he timidly asked.

"Wanted to see me?"

"Yes, I was thinking about other day!"

Oh no, he changed his mind for sure, I just know it Danny told himself in the back of his mind.

"Well, I was thinking of that incident outside and how you were telling me how you were wanting reports coming from Germany and I can't with good conscience have you working on the sidewalks selling newspapers."

"Sir if you let me, I swear I will make it up to you. I'll sell more newspapers I swear!"

"No, I made up my mind I don't think it's a good idea that you should be on the streets selling newspapers for me anymore."

"I understand sir. I don't blame you," Danny said as he hung his head feeling regret of trying to break in the newspaper factory.

"Starting Monday, I will have you doing chores for the lead production department. If they need you to fetch ink, then you go and fetch ink. And if they want you to sweep and mop, then sweep and mop, but your duties will no longer be needed selling newspapers. You sir have just moved up in the company!"

"You're not firing me!"

"Firing you? No! Promoting you? Yes!"

"I don't know what to say," Danny said as he stood in awe and overwhelming excitement trying to catch his breath from the thought he had lost his job.

"A thank you will be in order."

"Thanks, I don't know what to say."

"Promise me you won't let me down."

"I promise Mr. Owensby."

"So, what did you come to see me for?"

"I was wondering if you're still coming this Saturday to teach me more about how printing works."

Mr. Owensby walked to the back of his desk, sat down, and put on his glasses thinking to himself, I just promoted him he can clearly learn more from lead production, but if I tell him that my chances to see his Aunt Louise again could be ruined.

"I just offered you a job and you still want me to come to your place?"

What am I thinking? I'm successful and smart, Mr. Owensby thought to himself. Did I really give him the opportunity to back out of inviting me to his place to meet his Aunt Louise? I mean teach him about printing, I mean meet his aunt, my potential love interest?

Oh no, Danny panically thought to himself, this ain't good. He just offered me a job. There's no reason for him to come to my place now and meet my Aunt Louise, I mean teach me about printing, I mean meet my aunt, his potential love interest.

In that moment they both felt their spirits get sucked into the darkness of the black abyss with the terrifying scream of noooooooooooo! Saying did I just say that...? Yea often times someone might say something and regret it but the metaphor of them falling into a bottomless pit at that moment seemed to be well in comparison to how they both were feeling at that time. But luckily, we all have our moments of redemption, you know that beaming light at the end of tunnel, that one thing that could change any moment from worse to good. Well, it came in twinkling of an eye. It came with brilliance. It came in the form of chocolate cake!

"We have cake!" Danny blurted out. "Chocolate cake!" Trying to sell Mr. Owensby on the idea of cake like he did selling newspapers on the street corner.

That's all Danny could really say giving the moment's circumstance as he looked at Mr. Owensby hoping chocolate cake would somehow be the luring bait to get him to come over to his Aunt Louise's apartment that Saturday.

An inner sigh of relief came over Mr. Owensby as he thought to himself, great opportunity! Act like chocolate cake is your main motive.

"Yes cake, chocolate cake, I see no reason not to make it this Saturday."

"Thanks Mr. Owensby. I'm looking forward to it."

"Me too," Mr. Owensby nodded with his stamp of approval to their future meeting.

"Well, it's time for me to head home. I'll see you in the morning Mr. Owensby?"

"Before you go, you have a younger brother, correct?" Mr. Owensby asked regaining Danny's attention as he began towards the door.

"Yes sir, Mr. Owensby."

"Well, I just had a paper boy position open up. Do you think he might be interested?"

"You mean Har Har? I mean Harold, my brother Harold, sorry, Har Har is my little brothers nick name for him. It kind of stuck. Yes, I think he would be interested."

"Great, we will discuss it Saturday."

"Thanks again Mr. Owensby."

"By the way, can we not tell anyone I went soft on you boys after the whole window break in thing? I don't want people thinking they can do something bad and have no repercussions for it. You know like steal newspapers?"

"Yes sir, my lips are sealed, and I'm sorry sir, I really am."

"Just don't make me regret my decision."

"You won't sir, I promise."

And Danny meant it. He was in no way shape or form going to let Mr. Owensby down. He was the first man besides his dad that was making a positive impact on his life. Danny didn't care too much for the big city as he did for our farm, but one thing was for sure, Mr. Owensby was someone to look up to, someone who he was proud to say was a friend and a pillar to his life and ambitions. Mr. Owensby was a man of devout honor!

Once Danny left the office Mr. Owensby said to himself "That's twice he's mentioned chocolate cake. His aunt must make some really good chocolate cake!"

I was pleasantly surprised to hear later that day that Mr. Owensby had offered me a job as a paper boy. This was good. Not only did my brother get promoted, we now had firsthand access to the newspaper to catch up with what was happening with the war and the current events taking place in Europe. Anything that could benefit us on our mission was always a plus and a step in the right direction. Yes, our plans had holes in them, like, how were we getting to Germany, how can three young boys from the state of Georgia rescue their father, how could we possibly defeat the German Army? Hey, we were kids, we dreamed big! That's what kids do they dream big, and no dream is too big. We didn't know how we were going to do it, but we knew somehow someway we were going to make it happen and that's all that mattered.

CHAPTER ELEVEN

That Saturday was an important day. Unknowingly, that time, that day would have such significance and overall impact on all our lives. Funny how sometimes you can't see destiny unfolding right in front of you. It's not until you've crossed many crossroads and looked back that you can see where all the roads in life led you to. that one particular moment and you say to yourself wow, I see it now. My plan to play match maker between Aunt Louise and Mr. Owensby was no longer of any importance considering we now had access to all we were hoping to get from the newspaper, but Mr. Owensby was a good guy and if we went this far in our plan we might as well see it through. Honestly, I have no regrets.

Mr. Owensby's nervousness grew intensively as was anticipated. I guess he did take quite a liking to Aunt Louise. What was not to like? She was funny, charming, and hardworking. Besides, she was my aunt and the greatest aunt in the world. That Saturday Mr. Owensby showed, knocking on the door.

"Who can be showing up on a Saturday?" Aunt Louise asked inquisitively. Making her way to the door she opened it to find a nervous Mr. Owensby on the other side.

"Nice scarf you're wearing," Mr. Owensby said as the door

opened.

Aunt Louise cracked a smile and said, "I'm not wearing a scarf."

"Oh, yea right. Sorry, of course you're not. You're not wearing anything. I mean of course you're wearing something, just not a scarf. I thought you'd be wearing a scarf. Most women like scarfs. But you're not. But if you were, you would look great wearing it," Mr. Owensby said.

"Thanks," Aunt Louise said looking at him strangely with a warm smile, and proceeded to ask, "So how can I help you?"

"Oh, sorry we met at the hospital not so long ago. I'm Danny's employer. I was coming over to discuss some of the work involved at the printing press. I promoted him. He's been really interested in learning, so I thought I would stop by and give him some pointers."

"You didn't have to go out of your way," Aunt Louise said.

"It's no problem really. Besides, I needed a break anyways. So is Danny here today?" Mr. Owensby asked while leaning his head in, scouting out the room for Danny's presence.

"Yes, if you want, you can come on in. Forgive the way the place looks. I do have three nephews."

"You should see my office sometime. Looks like it got hit by a tornado. Your apartment is mild compared to mine."

"It's a work in progress to tidy up after the boys but I manage."

"They can't be that bad?"

"Danny, you've got a guest," Aunt Louise said. Then turning the conversation back to Mr. Owensby, "Oh no, the boys are perfect. They do their part around here. Let's just say it's not the Ritz or the Hilton."

"Hey Mr. Owensby," Danny said, greeting him with a hand-shake. "You remember my Aunt?"

"Yes, I brought it to her attention. I suppose she didn't remember."

"I'm so sorry, yes, you said we met at the hospital. Danny suffered a concussion and I'm the one having amnesia or I'm just slacking up on my southern charm."

Mr. Owensby thought to himself, just great, she forgot all about me, as he made his way through her tiny two-bedroom apartment.

"If I do say so myself, you didn't lack on much southern charm at the hospital," Mr. Owensby replied.

"Well, if you don't mind maybe I can brush up on my southern hospitality by offering you a seat?"

"You do like southern hospitality, don't you Mr. Owensby?" Our little brother Timmy asked, hoping it would show some spark of interest on Mr. Owensby's part.

"Yes sir, I sure do," Mr. Owensby replied. Then turning to Aunt Louise, he said, "I'm much obliged madam," tipping his hat, "Sorry, there I go not even thinking of taking my hat off."

"I guess we both failed at hospitality today," Aunt Louise said as she cracked a charmful smile.

"Yes ma'am, I do believe we both did," Mr. Owensby answers obliging with his own charmful smile.

"Well, we have the rest of the day to make up for it, now don't we? Speaking of hospitality, would you like some sweet tea or some water?"

"Water would be fine!"

"Be right back with your water."

"Hey Mr. Owensby, how long have you run the newspaper factory?" Timmy asked.

"A long time now."

"Do you ever meet any movie stars?" Timmy asked.

"Oh no, I never met any of those, but we do have spots of advertising for the movies."

"I love movies. I want to grow up and be a movie star. I wanted to be funny like Charlie Chaplain but I'm only eight. I can't grow a mustache!" Timmy said hanging his head.

"Well, you don't have to have a mustache to be funny. It's all about comedic timing!"

"What's comedic timing?" Timmy inquired.

"Well, how do I answer this one? It's like a joke only you have to wait for the right time to say the punch line."

"Oh, okay?" Timmy looked off trying to take in the information. "I think I understand what you're saying."

Aunt Louise entered the room with the cup of water and handed it to Mr. Owensby and asked, "So what are we discussing?"

"I was just explaining to your nephew about comedic timing. I don't think he got my answer."

"You remember the other night you telling me I didn't look like I had wings?" Aunt Louise asked.

"Yes ma'am," Timmy answered but was still confused.

"That was comedic timing. You used something that was relative to the topic and made a joke out of it."

"Oh, okay, so I got comedic talent that's cool! And like how you whispered saying I was eating your wings, that was comedic timing too?"

"Yep, you got it!"

"That's cool. Watch out Hollywood here I come!" Timmy said holding his head up high.

"Now that's the attitude to have!" Mr. Owensby said taking

a drink of water.

"And what about you?" Mr. Owensby asked Aunt Louise.

"Me?" Aunt Louise responds, Oh, well I just work overtime in a workshop that's about it."

"That can't be the only thing about you. I'm sure you have some great ambitions?"

"Yea I do, but my only ambition in life right now is to not burn anything when I'm cooking. I know New York has a lot to offer but I don't have the time for it. Besides, we are at war, and I don't want to be self-centered in life knowing people have it worse than me. If I am bodily abled to work and come home, watch out for the boys, not burn a meal in my book, I've contributed to society. To me that's true ambition. Not something extravagant or extraordinary but just humble ambition and I prefer it that way!"

"That's an honorable answer," Mr. Owensby replied and was more impressed with her now than when he first met her.

I guess everything she said or did grew on Mr. Owensby pretty quick. A week ago, he was just some employer working all day at the printing press and working long hours. But today he was sitting on our couch being the subject of a story taking place.

"But I can also swing dance to some jazzy saxophone," Aunt Louise said.

"Mr. Owensby you got to see my aunt dance." Timmy says with excitement.

"Ah, that's the last thing he would want to see," Aunt Louise said trying to downplay her dancing skills.

Mr. Owensby smiled and motioned to the floor, "Oh no, by all means I'd be much obliged. Besides, you have rather struck up my curiosity."

"Okay, but I'm going to need a partner in crime," then looking over to our little brother Timmy and stretching her hand out, she said in an English accent, "Sir, will you do me the honor?"

"Why, I will be delighted Madam," Timmy said in a New York accent.

"I'll get the radio,", Danny said turning the dials of a static radio landing on a station playing the latest in jazz.

Timmy and Aunt Louise took the living room floor while the saxophone plays a rhythmic tune. Aunt Louise took Timmy's hand they both kicked out their leg, turned it in, faced each other, kicked their leg out, did a marching step, then twirled Timmy around, and they both do a line dance swing. Danny and I joined in keeping up with the steps twirling around and laughing while enjoying life and its brilliant moments.

Mr. Owensby watched as he witnessed this family delightfully entertain him. He was not even there five minutes, and they were dancing, celebrating a moment in life, not just celebrating life, but living it to the fullest. He greatly admired it if nothing else, as he thought to himself maybe this is what he had been missing for himself. But he couldn't help to think maybe he was missing out himself cause Louise's appearance made it quite obvious what he had been missing in his day-to-day life. He was missing someone like her. There's nothing like a woman that can bring out the life in a man and clearly life was presenting it in the form of a swing dance and a jazzy New York song on the radio of an FM dial. She fit the part so well in her little black shoes that barely touched the floor, complemented by her white lacey socks that barely covered her ankles, and that yellow dress with her cooking apron on, a starlet smile that went well with her rosy lips, the curls of her shoulder length brunet hair, and the eyes so blue she must have stolen from the ocean itself. If anything, I can say Mr. Owensby was smitten. If cupid done his job, he sure struck Mr. Owensby that day with arrows hailing out of the heavens with sparks of light. Aunt Louise might not have known it or just didn't see it. But Mr. Owensby was convinced he was now in love.

"Get up join us!" Aunt Louise said loudly over the radio blaring.

Mr. Owensby came to his senses out of the trance as he was greeted with Aunt Louise's majestic smile.

"What?" Mr. Owensby asked.

"Come join us!" Aunt Louise put out her hand in a welcoming manner!

"I can't dance to well," Mr. Owensby replied regretfully.

"That's okay, just try, you don't have to be the greatest dancer just enjoy the moment."

How could Mr. Owensby resist taking part in celebration of life, this was his moment to impress Aunt Louise and to bond with us as well. He may not have been the most outgoing man, but a man can't go wrong with a little dance even if he had two left feet.

"I'm going to show you some easy moves," Aunt Louise said as she took Mr. Owensby's hand, "Now step in and out."

Mr. Owensby's heart raced inside him as Aunt Louise greeted him with a southern smile as he followed her instructions.

"That's great, you're a natural. Just remember to enjoy the moment. Let the music tell you what to do. Can you hear the music talking to you?"

"Yes, I can hear it!" Mr. Owensby replied with a welcoming smile as the music stopped.

They looked at each other and stopped dancing and lingered

into each other's eyes for a moment. Then she sighed and broke away.

"Well, that was exciting. So, who's willing to help me prepare evening dinner while Mr. Owensby discusses job details with Danny?"

"Do we really have a choice?" Timmy asked in his charming and cunning protest.

"Not really, but if you want to eat," Aunt Louise replied.

"Okay, I guess I'll help cook dinner." Timmy said hanging his head walking towards the kitchen.

"Well, you do know you'll be helping me make my chocolate cake."

"Chocolate cake? You got yourself a deal Aunt Louise!?" Timmy said as he perked up his head with a grin.

She knew just how to work us. We were helpless to say no to her when it came to the persuasion of chocolate cake. It was like her spoon was some magic wand and any time the chocolate powder and dough hit the bowl wonders happened!

"You know where the flour is, I'll get out the pan out," Louise said as she made her way to the small New York apartment kitchen.

In the middle of all the fun we had no clue what was later in store for us and how things would turn on a dime. As a kid you're never prepared for the worst. I wish I could say things went as planned or hoped for after that. We had dinner, spoke about the newspaper factory, and shared stories, a typical day one might have. But it all came vague with the knock at the door. Sometimes I wished we never opened that door. But without that knock at the door our adventures never would have happened!

CHAPTER TWELVE

I remember it to this day, unexpectedly opening the door without a care in the world. Then my heart sank within me at the appearance of two soldiers standing in their uniforms. They didn't have to say a word, I knew why they were there.

"Is he dead?" Was all I could muster up with tears forming in my eyes and a lump in my throat.

The two gentlemen looked at each other then looked back at me, as one of them said "We are not sure."

"What happened?" Aunt Louise asked as she took a seat with jittery hands expecting the worst.

I can't imagine how she felt in that moment. The weight of the world must've stood on her shoulders. Here she was struggling, trying to take care of us and now she just got the news she lost her brother.

"Madam all we know is Dewight Stanfield is presumed dead. There was some heavy fighting, his fox hole was hit on a mission, the Germans happened to capture a few soldiers. He is presumed to be dead or captured!"

"Those Nazi Germans, I hate them!" My little brother Timmy blurted out with his eight-year-old anger.

Though he never used such strong words filled with hate, I

couldn't help but feel the same pain and anger he was feeling. It was evident this was no accident. It was war and it made us feel vulnerable, emotional, and downright angry. Even though the war was over there, we were the ones who were being affected by it. Thousands of miles away and helpless to do anything about it. All we had to show for it was a few choice words like Timmy, "I hate those Nazi Germans!"

"That's not going to help matters none," Aunt Louise said trying to calm him down in her subtle way.

"But I hate them. They killed Dad! I hate them!" Timmy screamed as he took off running to his room, jumping into his bed and bursting into tears. "Daddy, please don't be gone, please Daddy?" Pleading with hope against hope my little brother cried on his bed of despair.

"You said he might have been captured. If he was captured, he might still be alive?" Danny asked.

"We can't be too sure at this point. It's all speculation!" one of the soldiers replied.

"Is there anything you can do?" Mr. Owensby asked.

"We are doing all we can. Unfortunately, there's not a lot we can do at the moment, but if we get confirmation he is alive we will let you know!"

"He has to be alive! You would know for sure if he was dead, but you don't know for sure, so he has to be alive!" Danny said.

"We are hoping for the best," one of the soldiers replied.

"So, what happens now, what happens if you don't find out?" Aunt Louise asked.

"Then the Army will declare him killed in action," the soldier replied.

Killed in action, those words shot right through me. I'd rather had faced the whole German army with a sling shot than hear those words. Heroes didn't die. At least that's what I thought, not just heroes but my dad. He just couldn't be dead and this had to be some nightmare and I'd be waking up soon. Unfortunately, it wasn't a dream, this was really happening.

That night didn't rest easy for any of us at the Stanfield household. I spent half the night staring up at the ceiling trying to sleep but the thoughts of Dad kept running through my mind as the scenes of the war played in my head.

I could see Dad in the fox hole as loud thunderous bombs went off shaking the ground as dirt flew through the air from its impact, the loud sounds of cannons blaring and the screams of men who ran into the battle in fear and with courage.

As I imagined the scene over and over the room grew darker and darker, shadowy figures hovered about as my heavy eyes fell asleep whisking me into a world of the dreams.

I could see the battleground and the soldiers fighting against one another as they exchanged gunfire. Then out of nowhere a fierce dragon swiftly flew above them as Dad stood to his feet, throwing away his helmet as the other soldiers ran for their lives and he waved towards the dragon smiling, welcoming him take him into the afterlife.

. "Daddy's dead, Daddy is dead!" I yelled from the top of my lungs as I trembled in fear sitting upright in my bed as the bedroom light came on.

"It's okay Har Har, it's going to be alright. It was just a bad dream," Aunt Louise said as she sat on the bed and pulled me into an embracive hug.

"It wasn't just a dream. Daddy's dead I just know it, he is dead!

CHAPTER THIRTEEN

A few days had passed, and the thoughts of Dad didn't stray far from our minds. I went to work at the printing company that week selling newspapers. Staying busy helped me to keep my mind off things but it was tougher on Timmy. He really didn't have an outlet to help him cope with the grief of losing our father, if anything he become more distant. Slowly he started separating himself from us. I would come home in the evening times and say hi and sometimes he wouldn't even respond nor look my way. Even Danny and Aunt Louise got the silent treatment.

"He's getting worse," Danny said as Timmy got up from dinner.

Timmy would just get up from the dinner table, not say a word, go to our room and stare at the ceiling for the rest of the night and fall asleep.

"We got to do something," I said to Aunt Louise thinking she would have all the answers.

But her silence gave evidence to her own grievance and distance. We all might have been living under the same roof, but we had become strangers at home. We all were weighing the battle of losing Dad. That two-bedroom apartment was once filled with strength and laughter and now it was filled with weakness of heart and we dared not to burden the others as if we were really strong enough to weather it all on our own.

We might had gone our separate ways trying to deal with the loss of Dad in our own little ways, but I knew I was right. We had to do something. We just couldn't set back and watch ourselves fall apart. We needed my brothers smile back, my aunt's humor, and my brothers' sense of adventure, and I was persuaded no matter what we were going to be family again.

The next day at work the ink from the press had spilled some and Danny was helping the press operator clean up the ink from the floor when I arrived back at the factory from a long day of selling newspapers on the street corner.

"What happened?" I asked.

"The press, it's not working dear lad. Its leaking ink every-where. It's never done it before," the press operator Scotty said shaking his head while trying to wipe the black ink up with old newspapers and clothes, dirtying his hands in ink.

"Need any help?" I asked.

"Yes. Go to the storage closet and grab a mop and bucket and fill it with some water," Mr. Scotty said pointing to the storage closet.

"Yes sir!" I said running over to the storage closet and flick-ing on the light. The closet was filled papers and bottles of ink, but no real sign of a mop much less a bucket. My eyes wondered through the miscellaneous items until my eyes fastened upon the mop.

"I found the mop, but I don't see any bucket," I said as I hol-lered over the loudness of the paper press.

"It's there young lad you just have to move some papers around. It's probably beside the counter," Mr. Scotty shouted back.

He was right, it was right there I was just looking too hard. I grabbed the bucket and ran to the water fountain next to the bathroom and filled the bucket with soap and water and ran back as I left a trail of soapy water behind me.

"Here I will take it," Danny said reaching for the mop, "it's my responsibility," he eagerly spouted.

It might had been his responsibility, but I couldn't set back and not help. It was my first week on the job and if those papers didn't get printed, I couldn't sell, and if I couldn't sell, I would be stuck home and all I would be doing is setting at home thinking of Dad. I needed this job; it was my therapy and that's when it hit me like a ton of bricks.

Timmy has no outlet for him to not be thinking about our current crisis. Losing Dad even affected his social life he hasn't even gone to the theater since it all happened. He loved the theater. He loved movies and stories. I thought to myself what if we stuck to our plan where we rescued Dad from the Germans? What if we convinced him maybe Dad isn't dead and what if Timmy was right all along about jumping on a ship and going to Europe? Maybe if we told him the idea wasn't so crazy after all it might give him other things to ponder on than the fact Dad might be dead?

Of course, this was our plan from the start but what if this was the fuel to the fire? What if this all happened for a reason? What if jumping on some ship was the answer to it all or am I starting to lose it? But I didn't care if I was losing it or not, I just wanted my family back. If we never went to Europe to save Dad, I was okay with it because that really wasn't possible, and I knew it but what was possible is making my eight-year-old brother believe it was. It was worth a shot.

Something had to be done, I couldn't do this alone. I needed the skills of a persuasive partner and there was no better partner to convince my youngest brother to embark on an adventure other than my adventurous brother Danny himself, or should I say Super Fly Danny!

"I got it; I know what we got to do."

"Maybe if we had another mop!" Danny replied.

"Yea, another mop would work, but I'm talking about Timmy!"

"Timmy, he hates mopping floors!"

"No, I'm not talking about that. You remember our little plan?"

"Yea, well that plan is ruined now. You can just forget about it and get back to work. Look around this is all we got now!"

"See, that's it. We can go to work here but Timmy can't. We can occupy our time but he's at home by himself all the time. He has no way of getting things off his mind."

Danny turned and looked at me and said, "I'm listening."

"'Well, you remember we was going to rescue Dad. What if we said we still wanted to make up plans to do it?"

"But Dad might be dead or captured by the Germans, you heard the soldiers tell us just like I heard them," Danny replied.

"But you see, he might not be dead. If we give Timmy a reason to believe Dad's alive, he just might be okay. All I'm saying is the thought of an adventure might do him good especially if he thinks we have a chance to save Dad."

"But what if Dad is dead, then what?" Danny answered.

"I don't know but if we don't try something, I don't know what will happen to him. It's worth trying, Dad would want us to try!"

That was always the cornerstone in a lot of the things we did. If something looked like it would have Dad's approval, we couldn't argue against it. We knew Dads' character and we all admired him and wanted to be just like him and when I said to Danny that Dad would want us to try to help Timmy, well that was like the holy grail of the conversation. I knew he had to agree to it. Besides, he was the one who was gung-ho more than me on our first but failed mission. He was so gung-ho he was willing to wear stockings on his face. There was no way he could say no, and honestly why would he want to say no anyways? This was for our brother and the hope to bring our family close together after all the devastating news.

"Okay but how do you want to do this?"

"Well, we need a trusted source that could be a big benefactor in our mission," I replied.

We both looked at each other and said at the same time, "Mr. Owensby!"

Chapter Fourteen

We knew we could get Mr. Owensby to help but we needed to convince him first. We knew it wouldn't be too hard to convince him considering the circumstances, but we needed to honest and sincere about our true intentions to help our brother Timmy with no hidden agenda. Yes, that meant telling Mr. Owensby about defeating the Germans.

There we were standing in Mr. Owensby's office, ink on our shoes and dried ink on our hands, hoping he would understand our motive.

"You can't be serious! Have you been sniffing ink?" Mr. Owensby replied.

"No sir, but if you see Timmy, he isn't talking and always distant since hearing about Dad," Danny answered.

"Yes, but trying to fight the Germans as kids is out of the question," Mr. Owensby replied.

"We know we can't go, but we can make our brother think we are going. It's to help him feel like he can do something for Dad. We are kids, we have imagination. If we don't use it, we grow old," I replied.

"So, you're not really wanting to go to Germany, just play pretend you're going?" Mr. Owensby asked.

"Yes sir."

"I would need to give this some thought," Mr. Owensby responds.

"Sir if you don't mind me saying, but me and Harold both respect you a lot, not only respect you but trust you. He wouldn't even have asked you if we thought you wouldn't be willing to help us. Look around Sir, this whole factory is built on stories, built on adventure. Someone lives an adventure, someone writes it, you print it, and the world reads it. If no one had an imagination, then where would adventure be? All we are asking is you help us on the adventure!?" Danny said.

Well, if Danny didn't always find the right words to say to Mr. Owensby, it seemed like he always knew what Mr. Owensby wanted to hear. Either that or Mr. Owensby just wanted someone to persuade him into a little adventure of his own. Maybe it was both of them I am assuming. Mr. Owensby often read a few books and read the paper but never left the office much. So, I guess when Danny explained in his perspective, he completely got what we were trying to do.

Mr. Owensby took off his glasses and began to contemplate the idea of helping us out. It seemed like forever until he mustered up any form of interest.

"So, this is all for Timmy?" Mr. Owensby asked.

"Yes sir!" we both answered!

"And what exactly do you have in mind?" Mr. Owensby asked.

"Well, I was thinking one of two things actually. We can tell Timmy we are going to save Dad and that we know where a German spy is and he has secret documents, and we need to get the documents to authorities. But we would need a place to act like we are secretly planning the details. I was thinking we could use the paper factory."

"And how are you going to convince him there's a German spy and you know that he is in New York?" Mr. Owensby asked.

"That's the easy part. We make a fake newspaper saying a German spy might be in New York with top secret documents," Danny answered.

"It could work!" Mr. Owensby said, "But do you know how much it will cost me to print one copy?"

"You can have my weeks' pay; I don't care how much it cost. We just need to make my brother feel like he has some kind of sense of purpose," Danny answered.

"It could be costly. It might average out more than a week's salary, plus I will have to talk to Scotty over in production and then there's paying him overtime just to print it."

"And I almost forgot, Mr. Owensby, we would need you to spend more time with Aunt Louise so she doesn't become too suspicious of our plan."

After hearing he will be spending time with our Aunt, Mr. Owensby quickly responded, "I think I can get it down to no cost!"

CHAPTER FIFTEEN

The rest of the week in our spare time we sat in Mr. Owensby's office strategizing the idea of how we can go about executing our plan with the help of the printing operator Mr. Scotty.

We had a map of New York laid out on his oak desk, a few newspaper clippings, and a drawing of how we would move from one position to the other.

''At exactly twelve thirty-five we will say we want popcorn, and we will ask Timmy if he wants popcorn once we're in the lobby. We will show him the newspaper we had printed telling him we got a lead, and that will give Mr. Scotty enough time to rent the hotel suite and put fake documents in his briefcase and hide it under his bed," Danny explained the plan further.

"Don't worry about the suite, a friend owes me a favor and I can get the suite for the day at no cost. All Scotty must do is show up," Mr. Owensby said.

"And we will leave the theater around twelve forty-five, give or take a few minutes. That would still give Scotty time to plant the documents."

"But you have to make sure to take pictures of the documents. If you don't it's not going to seem believable," Mr. Owensby replied.

It was so cool standing there at Mr. Owensby's desk along with him, Mr. Scotty, and my older brother making plans. For a minute there I felt a sense of pride and a feeling of importance. Here I was, me and my older brother standing with two grown adults conspiring a cooperation to get my brothers mind over the loss of our father. Though it felt slightly deceptive, but the root of the mission was pure in nature. None the less, we were doing this for our brother.

Standing there amongst the drawn-out map of the hotel and the entrance way strolled out across Mr. Owensby's desk I felt a sense of empowerment. It was like the feeling of a young man when he reaches manhood, like a tribal ritual where the young men would prove himself to the chief elders that they were men. We had no need to prove ourselves to the men standing there but more or less we were proving ourselves to ourselves. Though we were young we felt like men, yet we were boys amongst men.

And in that moment, we felt a form of strength and empowerment not knowing what that day had in store for us. As the true test of manhood awaited us, not just a test of manhood but sorrowful tribulation we would have to endure. Maybe standing there that day helped to shape and form us to believe there's nothing we could not accomplish in life.

Unfortunately, our plan never did come to fruition. That following evening brought our true test of manhood, our instinct for survival. Unknown to us, our lives were about to change.

CHAPTER SIXTEEN

Aunt Louise's countenance was of mere sadness as Danny and I entered our aunt's apartment that evening. By the look on her face and the presence of an older lady along with the local police it sure didn't give off any good vibes.

Our brother Timmy sat in tears on the couch already knowing the outcome of what was about to take place.

"What do you mean? I don't understand I am their aunt!" Aunt Louise protested.

"We understand but according to the state their father never gave you custody of the children," the case worker replied.

What is this? Is this really happening I thought to myself? When the lady said those words, I knew she was a case worker and she worked for the state of New York.

Here I was just a short time ago feeling like a man. Now here I am forced to accept the reality I am only a child, and my life and future is in the hands of strangers who thought they knew what was best for me and my brothers' well-being. I couldn't tell how helpless I felt. It was like swimming in deep waters with swift currents that just pull you under. And if anyone knew anything about swift currents it was me. I would hear talk about it down at the Uncle Tessy Dock and all its horror stories of young and old sailors getting taken under at sea. And the news of hearing Aunt Louise didn't have custody of us stole the very breath from me like that ole sea.

I would like to say I can remember much from that point on, but I can't, maybe I just blocked it out of my mind. The fact that one moment I'm here with family and the next we are being ripped apart to be placed in the care of the state.

But I can remember the emptiness I felt walking down the stairs looking over to the police car next to me and looking over to my two brothers as we entered separate cars and we looked at each other knowing we may never see each other again. This was our last day we would ever be together again.

I wanted to wipe the memory clean from my mind. Aunt Louise gave my brothers a hug and promised she will get us back. I can still hear Timmy crying out, "I don't want to go! Why are you making me go?" as the police officer closed the door.

I guess the officer must have done this a hundred times because it seemed as he was not affected nor showed any compassion at my brother's plea, nor was the case worker who now was power of attorney over what will happen to us.

I just remember riding away and Aunt Louise crying on the sidewalk. This couldn't be happening; we first suffered the loss of our father and now we are suffering loss of each other. Life wasn't fair, we were supposed be together, we were family and that's what families do they stay together.

CHAPTER SEVENTEEN

That evening it rained as we pulled up to a stone building with many windows. The yard seemed to be well kept, the bushes on the outside had been trimmed and maintained. Even though the appearance seemed to catch my eye admiring how nice it looked, but it wasn't home. It wasn't Georgia, and it wasn't my Aunt Louise's place. I wondered if my two brothers had been placed in such a place as this one. Maybe they were in a nicer place. At least they were being placed in the same orphanage with each other. They at least had each other, despite my circumstances I was thankful for that.

The police officer who had taken me from my aunt's apartment accompanied me as we entered the orphanage. The open foyer was nice as well, there was black and white tile that spanned a good thirty to forty feet with wrap around stairs that lead to the housing of the other orphans.

A catholic nun greeted me as I was looking around taking in my new surroundings, she was slim with a youthful face. Sister Milica is what the other children called her. She had only been working at the orphanage for just a few years now. She was an orphan herself growing up and spending a short time of her adult life out in the world she felt the conviction to give back to society. Maybe she saw that the orphanage was her only way to help better the world, she knew so many were lost in the world, and this was her way of helping them to find their way. And that's what she wanted to do, too just to give a little direction so others might find their way in life. Maybe it gave her a sense of self-peace or a self-worth, sacrificing for the good of others. Whatever her calling was it engulfed in the presence of peace and a warm gentle smile that greeted me with kindness at the door. She had a way of making one feel at home.

"Harold, is it?"

"Yes ma'am?" I replied with slight curiosity. How did this woman know my name knowing she never has met me before?

"I'm sorry for your loss. We have a few young ones here as well who've suffered the same as you, I'm sure you would fit in well here with others."

I didn't know if that was supposed to make me feel more comfortable about my situation but at least the other kids could identify with me and I likewise. But still I was the new kid, and I didn't know how others would receive me. I didn't only worry about myself but my brothers as well and how they were going to cope with their new surroundings and if I would ever see them again? Would I be able to contact them? And Aunt Louise what was she going to do, could she somehow get custody of us boys? So many questions ran through my mind, was I going to get fired for missing work at the printing company? Was Mr. Owensby going to be okay? What was going to happen? Would I be here forever? All I wanted was my aunt, my brothers, and my job back, but most importantly I wanted Dad back!?

"Yes ma'am, my name is Harold but sometimes my youngest brother calls me Har Har. It's short for Harold."

"I see they didn't give you much time to pack any belongings," Sister Milica said.

"No ma'am, they didn't."

"Well, we can see what we can do to get you some belongings if you'd like?"

"Yes ma'am, I think I'd like that."

"I would have hoped certain individuals would not have been in such a hurry and showed some compassion on those less fortunate," she replied turning to look at the police officer who had brought me to the orphanage.

"Compassion and patience go a long way does it not officer?" Sister Milica asked.

I think she might have struck a nerve with the officer. Looking up at his rough exterior I seen him get a lump in his throat and trying to muster up some words to bravely defend himself of his actions, but nothing came out.

"You may go now sir, I can take it from here," Sister Milica said gracefully.

Wow did she just make a grown man crumble to mere putty with her words? I never seen someone with such poise and wisdom. I suppose the officer must have felt some guilt because he had nothing to say for himself. At least she seemed to care for my needs, unlike the gentleman who brought me here.

"I like the name Har Har!" she replied and turning to look at the officer once again with a not so approving stare giving the hint it's time for him to leave.

"I will see what I can do to get some of his things," the officer said hastily.

"That would be a real generous thing for you to do, maybe next time you won't be in such a hurry?"

"My apologies ma'am, good day!" The officer said humbly

taking in account that he had been in a hurry and didn't take in the matter that us three boys might need some extra clothing or some personal belongings.

"My brothers, where did they take them? Will I be alone here without them?"

"There's another orphanage in upstate New York. I'm sure that's where they are headed," the Officer replied

"Thanks sir," I replied as I lowered my head in sadness at the thought of the distance between us, my heart sunk deeper than the Grand Canyon. As if the walls of my heart had mountains on every side and there was no way to see the top without a glimpse of light, the mere glimmer of hope to see my brothers again seemed alien to me as if that mountain of hope was swallowed up in doubts. Little did the officer know but these words shattered any hopes of seeing my family again.

That night as I laid in my new bed the light made its way through the widow that hovered a few feet from my bed. I prayed Lord please help my family, I don't want to be alone. I want my aunt, my dad, my brothers if you can please help me.

Funny how prayers sometimes aren't just prayers but it's us calling on a higher power greater than us. It's the substance that forms the healing of our souls, it's the breach of peace extended with in us calling out for us to have a chance to feel some comfort. It's the revelation within our spirit recognizing that we're not always alone and we have someone to talk to even in our darkest hours. Sometimes prayers don't come back the way we intended them to be or what we hoped for but it's the moment we call out that has substance and becomes the things hoped for.

I remember one time my dad and us were fishing on the Darren River down in South Georgia, and an old man's boat capsized at the waves of passing boat and it threw him overboard. He must have been in that water for some time until a passing boat had heard him cry out for help. I think sometimes about that old man in the water and how if he didn't call out no one would have saved him. That's just like prayer, if we don't call out who's going to answer?

I knew it would take some miracle lying there in bed but what else did I have? The odds were against me and if there was a miracle on its way it needed to hurry up. All I knew was that God had a lot of people to influence to make it happen. But in his vast wisdom he always has a plan if we see it or not! It's just up to us to notice along the way and give some thanks even if we don't yet see the end results, this is what we call hope!

CHAPTER EIGHTEEN

A little time had passed since that night, and I had no idea that little prayer I made lying in bed was about to make its way back to me. What I dreamed up in my mind was far from the reality that was about to take place, as matter-of-fact reality was far removed from my understanding. That answered prayer had something different in store for me.

It was lunch time as I sat with my friends when I heard my name being called at mail time. This must be a mistake; I've never gotten mail the whole time I had been here. I'm not even sure if Aunt Louise or my brothers knew where I was or had any information on my whereabouts. Surely if they had known anything I would have gotten mail from them by now.

"Harold Stanfield?" a young man called out.

Yes, I must not be mistaking he called out my full name as I sat in disbelief quickly raising my hand, shockingly surprised.

"Here I am," I said eagerly as the young man made his way to me. Each step he took towards me seemed like a lifetime as I held in my excitement and waited for my letter.

My mind rushed with so many thoughts, was it my brothers, my aunt, surely, she's writing me, who could it be, maybe they had got good news and I was getting out of here?!

As the young man arrived to where I was sitting, I noticed the letter in the envelope seemed rather bulky as if someone really took the time out to write me a long letter. As he started to hand me the envelope, I noticed fancy lettering which struck me oddly and I admired it closely when he handed it to me.

"Sorry sir, I am late, but I have been rather busy. I hope the letter is well received." The young man smiled as he walked away.

Who is this from I thought as the name of the sender had no address on it just the name, that read *The King of Adventure*. My curiosity was piqued even more at the name *The King of Adventure* and what all of this meant.

As I opened the letter, I discovered a familiar texture of paper. It was the same kind of paper they used down at the newspaper to print the daily news on. There were several blank pages of paper as it appeared to be cut in several different pieces to fit into the envelope and a message that read:

Whatever you draw or write, it will all come true, you're the author of your own adventures!

What did this all mean, I'm the author of my own adventure? I was rather puzzled at the message but none the less I was a kid and adventure was part my passion, maybe not as passionate as my older brother or not as daring as my older brother. I was the levelheaded one, the odd one out of the bunch. If I saw danger in anything I would flea in a heartbeat. Surely, they sent it to the wrong brother. I loved adventure but not enough to be a dare devil. I guess this king of adventure guy knew something I didn't, maybe he knew it was something I needed in my life outside these four walls. What could it hurt to draw something or make up some adventure and write it down? Heck I was a kid, using my imagination was second nature. Besides, maybe that's what I needed to use my imagination, something to be the comfort inside all this pain harboring at the shores of my life. Maybe the king of adventure knew I needed an escape from reality. After all, isn't that what stories do is give us an escape?

Later that evening laying in my bed my thoughts took place as I stared over to the envelope with the blank newspaper sticking out of the from the corners. It's like it was somehow calling to me, I wished I were back home in Georgia on the river with my dad and brothers like the times we use to go fishing, or better yet like those old big sail boats that I used to see sailing on the shorelines of the ocean. I could just sail away from all these troubles.

I could just imagine it, the wind hitting my face, the ocean blue water splashing upon the deck of the boat, the smell of the ocean, and the breeze that carried us away in the middle of the sea where nothing could ever take us away from each other ever again, no war, no orphanage only us and the sea. Yes, we would be the captains of our own destiny. That's it I said to myself, that's what I'm going to do I'm going to draw a sailboat.

I set up from my bed and for a brief moment I felt in my gut like something was about to happen. I didn't know what it was but just the decision of drawing a sailboat felt like destiny. I cannot place my finger on it, but something had stirred within me and there was no turning back. I had to do this for my own state of mind.

I grabbed my pencil, took the paper out of the envelope, opened it up, placed it out on my desk and began drawing the ship. It was like something guided my hand; the ship looked just like a ship you would see an artist draw. Everything from the sails right down to the bow of the ship, all in perfect detail. It was as if Van Gogh himself was taking hold and drawing it himself, or the spirit of DaVinci had taken hold of the pencil.

I stepped back, pushing myself away from the desk, dropping the pencil from my hands as it fell from the desk rolling onto the floor and coming to my sense's as I was in a trance.

"What just happened?" I said loudly in utter shock. How can this have happened? I stared down at the work of art I had just drawn knowing this just wasn't impossible.

Then all of a sudden, the room turned dark. I felt utter fear unlike a fear one normally fears, this was beyond any fear I ever felt. Darkness had darkness and that darkness had darkness. I cannot describe it but I knew something was about to happen.

When I woke from my sleep the next morning snuggled in my bed with sleepy eyes, I thought that was one crazy dream. Confusion set in as I set up in my bed and a mysterious noise made a thumping sound outside in the courtyard.

''What is that loud sound coming from outside?" I asked as I sat up from my bed intrigued, especially never hearing that noise before and taking in account of the strange event that had occurred the night before. My mind curiously enquired in the matter.

"What sound are you talking about, are you alright?" my roommate Dexter replied looking as if I had lost my mind.

"Yea, I think so. What happened?"

"Nothing happened, what are you talking about?" Dexter asked.

I suppose Dexter had no clue to what had happened to me the night before and I had no clue as to why was I waking up to some thumping noises coming from outside courtyard.

"Are you sure you're okay?"

"Yea, I think so!" I replied but was I really okay? Clearly

these events were not normal, the drawing, the darkness, now the thumping, maybe I wasn't okay, but I had to know what that thumping noise was.

"You're acting very strange today," Dexter said as I stood at the doorway trying to figure out what that noise was.

"Are you sure you don't hear that? It's loud, very loud," I insisted.

"No. I don't hear anything, what does it sound like?"

"A big thumping noise!"

"I don't hear anything but if it will make you feel better, we both can go and try to find whatever you hearing to ease your mind."

"Yeah, let's do that, Dexter."

As we made our way to the foyer and down the stairs of the orphanage, I froze not believing my eyes.

"Why are you stopping?" Dexter asked.

As I looked out the bay windows, I think Dexter was right. I found out exactly what the thumping noise was, and I think I just lost my mind too.

Those thumping noises were the sounds of wind blowing through the sails of a ship sitting outside in the courtyard. The same kind of ships that I used to see sailing off the ocean shores down on Tybee Island when my dad took me and my brothers to the beach every summer.

"Do you see that?"

"See what?"

"The ship in the courtyard."

"Okay, you have really lost it. There's no ship in the courtyard!" Dexter replied as he perked up one of his eyebrows behind his glasses.

"Well, I see a ship!" I said as made my way to the foyer and opened the door to the orphanage and pointed at the ship in the courtyard. "How can you not see it? It's a giant ship sitting right there on the grass?"

"Ships don't sail on grass."

"Yea, I know," I answered realizing maybe I'm just losing my mind.

"There's no boat Harold. Maybe you should go and see one of the nurses."

But there it was plain as day. My newly drawn adventure waited on me, parked out on the lawn. It all made sense now, it was the drawing after all. The King of Adventure did say whatever you write or draw will come true. And there it was with its sails flapping in the wind calling me, with my heart beating fast in my chest.

"Where are you going?" Dexter asked.

I turned back and smiled with a tear rolling down my face, overwhelmed with emotion, knowing my escape from all my troubles sat in the courtyard of the orphanage and the flapping of the sails were beckoning to me saying come aboard young man.

"I'm going on an adventure Dexter. I'm going on an adventure!" I replied.

I turned and made my way to my destiny, and as I came near the ship a stairway appeared out in front of me in the shape of clouds. I heard a horn blown and a voice shouting saying all aboard, all aboard, hurry the ship is about to depart.

As soon as I placed my foot upon the cloudy stair we were at sea. I could see the ocean. It was clear blue and in my soul was peace.

Chapter Nineteen

The orphanage I had been staying at was in a disarray after my disappearance and concern fell upon the nuns.

"What do you mean he is gone, Dexter?" Sister Milica asked.

"He just went out into the courtyard and disappeared," Dexter replied.

Sister Milica became really concerned, this is not the first time this had happened to kids at the orphanage. These events often happened where the kids would be gone for a few days and return not the same.

"This is another one of those bad omens," she said as she held her cross neckless in her hand hoping for the best.

Later that day was far spent with anguish. Sister Milica and the other nuns knew they would have a tough time explaining the missing ordeal to the head priest who was making a surprise visit that day.

Sister Milica and the other nuns stood at the doorway of his office, nervous to enter and face consequences of a missing child. They waited patiently on how they would devise their words to the head priest.

"Come in," the head priest said as he set at his desk looking over at the nervous nuns.

"So, you have something to tell me. Your facial expressions are giving you away, what seems to be the trouble?"

With a nervous stutter one of the sisters, Priscilla, spoke up. "We have a missing child again."

"Again?" the head priest asked.

"Yes sir, again. You see, sometimes a kid comes up missing and he or she is gone for a few days then they come back but not the same as before. They come back telling tall tales. Of course, that's how kids are, they tell tall tales"

"Really? Tall tales and what kind of tall tales do they tell you?"

"It really depends sir, some say they were on safari in Africa. Another said they were hunting treasure in the Amazon of South America. Some even said they were in a big house with all their family. Stories tend to change depending on the child."

"And who is this kid that's missing? I would like to see his room."

"His name is Harold Stanfield. He had been staying with his aunt in New York City, but he lost his father to the war and he was separated from his brothers. He is a good kid, never gave us any trouble," Sister Milica replied.

"I see, and now all of a sudden he just disappears?"

"Yes sir."

"And I do suppose there was someone who seen him before he went missing?"

"Yes, Sir his roommate Dexter said he disappeared in the courtyard and said he saw a ship."

"A ship huh? Now I find that interesting."

Moments later the priest and the nuns stood looking in my room inquiring about my missing presence as they looked around to find some sort of evidence to my whereabouts or some sort of clue to what might have happened to me. As the head priest observed the room, he noticed a torn envelope on the nightstand that read *The King of Adventure* that perked his interest.

"And you're Dexter, correct? Can you tell me what happened?"

"Yes Sir, Harold woke up and said he kept hearing a loud thump outside. I thought he had lost his mind."

"What do mean lost his mind?"

"I didn't hear no thump, then we went to see what was making the sound, the sound he was hearing, and we went outside to the courtyard and next thing I know he was gone."

"The night before, did he do anything strange or act strange at all?"

"No Sir, well he did draw a drawing of a ship. There's no way he could've drawn a ship that good. Come to think of it he said he saw a ship in the courtyard," Dexter said.

"I see."

"What do think this all means?" Sister Milica asked.

"I'm sure there's more to this story. If you don't mind, I would like to take a look around by myself."

"Yes Sir!" Sister Milica answered as she motioned to the other nuns to leave so the priest could examine the room.

When the small crowd of nuns, including the young boy Dexter, had left the room the head priest stood looking out the bedroom window, out into the courtyard where the ship had been sitting and smiled shaking his head. It was quite obvious to him what had transpired in the middle of the courtyard and why I was missing.

"You did it again didn't you? You did it again!"

Then he turned back looking to the chest of drawers with the opened envelope from the King of Adventure and tucked the envelope into his jacket pocket counseling the evidence from the those at the orphanage. He knew that the rest of the nuns or children wouldn't understand what was taking place, so it was up to him to keep the matter quiet until things returned to normal. He had seen this before, where kids from the orphanage had disappeared and came back with tall tales of great adventures. He himself was no stranger to adventures from the King of Adventure and as he turned to the door he said, "If an adventure is what you want, then an adventure is what they will get."

Chapter Twenty

While I took in my surroundings on the ship, a familiar voice spoke to me from out of nowhere.

"I see you made it. I was hoping you would join me on this adventure."

"Scotty?"

"Yes Sir, yours truly. So where are we going my Captain?" Scotty replied as he bowed taking off his sailors' hat.

"Are you the King of Adventure?" I asked with curiosity.

"Oh no sir my Captain, I'm not the King of Adventure, only you know that answer. I'm merely the servant of him."

"Did you send me the envelope?"

"No Sir dear lad, but I did happen to have part in preparing the letter for the King of Adventure. He did allow me to put it in the envelope and mail it out for him, though I must admit it was quit the honor to do so."

"So, you do know who he is?"

"Sir, only you know who he is," Scotty answered.

"What do you mean only I know who he is? You told me that he allowed you to put the paper in the envelop, so you must know who he is!?"

"Yes, and I must admit it was a great honor for him allowing me to do so, or else how would I get the chance to see your adventure unfold? Speaking of the envelope where is it?"

"I left it back at the orphanage," I said as I patted myself down knowing full well that I left it back at the orphanage not knowing moments later I would be sailing on a sailboat out at sea.

"Really, are you sure you left it back at the orphanage?"

"Yes, I'm sure of it Scotty!"

"Look into your coat pocket, Captain Har Har," Scotty commanded.

"But I'm not wearing a coat!" I answered doubting Scotty's words.

"Are you sure about that?" Scotty asked as he looked at me with a knowing eye and a slight grin.

"Yes, I'm sure!" I said. Then I looked down and sure enough I was wearing a captain's jacket just as Scotty had said, a sailor's jacket one that would predate back to the pirate days. It was dark blue with gold embroidery trim upon the pocket and cuffing on the sleeves.

"Your pocket!" Scotty said pointing to my jacket pocket. "Look in your left side pocket."

He was right, the envelop and paper were inside my left pocket along with my pencil I had from the orphanage.

"But how, this is impossible?" I asked.

How could this be I thought to myself, but the mere fact that I drew the ship into existence was beyond me and completely impossible. I couldn't help but doubt it all but here it was the letter and ship right in front of me.

"Nothing is impossible here," Scotty said to me as if he was reading my mind, knowing my very thought.

"How did you?" I asked pausing in disbelief.

Scotty shrugged his shoulder and said, "I just work here. I don't know how things happen, they just do but nothing happens here if no one writes it or draws it. That's what I do know."

"But you work at the newspaper factory," I replied.

"Oh yes, I do work there. It is a place where stories are told is it not?"

"Yes, it is I do suppose!"

"Wherever a story is I'm going to be there. Speaking of stories are you ready to start yours?"

"My story?"

"Yes, your story, your adventure, that's what the paper is for so you can write or draw your adventure. It's yours to write. Only you can tell your story. You're the author of your own destiny. So, tell me are you willing to write it and live the tale of many adventures, fight against imperial evil, sail across the seven seas, and tell the tale only few have told? The story is waiting on you young lad!"

As I held the paper in my hand I asked, "I can write anything, and it come true?" Yet my doubt was stirred with inspiration and inspired by his words as I greatly wondered at the possibilities.

"It's your story. It's as real as you believe it to be or should I say it's only as real as the ink on the paper, or should I say the adventure is as real as the writers who write it? So, tell me Captain, where shall our adventure begin?"

"I don't know," I said shrugging my shoulders while glazing down to the paper then back up to Scotty.

"Surely you have something in mind or else why would the King of Adventure have chosen you to write it? Or did you choose the King of Adventure?"

"You're confusing me Scotty," I said while momentarily pausing. I questioned, "What should I do?"

"You know what to do!" Scotty said with a mischievous grin.

"And what's that?"

"Write it!"

"What, write it? That's all I got to do, write it or draw it and it will come true?"

"Yes Sir, that's how it works. I don't know how it works it just does. So again, I ask you where are we going? Better yet what do you want?"

"I want to be with my dad and brothers again."

"Ah I see, so you have a desire, that's good. Now we must conquer the adversary to make an overcoming victory, so are you with me Har Har?"

"My brother calls me Har Har."

"Yes, I know. Actually, I know more than you think I know. But the thing I need to know is are you with me? I mean are you ready to face pirates, look into the eyes of a fierce dragon, take on a tyrant and save your father?"

"You mean I can save my father?"

"Isn't that what you wanted, to be with your family? Isn't that why you drew this ship? Isn't that the true desires of your heart, Har Har? If it is then let your pencil be your guide and make an adventure!"

"Okay, I want to make an adventure," I said as I opened up the paper and started to write. As soon as my hand began to move, light came from the paper with gold lettering in Latin. Then I heard two voices behind me say, "Where are we?" and when I turned my two brothers stood before me astonished taking in their surrounding of a huge ship that they both suddenly appeared upon.

"Har Har!" Timmy said as he ran up and hugged me. "Where are we Har Har?"

"On a ship out at sea, that's all I know."

"How did we get here?" Timmy asked.

"I don't understand it myself. All I know is I was just writing on this paper and you two showed up."

"Allow me to explain my dear lads!" Scotty suggested.

"Please do Scotty."

"Well, you see there's this king called The King of Adventure and he had a letter sent to your brother Harold and whatever he writes or draws on it comes true. Undoubtedly, he just wrote the two of you into the story so that's why you're here!"

"Wait a minute, I know you, you're Scotty from the newspaper company!" Danny said.

"Yes, that's me at your service," Scotty responded taking a bow.

"But how, I don't understand," Danny replied.

"Show them the paper dear lad and they may understand."

"See I was just writing. I think its Latin or something. All I know is I was writing, or something was writing it for me using my hand and then all of a sudden you both showed up. I know it sounds strange but what I think I understand is whatever we write or draw, an adventure comes true!"

"Show them and let them see for their self, Har Har," Scotty said.

"Look, here is the writing I wrote and it's somehow in Latin."

As I showed them the paper the words in Latin started to change from Latin to other languages. I saw what looked to be Spanish, back to Latin, to even English, and when it appeared in English it said, *and my brothers stood behind me startled and amazed.*

"You mean you can write anything?" Timmy asked with excitement.

"Yes Sir!!" Scotty answered with a nod and wink as he tipped his hat.

"Well, I want to be a warrior. Can I be a warrior or a soldier of some sort?" Timmy asked.

"Well, I don't see why not, Timmy?" then turning to me Scotty said, "Give the young lad the pencil and paper and let's see if he becomes a soldier, tell you the truth Captain I'm quite interested in seeing this for myself!"

As I handed my little brother the paper and pencil my intentions matched that of Scotty's. I wanted to see if the powers at be worked in my younger brother's favor as well as it had worked for me, I guess I just wanted to see it standing from the outside looking in. Sometimes in life we have to look from the outside to see what's going on within. I might have been smack dab in the middle of the greatest adventure in my life but if it wasn't shared with two of the greatest people I had ever known then what was it worth? My eyes eagerly fastened on my brother's hopeful experience, and it wasn't just his experience taking place it was mine as well, it wasn't just his adventure nor mine but ours.

Timmy placed his hand holding the pencil on the sheet of paper and just as it happened to me something took control of his hand and it began to write words on the paper in different languages, and when he was done we looked, and Timmy was dressed in a soldier's outfit that appeared to be a soldier's outfit of the 1400's. Timmy always looked up to Dad a lot so I think that's why he wanted to be a soldier cause Dad himself was a soldier fighting the German army, so I guess this was his way of honoring our father.

"Look I'm a soldier just like Dad. But this hat is kind of weird!" Timmy said as he tugged at the huge hat on his head trying to fix it. But it just kept slipping off his forehead falling over his eyes.

"Wait a minute, if Timmy is dressed in an old soldier outfit and Harold is dressed like a captain of a ship over a few hundred years ago and we're in some adventure and you can write anything and it comes true, tell me Scotty what year are we in?" Danny asked.

"You are in the 1400's, back when treacherous pirates ruled the seas, who savagely pilfered the lands in search of untold treasures!" Scotty answered in a pirate's voice.

Timmy's interest perked and he responded repeating Scotty saying, "Treasures and gold?"

"Treacherous pirates, I don't know if I like the sound of that!?" Danny nervously said.

"Yes, and a fierce pirate that goes by the name of One-eyed Steve," Scotty replied.

Timmy busted out laughing and said, "That's a funny name for a pirate!"

"Funny you say, but dangerous, very dangerous, even the sharks them self are afraid of him!?"

Timmy's eyes got big and round at the mere thought even sharks were terrified of One-eyed Steve. Even my old my brother Danny was shocked at even hearing about the sharks from Scotty, though Timmy might have had a moment of shock and disbelief himself that One-eyed Steve might be as fierce as Scotty had mentioned but opposition never deterred Timmy from any conflict. I don't know if he was just brave or just too young to be too scared. Well, I suppose he was a little scared at times but more the less he never showed any fear of confrontation. Needless to say, he was fearless to a point it was dangerous, and that's how he liked to live sometimes, hanging on the edge but never the type to let go of the edge but just tested his limits. I admired my little brother for this at times, if it had not been for these adventures I don't think I'd been so eager to get out of my own way of thinking. Needless to say, I think we were learning to become fearless in a fearful time, even when we sometimes felt the fear and was too proud to show it.

"If sharks are scared of him, he must be really bad?" Timmy said.

"Yes, he is bad. He even has a big black eye patch over his eye to prove it!" Scotty replied.

Timmy then began trying to hold back his smirky laughter but could not refrain it and blurts out, "An eye patch, that's not scary! You should have seen my lunch lady at the orphanage!"

"Scotty, why are you talking in a pirate's voice?" I asked.

"Well, who else will be the narrator of this great adventure arr..?"

"Arr..," Timmy said as he giggled joining in with Scotty impersonating a pirate.

"Arr.. arr..," Scotty said again.

Timmy laughed and said, "You're funny!" Then turning to me and said, "Isn't he funny Har Har, arr.. arr..?"

"Arr.. arr.. where shall we go Captain Har Har?" Scotty asked.

"Let's go and fight One-eyed Steve!" Timmy said as he grabbed the pencil and paper and before we knew it Timmy had written on the paper saying the sea was foggy and looming ahead was the danger of One-eyed Steve and his company of pirates.

"What did you just write?" I asked grabbing the paper from Timmy to reveal the writing of the dangers ahead.

"I don't know let's read it?" Timmy replied not knowing what he wrote.

"Oh no," I said putting my hand to my head, "we got to fight pirates?"

"And get their gold!" Timmy said with his adventurous smile.

Just as he got his words out, a big loud bang came from out of the fog that surrounded our ship.

"What was that?" Danny yelled as he ducked in fear knowing that this was about to take a turn for the worst.

"That is no other than One-eyed Steve!" Scotty replied as he held onto the bow of the boat as the boat swayed back and forth from the incoming waves.

"One-eyed Steve, you got to be kidding me?" Danny said.

"And his company of pirates, don't worry older brother I'm a soldier and I will protect us!" Timmy said holding up his sword.

"Glad to see your confidence shining through at this present moment," Danny spouted back as another blast fires off.

"Quick! We got to out sail these guys. I'll take the helm, Danny mend the sails, Timmy you're in charge of the cannons."

"But this ship doesn't have cannons on it, and we don't have a crew to help us fire the cannons back at One-eyed Steve. How are we going to fire without any cannons on the ship?" Danny asked as a splash of water hit him from a cannon ball hitting the water from outside the boat.

"Write it in the story!" I yelled as I took control of the helm of the ship.

Another shot blasted through the air landing in the waters next to us splashing water upon us.

"Hurry, hurry I can see them! They are gaining on us!" Danny screamed as he looked back to see in the foggy distance the shape of a ship gaining on us with pirates at the front of the ship holding out their swords.

"I got it!" Timmy said as he grabbed the paper and begin to write.

Just as before the paper began to shine with gold lettering that read, *gunmen stood ready along with crew members of the ship preparing for the battle against the treacherous pirate One-eyed Steve as they loaded the cannons and stood ready with swords in hand to defend Captain Har Har and the rest of the ship mates.*

"Did you write it?"

"Yes, I wrote it!" Timmy yelled.

"Are you sure?" and as soon I said those words I looked and there were crew members standing sword in hand ready to defend the ship and my crewmen stood ready with torches to light the cannons with fire.

"We will not let them take us Captain Har Har!" One of the crew members shouted.

I turned the helm of the ship with all my might straining with all the strength I had to turn my ship lining up the cannons to aim at pirate One-eyed Steve's ship. One careless move and we were goners. Everything had to be done right, there was no room for mistakes.

"Quick! Help me turn the ship to the right!" I spouted to one of crew members standing by in the bow of the ship.

"Yes Sir, Captain Har Har!" he replied without haste.

As we started to make the turn, over our heads fibers of wood shattered from the blast of a cannon ball ripping through one of the posts above us, nearly splitting in two one of the logs that the sails were connected to as the crew members ran for cover from the flying debris.

"Timmy as soon as I make the turn and I give the word tell the men to fire their cannons upon One-eyed Steve's ship."

Timmy looks at the ship gaining on us and screams, "They're

getting close!" Then he does a cross sign over his forehead and chest and screams, "Maybe this was a bad idea Har Har?"

"You think?" Danny says.

"Come on, come on!" I said arguing with the helm trying to turn it as I strained with all my might. "Yes, yes we've done it!" I said as we lined the ship up for the perfect view of firing.

"Timmy, fire at will!" I screamed as loud as I could. "You heard him, fire" Timmy gave command to the crew members.

Bang! Bang! Bang! The cannon balls fired through the air leaving a trail of smoke from the cannons accompanied with fire, sending one of the cannons in the front of One-eyed Steve's ship ripping the front of the ship wide open as water begin to pour into their ship. As their crew members scurried with buckets to capture the water that was gushing in from the sea through the hole in the ship.

"Direct hit! We hit them Har Har!" Timmy screams.

"Turn on ward to their ship. We will take them on!" I bravely commanded as the crew members stood ready with sword in hand.

"Prepare for battle mates!" One-eye Steve commanded as we made it close enough to hear. As soon as we made our way to engage, One-eye Steve looked and laughed and said, "You cannot win Captain Har Har!"

I was shocked. How did pirate One-eyed Steve know me and how did he know my name was Har Har?

"How does he know your name Harold?" Danny asked.

"I don't know, Danny!"

"You think you can come here and we not know who you are Captain Har Har? We know who you are, and you may have got us this time but there's always tomorrow! Don't think I will let you get away with what you have done to me!"

"What have I done to you?" I screamed.

"They don't call me pirate One-eyed Steve for nothing. Oh, you don't know do you?" He asked as he put his hand to his eye. "All I got to say to you Captain Har Har is an eye for an eye and I want your eye!"

"Never going to happen, fire upon them!" I commanded.

The smell of smoke hovered in the air with the loud sounds of the cannons firing away as another round of cannons were hitting and crippling One-eyed Steve's ship even more.

"Well, it's been fun but not fun enough, Har Har!" One-eyed Steve said as he held up a paper and pencil and begin to write, then vanished from out our sight.

As I stood in shock at his disappearance it was clear to me that The King of Adventure had sent him a letter as well and something told me this was not the last time I'd see the likes of One-eyed Steve.

The sea could be heard gently hitting the side of the ship making light splashing sounds while the sails flapped in the wind as the rope on the sails thumped lightly on the ships pole.

I stood there looking out from the deck of the ship trying to take in all of what just had happened and with heavy thoughts thinking what did he mean an eye for an eye, how could I have anything to do with his eye? This was my first adventure, and I didn't even know him from Adam!?

"Scotty, what was he talking about?"

"Who you mean dear Captain?"

"One-eyed Steve, he said an eye for an eye!"

"Only you can know what he is talking about, but you have not yet lived that part of the adventure and when it happens it will all make sense, but I can't tell you. You'll have to find out on your own."

"What do you mean Scotty, quit talking riddles!?"

Even though I understood what he meant, I haven't lived that part of the adventure yet and there was no clear answer from Scotty, and a clear answer is what I needed.

"Har Har the adventure is nothing but a riddle. Only you can solve your troubles and the only way to solve them is to live them," Scotty replied.

"How do I do that by writing my adventure?"

"Now you're starting to see the big picture Har Har. The story and ending are within you. You just got to trust it, trust what you really want will come to pass and it will happen. It's the heart of a man that forwards his journey. So now tell me boys, are you willing to see what lies ahead of you or are you willing to go back to the way things were before? This is now or never. The adventure lies in your imagination!"

"I don't want to go back to way things were," Timmy said,

"Me either!" Danny added, "I was miserable."

"Okay, let's do this!" I said.

"Tell me boys, what the one thing your heart desires the most? Better yet, what do you think brought you here?" Scotty asked.

"The King of Adventure brought us here!" I said.

"Yes, you're right, but that's not all is it Captain Har Har?"

"I know the answer you're looking for!" Timmy said.

"Do tell!" Scotty answered.

"We all want our dad back!"

There we stood, three brothers from Georgia in the middle of an adventure of a lifetime ready to take on pirates or anything that lay ahead of us. We were eager and full of hope. What use to look like a dark and grim path that life had so harshly and deceitfully played on us just seemed to fade away with the help of a little letter from The King of Adventure. All we knew was that we held the future in our own hands. So, we sought with hope and was filled with the sense of a new day upon us, and we were going to get our father back! We were going to be brothers and there was nothing that could separate us ever again and as I looked at my brothers on the deck of that ship, we looked into each other's eyes, and we knew we held our destiny in our own hands. There we stood brothers. And this was the beginning of the adventures of brotherhood.

Chapter Twenty-One

"I like it Grandpa, the adventure of brotherhood," Johnny said as he sat down listening to his grandfather tell his story.

"Well, it does have a little ring to it, I do suppose," Grandpa replied.

"So, what happened next? What was your next adventure?" Johnny asked.

"Well, the next adventure took place in the dark ages."

"This is my favorite part," William said.

"Yea, you always liked Draggy," Grandpa Harold said as his son was eagerly listening as he did when he was a child.

"Who's Draggy?" Tomas asked.

"Draggy was a fierce fighting dragon. He helped defeat your grandpas' enemies, I mean not that it's real it's just a story," William replied passionately.

It had been years since he heard any of his father's stories and for a brief moment William felt like he was five years old again reliving his childhood through the stories of his father.

"Yes, he was a fierce fighting dragon and my best friend," Grandpa Harold said.

"How did you become friends with a Dragon?" Johnny asked.

Well, our intentions had not changed much. We wanted to save Dad from the Germans. Months had gone by and we had heard no news of his whereabouts or if he was dead or not, and the only way we had a chance to save Dad was for us to go to Europe.

Just like the previous adventure we knew we had to do something. Little did we know we would end up in the dark ages.

Our ship had landed on the shores of England, it was a rough time with many people in a disarray and poor.

The locals had long time feared the presence of a fierce dragon who tormented them with his presence. The towns' people were starving and believed the dragon brought evil on their land. Many attempts were made to destroy him, they called to their king for help and the king sent his knights, but the knights could never prevail against him in battle. He out witted them all in battle cause the battle could not be won with might but with cunning of the mind, and the one who knew the dragon's weakness could be the only one to beat him.

Now, as our boat landed a knight in armor awaited at the docks for us, his body armor glistened in the sun, his sword was mounted to his side.

"Oh, there you are. You finally made it. We sent out a letter for your arrival."

"Letter, we never revived a letter?" I replied.

"Surely you received a letter. Look in your jacket pocket."

"But I haven't one," I said as I touched my coat pocket and sure enough there was a letter.

"Scotty?" I inquired.

Flipping up his face shield Scotty reveled his face, "Why yes sir Captain, it's me Scotty at your service."

"But how did you know we would be here?"

"Do you think you're the only ones The King of Adventure has been sending letters to? He knows what he is doing, even if we don't know it now, he sees the outcome far ahead of us. He even knows how this little adventure might affect you fifty years from now!?"

"So, what's this adventure?"

"It's an adventure of wisdom versus strength. A man is not as mighty as that which is sweet!"

"What do you mean?"

"You will be facing a dragon, a fierce dragon and once he is defeated you will see his true form."

"I don't know about no dragon. I'd rather face a bunch of rats!" my brother Danny said.

"Speak for yourself, I hate rats too!" I replied.

"Dragon? Really a real-life dragon?" Timmy's excitement grew.

"Yes, a real live dragon with fangs, claws, and scales," Scotty replied gesturing like a dragon with his hands and facial expressions.

"Does he have a tail as well?" Timmy asked.

"Yes, even a tail, a long tail!" Scotty replied,

"How can we fight against a dragon?" I asked.

"Have you learned nothing yet, Captain Har Har? As long as you write it and draw it, it comes true," Scotty replied.

"Wait, if we are going to fight a dragon shouldn't we at least be dressed like we could fight him?"

"Excellent point you have their Danny, like I said all you have to do is…"

"Write it!" Timmy said cutting off Scotty's words as he grabbed the paper and begin to write.

As soon as Timmy began to write, suddenly we all were

dressed in knight's armor.

"Now this is cool! You gotta try this," Timmy said as he flicked his face shield back and forth.

Timmy was like that at times when he was excited. He got extremely excited and when he was sad, he was extremely sad and of course my older brother Danny couldn't help but join in the excitement flickering back and forth his face shield.

"Hey, look! We're wearing a knight's armor, but we need a sword and shield," Danny said.

"Coming right up!" Timmy said as he drew another drawing with us holding both a sword and shield.

"Now you're ready. All you have to do is face the fierce dragon," Scotty said.

"Where is he?" Timmy said holding up his sword.

"Through the valley on the other side of the hill and remember this isn't a fight of strength but wisdom."

"How can we fight him with our wisdom? We have swords, surely we can defeat him in our armor?" Danny replied.

"It's a test of wits as opposed to strength. Without wits one may never possess strength!"

"So, how do we do that?" Danny asked.

"You must figure out the riddle set before you."

"And what is this riddle?"

"I have told you a man is not as mighty to that which is sweet."

"A man is not as mighty to that which is sweet, I don't get it!" Danny said.

"Don't worry about that now, you will figure it out. The King of Adventure already knew you would figure it out or he wouldn't have sent you on this mission. When the time comes you will know what it means, and you will defeat the dragon!"

CHAPTER TWENTY-TWO

As we journeyed into the unknown facing the fierce dragon with fear accompanied with courage, we made our way through the ridged rocky valley to the dragons' lair. The winters' wind of England made a chill upon my skin and ran through my bones. Maybe it wasn't just the cool wind that brought the chills but the fact this was dangerous. And the eerie feeling something bad was about to happen lingered all over my skin raising the hairs on the back of my neck. However, my fear was mingled with excitement, and this was an adventure worth embarking upon. How many people can say they fought a dragon and won? Clearly The King of Adventure knew we would defeat the dragon or else he wouldn't have sent us. There was no way he would've put us in this situation unless he thought we would defeat him. At least my thoughts comforted me in the matter believing in The King of Adventure. As we made our way to the pit of victory or failure, surely nothing would go wrong, right?

The screams of a monstrous creature echoed in the hillside as if it was calling out to its dinner. It was not an eerie scream but a violently hateful scream. The kind of eerie feeling you get as a child when your foot is hanging off the bed and at any moment in the middle of the night the boogie man is going to come out from under your bed and grab you by the foot and drag you down into the dark abyss of the under the bed monster world. The only thing was, instead of moving your foot back on the bed and making yourself free from the boogie man that waits for you in the middle of the night, we were dangling both of our feet off the bed in the face of the boogie man. But it wasn't the boogie man we were facing. It was a fierce dragon, and this valley was our bed of despair.

If I had known what that day would've entailed, I might had given a second thought of ever setting foot on that ship or even embarking on an adventure with my brothers. But sometimes we do not see the forest through the trees and I for one didn't see what was lying ahead of us. Even though that eerie feeling grew stronger and stronger every moment as we drew closer and closer to the screams of the fierce dragon.

"He is getting closer." Danny said as he held up his sword looking round about in the air from what his helmet would allow him to see.

"I can't see anything; can you see anything Danny?" Timmy asked.

"No, I don't see anything!"

Then out of nowhere a gushing wind came blowing in knocking us off our feet as the loud sound of flapping wings echoed above our heads with a screeching terrifying scream of what could only be the fierce dragon. As a shadow covered us from the sun and everything all of a sudden went dark the wind could only be described as if someone had blown a breath of air on us. Looking back, I have no other conclusion, it was the breath of the dragon that had knocked us down.

"It's the dragon!" Danny shouted as he tried to stand and another wave of wind came gushing in knocking him down. Then the sound of his wings faded to near silence like how a train rolls down the track slowly disappearing in the distance. First you hear its loud roar then it's gone.

When I had noticed the sound had left, I stood to my feet gripping my sword waiting on the second wave of attack. The dragon might have surprised us the first time but now we were prepared, and the element of surprise was not on his side.

"Come on dragon!" I shouted with fearfulness waving my trembling sword as I looked upwards into the skies in every direction.

I knew I didn't want to fight him, but I knew if he came back, I sure was going to give him a fight. He might destroy me, but he was sure going to regret ever messing with me. That is one thing I knew for sure at the time or at least that's what I was feeling. Sometimes bravery is accompanied with fear or else it is not courage at all. If a man don't fear what might hurt him, he don't respect his own courage and courage is not built out of bravery but built out of what needs to be done, and in that moment, I knew only one thing I could do is stand up to the dragon even when my bones clearly said to me run. Maybe that's why I screamed at him maybe my screaming at him was my way of convincing myself I was ready to fight and maybe I just was trying to convince the dragon he didn't want to fight me. I was hoping for the latter of the two if not both.

"Harold," Danny softly said in a fearful tone. Then he began beckoning with a louder tone, "Harold will you just stop for a moment?" In an almost demanding scream.

"What?" I responded with an agitated tone.

"Look!"

We both gazed upon an empty knight's uniform as our brother Timmy was nowhere in sight. Undoubtedly the dragon had taken our youngest brother. The sorrow we felt at that moment was unbearable, coming to the harsh reality our brother is no longer with us. We just lost our father to the war now we just lost our little brother.

Chapter Twenty-three

Distraught and anguished at the thought of Grandpa Harold losing his brother to the dragon just put Johnny in an uneasy feeling. He loved everything in the Grandpa Harold's adventurous story right up to the point of him losing his brother. Johnny hated his older brother Tomas but now he was hearing what it was like to lose a brother and he couldn't help but feel compassion for Grandpa Harold's younger brother and oddly enough he put himself in his grandfather's shoes and wondered what it might feel like if he lost his brother Tomas, even though he had wished earlier that someone would just throw that football right into his bahoogies.

"But Grandpa your brother can't be dead!" Johnny said.

"Just calm down I will get to that," Grandpa Harold answered.

"There's no way anyone can survive the jaws of a dragon! Why did he take him, he didn't do anything to him?" Johnny asked.

"Ahh yes, but he knew we were there for him. One thing about dragons is they're very protective of their territory," Grandpa Harold replied.

"But that still don't make it right Grandpa!" Johnny said and with anguish as he turned to his dad and asked, "How can you like this story out of all of them? I don't get it, why would you love a story about a dragon who stole your dads' brother from him and probably killed him?"

"Just wait Son, the good part is coming up. You're gonna love it," William answered.

"I can't love a story where one of our family dies!" Timmy replied.

"He didn't kill him!" Tomas said trying to reassure his brother there was going to be a good outcome in Grandpa Harold's story.

"Have you ever met Uncle Timmy, Grandpa's brother? Neither have I, so how do we not know he wasn't killed, or even Great Grandpa when he was fighting the Germans?" Johnny answered with anguish.

"Grandpa, Uncle Timmy isn't dead, is he?" Tomas asked hoping his little brother Johnny wasn't right at his assumptions.

"Oh no, but we thought he was dead. I tell you boys there's nothing worse in the world than the feeling we felt thinking our brother was dead."

In that moment Tomas started realizing maybe he had been a little selfish when it came to his younger brother as he looked down to his brand-new football. It was his greatest passion but he had let a passion come between him and his own brother. Many times he played with his friends but never let his own brother play with him. He played in the rain, in the mud, and bonded with his team mates but now he began to notice it wasn't just about a game it was about the bonding of it all and there's no bond like brothers. Cause once the game is over, they're the ones who will be there when the lights and the glory are gone. There's no score board to call the points, just family and that's the only goal one needs in life.

"Grandpa, I don't know how you could've borne the thought of losing your brother. I mean that had to be the most horrible thing any brother could go through," Tomas said.

"Oh yes, losing a brother is hard and it's even harder on someone when they just don't know how much you care. It was always important for us to show each other how much we cared for each other, for us just being in each other's life was the way we showed it," Grandpa Harold replied.

Grandpa Harold may have looked like some old guy in his overalls, ball cap, and mud on his shoes from working out on the peanut farm, but there was a wise man under that ball cap. He knew he had struck a nerve in the two boys. I guess you can say Grandpa Harold had a way with words. The story wasn't only about him and his brother but a story to bring his two grandsons closer together. I guess you can't judge a book by its cover, even if it looks like an old man in a ball cap and overalls. Sometimes wise men come in all shapes and sizes. Grandpa Harold's wisdom often came from the heart and the imagination of heart. He often said there is no telling what the heart can do if we allow it to dream up something great. Maybe Grandpa Harold was dreaming up something great, maybe he was just dreaming up two brothers getting along.

CHAPTER TWENTY-FOUR

"He is dead isn't he, just like Dad?" Danny said as he teared up with anger throwing his helmet to the ground. He continued saying, "I want to go home. We shouldn't be here, we should be back in New York!"

"We can't go home, we got to find Timmy."

"We aren't supposed to be here, this isn't supposed to happen and especially to Timmy," Danny said as he fell to his knees and cried, "First Dad, now Timmy?"

"We will find him," I said as I extended my hand out hoping he would be inspired by my courage.

"How are we going to do that? We don't even know where we are. We would be better off in the orphanage than in this place. If this king of adventure never wrote you, we never would have lost our brother."

"We can use the paper to find Timmy," I replied.

"What, are you serious? Using the paper to find Timmy, that's the whole reason Timmy's no longer with us," Danny spouted as he stood up and grabbed my pouch from my side opening it up, ripping a page, wading it up, and throwing it down.

"Have you gone mad?" I retaliated.

We never once had an argument, and I didn't want to start one now. But I had to make him realize this was the only solution we had. If we didn't have the paper to write or draw on then there was no way we could find Timmy and no way of getting back home. It was expedient to convince him things were going to be okay, even though I was not feeling it myself.

"Look Danny you're my brother and I've always looked up to you, but in New York all we wanted was make Timmy happy after we lost Dad. And after we lost Dad, we all lost each other, and I'm not willing to lose you or him again. We got to try to find Timmy and I believe we can, but nothing happens if we don't try. You know Timmy would do the same for us!"

"I'm sorry!" Danny said as he wiped a tear from his eye and looked downward. "So you think he might still be alive?"

"He has to be right? I don't think all this is by accident, the letter or the adventure. Think about it, if I had not gotten the letter from The King of Adventure we would still be stuck in some orphanage right now not knowing where each other's at and might not ever see each other again! Honestly, I think that's the reason The King of Adventure chose us to go on an adventure in the first place. Maybe he wanted us all to be together again and maybe that's what this is all about? Just imagine it, three brothers against all hope having the chance to be family again. If we got to believe in something why not believe in this? When you came up with the plan to break into the paper factory did I back out? No, I didn't. I was scared but I went along with it because we had a purpose and a mission and if there has ever been a greater purpose than now, I don't know what is!"

"And what's that purpose?" Danny asked.

"We save our brother. There's no way he's dead. The King of Adventure wouldn't let anything happen to him. Remember,

Scotty said The King of Adventure sees things a far off. Then we have to think like The King of Adventure!"

"So, you're saying we got to see us saving our brother like some Nostradamus kind of thing?"

"Yes, can't you see all this had to happen for us to come closer, to be near each other? This is just part of our adventure, I am sure of it. Maybe this wasn't only about a dragon, maybe this was about brothers bonding with brothers, just like we had back home and got separated. Maybe we have a second chance to make things right!"

Somehow, I knew my plea would convince my older brother. After all, he did love the both of us and if it meant us being together, he would make the sacrifice. We knew for some reason destiny chose to take our brother and we were bound and determined to get him back and that was our destiny!

"So how do you suppose we do that, Har Har?" Danny asked.

And it was that moment a streak of brilliance overcame me. Maybe our little brother Timmy's genius ways were rubbing off on me I thought to myself.

"That's it!" I said excitingly."

"What's it?"

"Our little brother Timmy is a genius!"

"What are you talking about Har Har?"

"That's it!"

"What is it? You're losing me."

"You called me Har Har!"

"And what's your point? Where's the genius in that, I don't get it?"

"Our nick names, I'm Har Har and your Super Fly Danny!"

"What are you talking about?"

"Don't you get it? That's how we find our brother."

"Now I'm really lost, how is our names going to find our little brother?"

"It's not the names, but the character of our names."

"Okay, I'm lost again!"

"You see, we can draw anything or write anything right?"

"Yes, and your point is?"

"Well, you are Super Fly Danny, all you need is superpowers to fit your name."

"You mean make me a superhero?"

"Yea, why not? You already have the name, we can give you superpowers like flying."

"Or use this stick to shoot laser beams at our enemies," Danny responded with enthusiasm.

"Yes, now you're thinking Danny."

"I totally get it now. Yea, our little brother is a genius, isn't he?"

"Yea, and you know what he would say if he was here?"

"Yea, he would say 'Yea, I know I'm a genius.' So what about you Har Har, what will you be?"

"I don't know, I haven't thought about it. All I can pretty much do is draw. It's not like that has great potential."

"Are you serious? You gave me a pep talk and you're not even giving yourself the benefit of the doubt. You'll be called the artist and the writer."

"I like it!"

"So my artist brother, when are you going to draw me a cape and write down my superpowers?"

"Say no more," I replied.

I drew a cape and wrote his powers on the paper and as soon as I did golden like lights shined about him and a cape appeared with a stick in his hand.

"Whoa, look at me!" Danny said as he stood in amazement in a superhero's outfit.

"See, I told you we can do this. Nothing can stop us as long as we use our imagination."

"So how do I fly?"

"I don't know, maybe you got to take off running?"

"Yea, maybe you're right."

Danny took off running, leaped, and fell face first into the ground.

"Maybe it's not working. Maybe it won't let me fly?" Danny said.

"We wrote it and I drew it, it has to let you fly. That's part of the deal."

"What am I supposed to do?" Danny asked as he opened his arms beckoning for an answer.

Then all of a sudden his feet lifted off the ground about a foot.

"I don't know but I do feel a little taller for some reason!"

"You're not taller, you're in the air Danny!"

"Are you serious you mean?"

"Yes, you can fly, try it out!"

Danny looked up into the sky and took off into the air with the wind at his face and his cape flapping in the wind, overlooking the hills and valleys, flying across the countryside taking in its majestic beauty.

"I'm flying! I'm really flying! I can't believe it, this is awesome!"

As I stood watching my older brother fly in the distance a familiar voice spoke from behind me.

"So you figured out he was supposed to fly. I didn't think

you'd figure it out this soon."

As I turned Scotty stood there in his knight's outfit.

"Scotty, you knew all along he was able to fly?"

"Of course I did. You know I do know some things, not all things but some. But I can't tell you, you have to figure them out on your own."

"I think this is the first time you didn't speak a riddle to me Scotty."

"Well Sir, don't you fret none, there's plenty more riddles to come. But right now there's only one riddle you need to figure out."

"How am I going to figure it out?"

"You will trust me, just like you figured this one out or shall I say someone you know will figure it out."

"There you go again speaking riddles Scotty."

"Riddle me another one," Danny said as he landed on the ground.

"About the time you learned to fly, dear lad," Scotty replied.

"You knew all along?" Danny asked.

"I sure did. I know a lot, but you have to figure somethings out on your own or else it's just not that fun. Plus, someday you will have a great story to tell others."

"So boys, are you ready to set out on your great adventure?" Scotty said in an English accent.

"How are we going to find the dragon?" Danny asks.

"Sir, you already know!" Scotty replies.

"What do you mean, I already know?" Danny asked.

"You figured out how to not walk, now you got to learn to see."

"We got that figured out too. We got to see things from afar like The King of Adventure," Danny replied.

"Then in the air you shall see afar off. All you have to do is look and you will find your brother and will be on your way to new adventures that lie ahead of you."

"I got it, I'm supposed to find the dragon by flying. He is right Har Har, there's no way we would be able to find Timmy on foot, in the air is the only way to look for him."

"You're wise beyond your years there lad. So tell me boys, are you willing to go on a great adventure, the likes that some have dared to adventure?" Scotty asked.

"Yes Sir, more than ever," Danny replied.

I don't know why Scotty always said that to us. Maybe he was encouraging us to take a risk or just to inspire us. None the less, he always got us energized to take the next step even though we didn't really know what lay ahead of us. Looking back, that day taught me if we believe in our future anything is possible and the sky is the limit. And from that moment on there was no limit in what we could do.

Chapter Twenty-five

Timmy fell to the ground as he was released from the dragons' grasp landing on a grass covered field beside a small cave that looked to be the home of the dragon. The dragon locked eyes with Timmy, staring him down with a fierce and piercing look as if he were hungry and ready to devour him and Timmy knew this could be the end of his adventure.

The dragon had scales that interlocked across his body, a few large horns on his forehead, and a muscular physique. His appearance of strength was mightier than a thousand strong armed soldiers. He looked like he could break and snap a tree in half with just his powerful claws but strangely enough the dragon didn't snap him in half, just carried him away to his cave.

Many things ran through Timmy's mind, especially our lives back home in Georgia. The biggest thing he ever faced was losing our father to the war or having to leave our home in Reidsville. But this somehow seemed bigger. At least staring death in the face was bigger than all he had been through. What more could an eight-year-old go through in life without breaking down? Losing Dad was tough but now his life might end. He was six feet apart from life and death and it wore a crown of horns.

They say you see your life flash before your eyes. Timmy

never said his life flashed before his eyes, but he did tell us years later as he stared into the dragons' eyes all he could think about was Reidsville and Dad. Somehow his mind ran wild to the time Dad had just plowed the field and we were planting cotton seeds. Dad had a few seeds in his hands and made his little speech like he sometimes would.

"Sometimes we have to plow the field get all the bad things out of the way so we can plant a seed, but as long as all the bad weeds are in the way it just doesn't grow to its potential. So you got to pluck the weeds up by the root or we just might lose everything. It's better to put in some hard work to reap bountifully than to not labor and get nothing in return," our dad would always tell us.

Timmy thought any minute this dragon could just pluck him up and cast him like the weeds but for some reason the dragon had spared his life. Maybe the dragon meant him no harm but there was no proof that he didn't mean him any harm either. He didn't know why Dad's words crossed his mind in that present moment. Maybe there was a significance to it in the present moment or he just had to put his mind to work to figure out Scotty's riddle.

Timmy knew this could be his last moments in life. There was no way this dragon was going to let him go, even though his mind was already hoping for escape as he shook and trembled in fear. But there's no escaping from a creature mightier with strength and swift in flight. There was nowhere he could run. Timmy knew there was no hope of running, even if he tried. The dragon could just snatch him up at any time if he tried to attempt such an act. All he knew was he should keep quiet and maybe the dragon would grow weary of him and not hurt him and pluck him out of the land of the living like some weeds in a field.

As he closed his eyes, he could hear Aunt Louise in the kitchen mixing her cake in a bowl and the smell of chocolate lingering in the air.

"Can I lick the bowl, Aunt Louise?" Timmy asked.

Timmy always liked licking the extra chocolate batter from the cake bowl as Aunt Louise got ready to cook her famous chocolate cake. Looking back those were some of the greatest times growing up. Sometimes you don't know it then but when you get older you look back and think, wow, those were the best of times.

"Yes, you sure can Timmy" Aunt Louise replied.

"I love your chocolate cake Aunt Louise, it's the sweetest cake in the whole wide world."

Timmy jolted at his own words, opening his eyes and looking at the fierce dragon that stood before him. It was in that moment our little brother had a defining moment. Yes, I said it before and I say it again, our little brother Timmy is a genius. He knew just how to defeat the dragon.

"Oh my god, I'm a genius!" Timmy spouted.

CHAPTER TWENTY-SIX

"Told you he's not dead Johnny!" Tomas said listening to Grandpa Harold's story.

"You were right, he's not dead but I don't get it, how is he a genius?" Johnny asked.

"Well Son, I'll get to that!" Grandpa Harold replied.

William clapped his hands with excitement and eager to hear the tale of draggy as he did when he was a child all his childhood. Feelings started to run away with him like he did when he was a kid and he couldn't help but blurt out, "Oh good we are getting to the good part," William said with boy like excitement.

William's excitement grew as he eagerly awaited the reveal of Draggy. When he was a kid, he identified strongly with the dragon as well as his uncles in his father's story. He often thought what life would be like outside of his own life where things happened if you imagined them. Many nights he closed his eyes hoping one day he would open them and Draggy would be there to take him on a great adventure. But then William got older, and he stopped closing his eyes. But today William was starting to open them again and was dreaming with his imagination wide awake.

"Yes Son, you always loved what happened next," Grandpa

Harold said.

"Wait a minute, the dragon is Draggy isn't he?" Johnny asked.

"What makes you think that?" Grandpa Harold asked.

"Well, you said Draggy was your best friend and Dad always loved hearing about Draggy and Dad's getting excited over what's about to happen, so he has to be Draggy!"

"Yes Grandpa, he has to be Draggy. Unless there's other dragons in the story?" Tomas said.

"I see, looks like my brother is not the only geniuses in the family," Grandpa Harold replied.

"Yes, we are genius's Grandpa," Johnny said as he went to high five his older brother Tomas.

"I guess I can't pull the wool over your eyes, can I?" Grandpa Harold said.

"Well, you did make me think Uncle Timmy was going to die from the dragon!" Johnny responded.

"So what happened next, Grandpa?" Tomas asked.

"Well, as Timmy stood looking deep into the fierce dragon's eyes knowing he was a genius, knowing he had figured out a way to defeat him without weapons even though how mighty he appeared to him, he knew nothing is mightier than that which is sweet."

"I don't know Grandpa, it's hard to call him a fierce dragon now knowing he's really Draggy," Tomas said.

"Bear with me young fellas, just imagine he is fierce. Put yourself in Timmy's shoes for a moment like you know that your life is about to end, can you imagine it sons?"

"Yea Grandpa, I can imagine it, and he stinks really bad too!" Johnny replied, as held his nose playing along.

"Yeah, and not only does he stink but he has bad breath, and one ear is crooked." Tomas said.

"Oh, but can you feel the fear Timmy was feeling? That's what you need to feel. Can you imagine how dark the cave was?" Grandpa Harold asked.

"It had to be dark and the only light you could see was from outside being blocked from his towering figure," Tomas replied.

"Now you're using your imagination!"

CHAPTER TWENTY-SEVEN

"Chocolate cake! That's it, that's how we defeat you! No one can resist Aunt Louise's chocolate cake!"

What we had imagined to be a fierce dragon turned to mere putty at the sound of chocolate cake. The dragon's tail even started waging. What one would have thought would have been such a mean creature was just a lonely ole dragon wanting to have a friend and if bribery of chocolate cake would open the door to friendship, well, they both had motives and chocolate cake happened to be their declaration of peace.

"You're not a fierce dragon, are you?"

The dragon shakes his head no and smiles licking his lips like a dog begging at a supper table hoping for some bread to fall or hoping his master will see him and hand him some food.

"Your nothing but a big ole baby, aren't you?"

The dragon shakes his head yes up and down and wags his tail even more at the excitement of Aunt Louise's chocolate cake.

"So that's what Scotty's riddle meant, there's nothing mightier than that which is sweet. We don't fight you by strength, but we befriend you with chocolate cake!"

The dragon's eyes got wider to the sound of Aunt Louise's chocolate cake and he wagged his tail even more like a dog ready to chase after a stick that has been thrown. We had not had a pet since we had left Georgia. We had a few cows, chickens, dogs and a cat that totally ignored us, but a dragon was a different story. The cows loved the corn, the dogs well they would eat anything, and the cat was so picky it turned his nose up at everything. But we never had a dragon as a pet and luckily Timmy knew just what he liked. I've said it before, and I'll say it again, our little brother is a genius.

"I'm sorry but I don't have any chocolate cake on me."

You could see the excitement of the dragon turn to a saddened appearance as his eyes turned to a saddened look and he began to pout his lips and turn away, slowly moping to the corner of the cave where he laid down as his eyes began to water.

There's no telling how long Draggy lived in that old cave without any friends, the towns' folk were terrified of him, but he wasn't a bad dragon he just got a bad reputation for being a dragon like all the other dragons that people have encountered through time. He wasn't like them, he was good and playful. He had a good heart, but he just never had anyone to show his goodness to and here was Timmy. One minute he was terrified of Draggy then the next minute he figured out he wasn't there to hurt him and all it took to lighten up a dragon's world was some good ole chocolate cake.

"I might not have chocolate cake now, but I can get some. How does that sound?"

Draggy pops his head up like he'd just seen a roll of bread fall from the table and began to frantically wag his tail again. It's like he had been waiting all his life for a piece of chocolate cake or maybe he was just waiting his whole life for someone to care for him. Either way he was going to get some chocolate cake and a lot of love from three boys who needed a friend larger than life.

"Would you like that? Would you want some cake?"

Draggy shakes his head yes and stands to his feet and starts sniffing the air hoping to find a scent of chocolate cake as his tail knocked over a treasure chest on the other side of the room that had probably been there for ages. I remember hearing a tale back home from one of the kids at school about how he read in a book once that dragons guarded treasure and kept it hid from people who might use it for evil or safe guarded it for a king. But Timmy barely gave any notice to it he was enjoying the moment of making a good friend.

"Why are you sniffing dragon? I don't have the cake with me?"

When Draggy heard this, he came sad again and started to mope and laid back down.

"But I can get it for you," Timmy said.

Then Draggy became playful again laying on his side, turning over like he was doing tricks then began to crawl his way on the floor to Timmy dragging his legs and tail behind him.

"Look at you dragging your legs, a dragon dragging his legs. I think I will call you Draggy, how do you like that?"

Draggy shook his head up and down and put out his paw and went to shake my little brother's hand. My Little brother made a great friend that day, who later became our best friend but at the time we had no clue he had made friends with Draggy and that he was okay. But to us he was in danger of a fierce dragon and we were about to go save him. Little did we know all it took to win over the dragon was that chocolate cake. I guess we didn't need our knights' armor after all but none the less, we dressed for the occasion. If you asked me, we'd have been better off just dressing up in an apron with a bowl of cake mix, but sometimes you learn as you go. If he had not taken our brother, we would have not stumbled upon Danny's super powers or mine. I guess destiny has a way of making itself known sometimes even though we were trying to write it on our own.

Chapter Twenty-eight

"What, for real? Chocolate cake? That's how he beat the dragon?" Johnny asked.

"Yes, that's all it took was Aunt Louise's chocolate cake and if you ever had her cake, you'd known just what I'm talking about," Grandpa Harold replied.

"So, he wasn't a fierce dragon after all just some playful dragon wanting a friend?"

"Yes sir, you see sometimes in life all someone wants is someone to be a friend. You know Draggy is a lot like us all at times. We get mistaken for something we're really not and it just takes one person in the world to see the real us and when that one person sees the real us, we become happier than life itself. Every good thing that's inside of us is just waiting to come out in us. Some of us have a song hidden in us, some might have the funniest humor in the world, everyone has their own treasure inside of them waiting for the world to see. It just takes someone to take the time and notice it."

"I'm Draggy ain't I?" William said.

"What do you mean you're Draggy?"

"I've been hiding in my own cave in life. My work has been my cave and I haven't taken care of what's important in life."

"What are you saying, hon?" Carolyn asked.

"You and the kids you're what's important. I've been so busy trying to give you a life but I haven't been in your life."

"I know you've done your best, hon."

"I can't believe it, my dad's story made me look at my own life and what's important. God, I loved hearing about Draggy when I was a kid, and now I realize how I'm so much like him."

"Son, we all have little bit of Draggy in our lives. Sometimes we all hide away, and sometimes we all are waiting to shine in life too, but we have to be open about what makes us happy the most in life," Grandpa Harold replied.

"What's that Grandpa, chocolate cake?" Johnny asked.

"He's talking about family Johnny. Grandpa is talking about family!" Tomas said.

"Your right Tomas, Grandpa has to be talking about family," Johnny answered.

Grandpa Harold was wise, but this was the last thing he expected. He had no idea his metaphor would strike a chord in his son's heart and he had no idea his son would compare himself to Draggy, like he was the one hiding away from his own family. Grandpa Harold may have been telling the story but deep down his son was living it in his own way. I suppose Grandpa Harold learnt something that day too. Maybe we are more like the stories we hear than we really think. Yes, he told those stories a lot, about him and his brothers, but this was the first time his son was teaching him a thing or two. I guess the only wise man in the family wasn't wearing the ball cap and overalls, it was a son who was listening again, and William was listening with his heart this time around.

Carolyn was humbled by her husband's confession. She could see some truth in what he was saying. Many times he told her his father told stories, but this was unlike any story she ever heard, at least not one that made such an impact on anyone. A dragon might have been a far fetch from reality but it didn't matter. It was that playful dragon and his little cave her husband recognized as a symbol to his own life and he was waiting for someone to see him. Maybe she felt as she had been blind herself in many ways not noticing what he was trying to do for them. She knew he worked hard but she never seen it as if William was hiding away. William wanted a better life for his family and he didn't see how it enslaved him until now and the family he was working for was the one thing that would rescue him from it. That's how life sometimes goes, we enslave ourselves for the better and lose what we are working for. But today was like no other day. Yes, Carolyn's son Tomas might have received his present for his birthday but the greatest gift they all were really receiving was one another. A father learning to be a father to his sons, a husband learning to be a husband to his wife, and that was what it's all about in life, the gift of family.

Grandpa Harold sat in silence not saying a word as his son put his hand on his wife's hand coupling their fingers together and he thought to himself, yes, I raised you right, proud at the moment seeing his son being a gentleman.

"I'm sorry Dad for the way I've treated you."

"It's okay Son, tell me one thing, Son."

"What's that, Dad?"

"Are you ready to use your imagination, Son?"

"More than ever Dad, more than ever!"

"So there we were, standing ready to search for my brother and slay the fierce dragon. My brother had just got his superpowers, but one small detail was standing in our way."

CHAPTER TWENTY-NINE

"We got a problem," I said.

"What do you mean, Har Har?" Danny asked.

"Well, you can fly and I can only walk, and there's no way you can fly with me hanging on your back. I hate to say it but you might have to go looking for Timmy on your own."

The thought of separating us hit Danny hard. He was our older brother and he at times felt like he was the one who had to keep us all together and for us to be split up wasn't something he wanted to do, especially when he felt it was his responsibility to watch out for his two younger brothers.

"There's no way I can leave you, Har Har, not after everything that's happened."

"But you got to go, Timmy needs you," I insisted.

"But what about you?"

"Don't worry about him young lad, I will watch over him. Just find Timmy, and all will be well," Scotty reassured Danny.

"I saw a small village up in an eastward direction, up past the hillside. If we can meet there that would be good."

"Did you see anything besides the village while you were flying?" I asked.

"No, I didn't see any sign of Timmy or the dragon, just the

village. I think I will have to scour the landscape for miles if I'm to find anything, it might take me hours," Danny answered.

"Let's hope not because we only have a little time left and it will be getting dark soon. And if you do find him don't do anything on your own. There's a chance you can't even save him even if you do have superpowers," I replied.

"You're right, it's best to save him together. Two is always better than one."

"Yes, two is better than one. Besides, it might do us good to go to the village. I'm sure one of the town folks will know where the dragon is, and it would not hurt for us to at least try to find out what we can."

"Okay, so it's settled. I'll meet you at the village, and if you don't hear from me…"

"Yes, I know and if we don't hear from you, we will come looking for you. But try to be back before nightfall."

"I will, Har Har."

"We're brothers, we don't leave each other abandoned!"

I could see a sense of pride come upon Danny's face as if everything I said was everything he was thinking and feeling, and that prideful look was accompanied with small water forming from his eyes giving evidence to how he was feeling inside. It's moments like these in life when you find life so precious and moments like these you know what's important. It's these things that make us who we are inside, where our light shines with hope. Even in despair we find courage, and with courage we believe we can conquer any mountain. And Danny's mountain was the fear of us being apart. It was unbearable for him to admit he was scared at times. But he proved his strength many times like being strong when dad left, or the time when he took that job with the newspaper to earn extra money to take care of his brothers, and that tear forming in his eye was saying I just want us to be to-gether. Sometimes his actions spoke louder than words and I was always listening.

CHAPTER THIRTY

As my brother departed for the skies, flying away searching for our younger brother, I felt as if my world just flew away from me. Yes, the dragon took my youngest brother and flew away with him and now destiny had given my brother the powers to fly and for some reason it felt like he had found his own wings. Sometimes a person just needs to see the world from a different view and when they do it changes them forever. I would like to believe that day changed my brother but come to think about it he always flew in his heart. He soured above the pain many times, it was just this time his feet were off the ground.

"So, are you ready there, dear lad?"

"Yes Sir, Scotty," I replied.

"Don't worry about him lad, things will work out. You have many adventures yet to come, so fret not my dear lad."

"I am not worried as much as I wonder what the future holds for us."

"I was a young man like you as well when I went on my first adventure with my two brothers, and I had the same concerns as you dear lad."

"What, you were given a chance to go on an adventure with your brothers too?"

"What, did you think you were the only one The King of Adventure has chosen?"

"No, I'm not saying that. I just had no clue."

"I see, so you didn't think I had been on tall tales as well? To tell you the truth young lad, there's many of us!"

"How many Scotty?"

"Who knows dear lad, who knows?"

"So why did he choose me?"

"Sir, only you can answer that."

"You say I know, but how can I know if I do not know?"

"Answers, answers, answers, will all be answered when the question is in the ears of those who may reveal to you what you seek."

"Another riddle Scotty? I was starting to understand better, now you're just confusing me!"

"You will understand before long but right now we need to go to the village, and dear sir, there's no riddle in that."

"Your right, we need to go."

"So, are you ready dear lad to take on the fierce dragon, fight pirates, and change the world?"

"Yes Sir, Scotty!"

"Then let's go, dear lad. We shall be there quickly."

Scotty began to stomp his right foot on the ground then his left and began to start running in place as dust began to form little clouds from under his feet.

"Sorry sir, I do got to warm up. I haven't had my legs work too well all morning."

As Scotty begin to run in place his legs gained speed faster and faster until smoke was coming from the ground so fast you couldn't even tell he was running in place. It looked like how the blades of a ceiling fan runs round and round and you can't keep up with the motion with your eyes when its moving at such a fast rate.

"Your legs, they're moving fast Scotty!"

"Yes dear lad, apparently they do, so you might want to hop on once I'm ready to go."

All of a sudden Scotty disappeared and two white horses with a stage coach behind them appeared. As I stepped onto the stagecoach and was seated we took off like a bolt of lightning to the village.

CHAPTER THIRTY-ONE

A little time had passed since Aunt Louise and Mr. Owensby had been in each other's presence but love was brewing in New York like the smell of coffee in the early morning. It was lingering in the air. Our plan to set up Aunt Louise and Mr. Owensby might have suffered quite a set back with us going to the orphanage but it all seemed irrelevant considering that the spark had already been lit and what may seem like an innocent friendship taking place undoubtedly was the start of something great.

Aunt Louise couldn't bare much of the burdens of losing a brother to the war much less not being able to keep her promise to watch out for her nephews. The heavy burden was way too much for her to bare but she found comfort in the lending extension of friendship she found in Mr. Owensby.

Mr. Owensby was a good man. He took us under his wings so it was no surprise he took to Aunt Louise like a moth to a flame trying to help her find us boys. I would like to think maybe he was trying to help her just to get back the best employees he has ever had, but to be honest I think he saw a lady he was quite stricken with and couldn't help but to extend his hand of kindness.

Mr. Owensby had had his secretary Tabitha call around all of

New York looking into finding our whereabouts. After receiving all the possible information, he entreated telling Aunt Louise and they had decided to take a trip to the orphanage in New York to see what could be done on our behalf. It was no big concern for Mr. Owensby to go out of his way for Aunt Louise. He liked the fact he was doing a good deed, not to mention it gave him time to get to know Aunt Louise. They did have a rather unique connection, they both were charmers to say the least and quite eloquent with hospitality.

"This must be it," Mr. Owensby said as they pulled up to the orphanage.

"This is an orphanage? It looks more like a mansion," Aunt Louise said.

"Are you nervous?"

"I'm not nervous, I just don't know how things will turn out. This is not what I imagined, nor what I expected. I feel like I'm fighting the war for my nephews."

"You're not alone in this, you do know that?"

"I promised to take care of them."

"And you haven't broken your promise. You're here aren't you? If you ask me that's more than keeping your promise."

"Thanks, I needed to hear that!" Aunt Louise said.

"And I needed to say it. I know you love those boys and if there's anything I can do to help…"

"You're doing it now, everything that you're doing…thanks."

"You're welcome and if there's anything you need…"

Aunt Louise would've said I know to Mr. Owensby but she didn't have to, her eyes said it for her, and Mr. Owensby's words were really saying he really liked her and when he looked into her eyes it told him everything he wanted to hear.

Sometimes people meet under the strangest of circumstances and sometimes destiny plays a big part in it. Never the less, something magical was happening. Maybe it was serendipity or maybe it was New York or maybe it was... well let's just say it was New York.

Chapter Thirty-two

The stage coach came to a halting stop at a village with a cluster of little stony houses with straw for roofs. And when I stepped out onto the street, suddenly the stage coach disappeared and Scotty stood wiggling his feet trying to fan off the smoke from his shoes.

"Ouch, ouch, ouch, my feet get hot every time I do that!" Scotty said trying to cool his feet.

I figured the town folk would find it strange that a stage coach had disappeared, and some man had appeared in its steed but the town folk just shrugged it off as if it was like it was nothing and went about their business.

"These shoes are going to need some mending if I keep running like that!" Scotty said.

"Scotty, I don't think this is a friendly town."

"What makes you say that, dear lad?"

"I pulled up in a stage coach and it disappears, and no one even paid us no mind."

"Well, I'm sure it's not the first time they have seen strange things about. After all, they have a dragon here and nothing can be more outstanding to see than that."

"I guess you're right, Scotty."

One of the young ladies who stood by overheard and answered, "Did you say dragon?"

"Yes, we are looking for a dragon can you help us find him?"

"What are you two doing looking for a dragon?"

"He took my brother and we're trying to find him, so me and my brother can rescue my brother."

"I don't know where the dragon is but I'm sure the town's giant might know where he is."

"You look strangely familiar?" I said as I studied the young lady's face trying to place where I'd seen her.

"Why, it's me Sister Milica from the orphanage!"

"Sister Milica, what are you doing here?"

"After you went missing the priest didn't seem as concerned about you as I was. I couldn't just tell him The King of Adventure sent you on an adventure."

"How did you know I would be here?"

"Not here exactly, but in this place of the adventure."

"What do you mean?"

"You're not the only one whom The King of Adventure has chosen."

"People keep telling me this!" I replied.

"I was once given the opportunity to go on an adventure from The King of Adventure when I was a young girl back in Serbia, and when Dexter mentioned that you saw a ship I knew what was going on."

"So how did you find me?"

"I drew you and it brought me here. I knew I had to come here to see if you were here.".

"But where are we?"

"All I know is this is just a piece in the puzzle of your adventure and the only way to find one of the missing pieces is for you to meet the giant."

"A giant?"

"He might know where the dragon is."

"Where can we find him?"

"There, in the large house upon the hillside but he might not be there right now."

"Do you think he will help us?"

"I don't know but it never hurts to ask."

"Then that's where we need to go, Scotty. And will you go be going with us Sister Milica?"

"I have to get back to the orphanage."

"Thanks, Sister Milica."

"You're welcome. Oh yes, I thought you should know you need to open your treasure. It will show you the way."

"My treasure?"

"The one upon your ship!"

"I didn't know we had a treasure."

"Everyone whose an adventurer has one. It's the one thing that truly guides us. Without it all hope is lost. You will understand when you open it, all things will make sense then."

"That's why One-eyed Steve attacked?"

"You were attacked by One-eyed Steve?" Sister Milica asked.

"Yes, you know who he is?"

"I have heard of him, but I don't know who he is. I do know that even the sharks are afraid of him."

"He can't be that bad, can he?"

"All I know is don't lose your treasure, if you do you lose everything."

"What do you mean everything?"

"I said enough, I must go."

Sister Milica took out her paper and begin to write upon it

and disappeared from our eyes. Just when I was starting to understand, I was starting to not understand. It was if those who were there to guide me were the ones who confused me. I know they didn't want to confuse me none but what did she mean that if I lost the treasure all hope was lost. And how was I going to defeat the dragon? I didn't even understand the riddle. I knew I'd figure things out in time but time was running out and I needed to find my brother. The last thing on my mind was some treasure chest even though I thought riches would be wonderful, but nothing was more valuable than my own brother. Riches are good for those who love it but brothers are forever. Riches come and go but family is forever.

Chapter Thirty-three

Moments later Aunt Louise and Mr. Owensby inquired of our whereabouts in the orphanage. Even though they were on the right track of finding out where we were, the greater problem arose of my current whereabouts. Yes, they may have showed up to the right address to where I was staying but I was missing and that just wasn't something an orphanage would just let anyone know about. If it got out that children were coming up missing then the State Department might come in and hold them all accountable, so the nerves of the whole staff was on edge.

"Excuse my name is Mr. Owensby, is there anyone whom I may be able to talk to?"

"Yes Sir, how may I help you?"

"Yes Madam, my name is Mr. Owensby. We are looking for a few young men Harold, Timmy, and Danny Stanfield."

"Did you say Harold? He goes by the name of Har Har?" Sister Milica inquired.

"Yes, and you are?" Mr. Owensby asked.

"I'm sorry, I'm Sister Milica, forgive me. I just got back from a small journey."

"So, you know my nephew, Harold?" Aunt Louise asked.

"Can... Can... you give me a moment?" Sister Milica replied

as she stuttered not knowing how to give a proper answer in the matter with trembling hands.

"Sure, we will be right here waiting," Mr. Owensby replied.

Sister Milica excused herself with a gut feeling that things were about to make a turn for the worse. She just left me and Scotty back at the village, now she has to make sure Aunt Louise don't find out while telling the head priest what was going on at the front desk. It wasn't like she could tell the head priest she knew all about what was going on with me and where I was. It was her responsibility to watch out for me, it wasn't like she could come right out and say I was at a village looking for a giant to recuse my brother from a dragon and it wasn't like the head priest would believe her anyways.

As she made her way to the head priest's office her heart was in her throat and the world was on her shoulders as she knocked upon the door of the head priest's office to reveal the discomforting news.

The head priest sat admiring the envelope from The King of Adventure and his mind drifted away to when he was a kid himself sitting in the orphanage as he himself heard the thump of the sails flapping in the wind and he imagined himself at the bow of the ship raising his sword in the air yelling into open seas as he made his way to his own adventure. His day dream was interrupted from a hasty knock at the door and he scrambled to hide the envelope from The King of Adventure.

"Come in...the door is open," the head priest answered.

"Sir, there's a man and woman here looking for Harold Stanfield."

"Who?"

"The young man who is missing," Sister Milica replied.

"Did you tell them that he is missing?"

"Sir, do you think I would tell someone's family that their relatives are missing? What should we do?"

"This is not the first time this has happened. Keep them busy. I will be there in a few minutes. Give them time to get comfortable and I will bring them to my office and take care of the matter."

"Yes Sir!"

As Sister Milica left the head priest's office the head priest stood up, put the envelop in his pocket, and turned to look out the window as if he was looking out to see the ship out on the court yard himself. Undoubtedly he had some sort of connection to the envelope and he just wasn't trying to hide the evidence of the envelope from the sisters at the orphanage but was hiding something bigger. And now he had to explain the whereabouts of a missing orphan and that the head priest had believed what might have taken place. There's no way he could tell them, besides, there's no way they would believe him anyways. The head priest was coy in his words and he had a way of deferring the attention of bad situation into a mere easy situation. He knew if Aunt Louise left there mad, she could turn things bad for the orphanage knowing I was missing. So, he had to put on some charm so he might appease the daunting emotions that vexed Aunt Louise.

It must have felt like miles as Sister Milica made her walk back down the hall to where Aunt Louise and Mr. Owensby awaited in the front hall. She traveled many places in her time working for the Catholic Church and walked many miles doing charitable deeds for the less fortunate, but that hallway was longer than all of those miles she had ever journeyed, and this was a journey she wasn't willing to adventure.

"I just spoke to the head priest, he will be here in a few

minutes to speak with you."

"Thanks madam," Mr. Owensby said tipping his hat to Sister Milica as he and Aunt Louise left to sit down in the waiting area.

"Something is not right," Aunt Louise said.

"What do you mean?"

"Notice how she left when you mentioned Harold?"

"I'm sure that is normal, and you have nothing to worry about."

"Did you see her hands tremble as if something has happened."

Aunt Louise's intuition was right, I wasn't there, and it caught the orphanage off guard when Aunt Louise and Mr. Owensby showed up without any prior warning even though I wasn't hurt or in trouble. But my disappearance could raise a few eyebrows and the orphanage could not risk any accusations.

"Excuse me, I hear you're looking for one of the children here," the head priest said as he extended his hand with good jester.

"Yes Sir, my three nephews Harold, Timmy and Danny Stanfield."

"And to whom, may I ask, am I speaking?"

"I'm their Aunt Louise Stanfield and my friend Mr. Owensby."

"Sorry, forgive me for not introducing myself. I'm the head priest, Steve Madison, here at the orphanage. How may I help you?"

"We are looking for my nephews. They were taken from me, and my friend got word that they might be here."

"That's not normally public information. I'm not sure where you got your sources," the head priest replied.

"I own a newspaper printing press, I have friends every-where," Mr. Owensby answered.

"I see, well I'm not familiar with every one of the children here at the orphanage but I'm sure we have some documentation in my office to see if one of your nephews is here or not."

"That would be delightful. I have been trying my best to find out where they are. I promised their father to watch out for them," Aunt Louise said.

CHAPTER THIRTY-FOUR

Aunt Louise and Mr. Owensby sat across from the head priest sitting at his desk. The uncomfortable hardwood seats didn't give much comfort along with the uneasy feeling that was perplexing Aunt Louise as they sat in the head priest's office.

"Sorry it's been quite a long day. We have had rather a long drive. You mentioned you might have some paperwork providing information if Harold is staying here?" Aunt Louise asked.

"Yes, as a matter of fact, come to think about it I do recall he is here. I'm sorry it's been a long day for me as well."

"Do you think I can see my nephew? I'm sure he would be pleased to know I'm doing everything I can to get him out of here."

"I would love for you to speak to him, but unfortunately, he is not here."

"What do you mean he is not here? You just said he was here."

"Sir, maybe I can reintroduce myself, I am Mr. Owensby. I own a newspaper in New York City, and I don't know how you run things around here, but the way I run things at my newspaper is I'm always on the hunt and my writers are always looking for new material to write. And a missing child in an orphanage would cause a great stir would it not to say the least?" Mr. Owensby said.

"Well, yes I could see where that would not look to glorious in the sight of the readers on the behalf of the orphanage, but rest assured he is doing well."

"Well, where is he then?" Aunt Louise asked.

"He is out on a field trip. From time to time a few orphans are selected to go on a small adventure from The Adventure King."

"The Adventure King you say, now that sounds like a far more interesting story than a kid going missing at an orphanage," Mr. Owensby replied.

"Sir, you have no idea how interesting it is. I can't go into many details but every kid who goes on this little field trip always comes back with tall tales and it changes their lives forever."

"I have an employee who works for me and he has mentioned some king of adventure and these outlandish stories when he was a child."

Mr. Owensby and the head priest conveyed back and forth on the conversation about The Adventure King. In the back of Mr. Owensby's mind he was recalling Scotty telling him stories about when he was in an orphanage and would go on adventures. As the two men strategically framed their words, each subtlety quite aware the other knew way more than they were letting on as they suspiciously pried the matter.

"And this employee of yours, what did he tell you?"

",Many things and from what I understand Harold won't be back anytime soon will he?"

"And your employee's name if you don't mind me asking?"

"Scotty, his name is Scotty."

"Well, I feel rather rebuked. Maybe you already have the answers you're looking for and perhaps you're right, he might be gone for a few days. However, The Adventure King does take his time shaping and molding young men's lives. It's a virtue I wish every young man could experience."

The head priest couldn't just come right out and say The King of Adventure sent your nephew a letter telling him whatever you write, or draw becomes true. There was a certain code The Adventurers embarked on that they would never let the outside world know unless it would have a powerful significant outcome in the future, and it made him wonder why Mr. Owensby's employee, Scotty, would tell Mr. Owensby about his own adventures growing up. He knew there was more to this story than Mr. Owensby was letting on and just what it could be? Could it be he owned a newspaper business and Scotty felt he needed to share it with someone who might share it with the world? Or did Scotty just need a friend to confide in? Either way he knew Mr. Owensby knew more than he was letting on. But just how much did he really know?

Aunt Louise might had not known what was really going on in the conversation about who The Adventurous King was but from what she gathered he seemed like an alright guy to help young orphans out such as myself.

"I have two other nephews, are they here as well?"

"I'm sorry but I'm not sure on that. I do know about Harold and I seriously doubt they are here at this orphanage or else I would've heard of it on Harold's departure."

"What can make you so sure they are not here?"

"It was brought to my attention that Harold had been selected to go on the field trip from this orphanage, but I haven't got any word on his brothers so I'm assuming they are at another facility."

"What are you saying? That they aren't here as well?"

"But The Adventure King never splits up family. As a matter of fact, his whole premise is about bringing families together and wherever Harold is his brothers will be with him also."

"You mean they're on the field trip together?"

"He wouldn't break up a family. Oftentimes The State breaks them up but he brings them together."

"And how long will they be on this little field trip together?"

"That I can't tell you."

"I think what she's trying to say is she really doesn't have the luxury of waiting around to see her nephews," Mr. Owensby responded.

"I understand, I'm at the mercy of it too, but rest assured they are in good hands and they will be back soon."

"You mentioned the other two might be at a different orphanage?" Aunt Louise asked.

"It's more than likely."

"And how can we find out where they might be?"

"I'll make some calls. Is there a number I can reach you at?"

"Yes, matter of fact, you can reach her through my new paper business. We are in the book under Owensby News. We are small, but we are known. We do a lot of printing for New York Times."

"Well, that should be easy to remember. I'll have one of my nuns call you as soon as I find something out."

"I would like to thank you for your time Sir, it's been quite hard on me these past few weeks, especially with the loss of my brother and the loss of my nephews. I'd been in a greater disarray if it had not been for Mr. Owensby's help."

"We all need friends in this day and age. Don't worry I will keep a good eye on them."

"Thanks, and your name again?" Aunt Louise asked.

"Steve, Steve Madison," the head priest answered.

CHAPTER THIRTY-FIVE

For the last several years One-eyed Steve had been raiding ships and taking the treasure chest from other ships that have sailed in from the adventures that the king had granted for others. And he has been burying the treasure in various locations so no one could find them. Even though One-eyed Steve had no lust for the treasure itself, he buried them so no one else can devour them.

"Holes, holes, holes in the ground, that's all I see," One-eyed Steve spouted off.

"Sir, we are trying. We can't find the treasure anywhere."

"It was all here Julius, keep looking," One-eyed Steve demanded.

"I don't know what to tell you Sir, but we can't find not one treasure chest."

"Keep digging, it's bound to be here somewhere!" One-eyed Steve commanded.

"Sir, we have been digging all day. Maybe someone has come and found all the treasure chests and dug it up for themselves."

"Arr.. who would dare steal treasure from most treacherous pirate in all of the seven seas? Do they not know even the sharks are afraid of me?"

"Unless it was someone who was fierce themselves."

"Who can be more fierce than myself, Julius?"

"Umm, umm, no one Sir, but perhaps…"

"Perhaps? There's a perhaps in the equation?"

"Well…"

"Spit it out Julius. Let's hear your theory, it's not like it would have any true merit at this present junction but none the less, I will humor you in the matter."

"Well Sir, there is one whose more fierce and mightier than you but…"

"Silence Julius, mind your tongue. How dare you brave yourself in such a manner, accusing me of being weak to a fiercer adversary."

"My apologies Captain, but you do know a fierce dragon lives here in these parts."

"A dragon you say, Julius?" One-eyed Steve said tugging at his goatee.

"Yes, and we all know that dragons are very fierce and powerful, and they love to gather treasure."

"So, you're suggesting that a fierce dragon came and took the treasure?"

"It is possible sir."

"I doubt it Julius, even dragons are scared of me."

"Well undoubtedly not Sir."

"Silence Julius, we all know dragons are scared of me."

"Well, the treasure isn't here and there's a dragon, and if he was scared of you, he wouldn't have taken the treasure."

"Stop saying that he took the treasure Julius!"

"We have been digging all day long, what more proof do you need Sir?"

"Fine, fine, fine, have it your way Julius. The dragon took the treasure, whoopty doo, get back to digging!"

"But Sir, if we keep digging and he took it we are just wasting time and we got until the next full moon to find it or...."

"Don't say it. I don't even want to think about the consequences."

"If we don't find the treasure by the next full moon all the memories will be lost."

"A fierce dragon you say?"

"Sir, look, there's footprints over here. They're quite large!" one of the crew members shouted.

As the pirates gathered around to exam the large foot prints, looking to what might have stolen the treasure, everyone's heart begin to sink cause they knew that if they didn't find the treasure by the next full moon that the memory and imaginations of many would perish. Not only theirs but all who had ever went on an adventure from The King of Adventure and time was sadly running out. They needed to do something and fast but it was quite obvious the treasure had been stolen and was now in the hands of a new adversary that had no fear for One-eyed Steve.

"It's a footprint of a dragon," one of the crew members said.

"I know what it is," One-eyed Steve replied.

"A fierce dragon no doubt," Julius said.

"Well, then we will find this dragon and make him pay, One-eyed Steve replied.

"Sir, dragons are dangerous. You're not suggesting we fight him, are you?"

"Are you afraid to fight a dragon Julius?"

"Well Sir, they do breathe fire and can easily destroy a village."

"You forget, Julius, we have nothing to fear."

"And what makes you say that, One-eyed Steve?" Julius

asked.

"Do you not remember, Julius, whatever we draw or write it comes true?"

CHAPTER THIRTY-SIX

Johnny's mind began to wonder as he set listening to Grandpa Harold and the thought of what One-eyed Steve said and them pursuing the fierce dragon whom they presumed was dangerous. He knew One-eyed Steve wasn't going to be kind to Draggy and if anything, he knew Draggy was in trouble. But what really concerned him the most was why would The King of Adventure allow such a mean pirate to have the same opportunity to do the same things Grandpa Harold could do? Why was he allowed to write and draw whatever he wanted and it come true? It just didn't make any sense.

How can The King of Adventure allow such an evil pirate to do whatever he feels like, steal treasure from ships and hide it and then just make war against a good dragon? Johnny couldn't fathom this idea, it was bizarre to him. But Grandpa Harold knew just the right words to say to get him inquisitively involved in asking questions. He knew if he was asking, he was using his imagination and he knew it was going to make him think. And if he thought, he might just learn to see things different than the way he had been thinking and he might find his own peace within and he might see a better outcome and not be blind to his own way, not only him but his brother Tomas as well.

He knew a little tension often times made brothers bond. They might not be on an adventure themselves, but Grandpa Harold was taking them on an adventure with his words. He knew how people bonded over stories, and he longed to see his grandsons' bond, and that was just an honest motive of Grandpa Harold.

"Wait a minute Grandpa, One-eyed Steve he was sent by The King of Adventure too?" Johnny asked.

"It will all make sense in the end. You will just have to be patient," Grandpa Harold replied.

"But Grandpa, now One-eyed Steve wants to fight Draggy and he thinks he's fierce. But he isn't fierce, he's a good dragon and One-eyed Steve is bad and not only that your brother is with Draggy."

"Oh yes, I see where you're going with this. You're afraid that One-eyed Steve could hurt my brother?" Grandpa Harold replied.

"Yes, Grandpa there's got to be a way for you brother to escape One-eyed Steve!"

"He's not going to hurt Grandpa's brother, ain't that right Grandpa? One-eyed Steve won't hurt him or Draggy right?" Tomas asked.

"But didn't you just hear what Grandpa just said? One-eyed Steve had been raiding ships and taking the treasure chests from other ships that have sailed. He has been burying them in the ground so no one else can find them and One-eyed Steve said whatever you write, or draw comes true. Undoubtedly, he has powers just like Grandpa and his brothers. One-eyed Steve can write or draw anything and it will come true so he can easily defeat Draggy."

"There's no way he can defeat Draggy, he's a dragon," Tomas

said.

"But Draggy is not mean he is a good dragon, and they want to fight a nice dragon and hurt him," Johnny insisted.

"But you forgot one thing Johnny," Tomas said

"And what's that?"

"Nothing is mightier than that which is sweet."

"What do you mean Tomas?"

"Just cause Draggy is good don't mean that One-eyed Steve can beat him. He doesn't have the answer to the riddle."

"What are you saying Tomas?" Johnny asked.

"One-eyed Steve doesn't have one thing that Grandpa's brother has."

"What's that?"

"Chocolate cake!"

"Oh yes, I forgot. You're right, there is no way One-eyed Steve can defeat Draggy, he has no chocolate cake. One-eyed Steve's powers can't defeat him."

Often times the two grandsons had opposing views, but somehow they began to merge in ideas and understanding each other as if each one was teaching and inspiring the other brother. Johnny saw the story as what could go wrong and his brother Tomas saw how things could go right. I guess iron does sharpen iron, and those two boys were sharper than iron when it came to Grandpa Harold's story.

CHAPTER THIRTY-SEVEN

As Aunt Louise and Mr. Owensby made the long drive back to New York City that day many things played on Aunt Louise's mind, especially about the field trip and what Mr. Owensby had said to the head priest regarding Scotty and his tales about his adventures growing up and how they could be connected. The way the two gentlemen talked, it was as if this was more than some act of kindness on The Adventurous King's part and curiosity had got the better of her.

"There's something you're not telling me."

"What do you mean Louise?"

"Back there at the orphanage you mentioned Scotty and adventurers he had when he was a kid. You're not telling me something. You know more than you're letting on and when the priest mentioned The Adventure King you didn't seem so worried about my nephews."

"Your going to think I'm crazy if I tell you."

"I might already think you're crazy, why don't you try me?"

"I don't know where to begin."

"Why don't you start from the beginning, from what you do know or at least what you think you know."

"Do you believe there's something greater out there than

us?"

"You mean like God?"

"Yes, like God and destiny and things we can't explain."

"If you're going to say my nephews were abducted by aliens I'm going to really start to think you've lost it."

"Yes, that's what I'm thinking, green little aliens landed and took them and are holding them ransom for your chocolate cake."

"It's official, you've lost it!" Aunt Louise said with a teasing smile.

Mr. Owensby had his moments of silliness. He often found ways to make Aunt Louise smile even when she was facing the toughest times in life. Sometimes a man doesn't always have to be so serious about life. Life does what it does, its just up to us to make it better and sometimes a little silliness can make life better. A smile is quite the antidote to whatever ails us.

"Well, you might think I'm really crazy if I told you."

"Well let's hear it crazy man!" Aunt Louise said with a flirtatious slap on Mr. Owensby's arm.

"So now it's official, I'm crazy?"

"Slightly, but I will let you off the hook a little until I hear what you have to say."

"Well, I think I've grown rather fond of you calling me crazy. I wouldn't want to risk you thinking I'm not crazy," Mr. Owensby turned to her crossing his eyes.

"I'm going to think you're crazy no matter what, so let's hear it."

"Well, when I was a young boy I got lost in the woods and this old couple found me and I spent a few days in an orphanage myself until my parents could locate me. There was this young boy in the orphanage, and we became friends. One day he told me about an adventure he had and asked if I wanted to go on an adventure with him."

"Wait, are you saying you went on an adventure with him?"

"That's the thing, I was a kid and I'm not sure if what I thought had happened really happened. You know how you wake up and you're still in a dream state? Well that's how I see in my mind's eye what happened, I can't really explain it."

"So, what happened?"

"He proceeded to pull out a pencil and paper and asked if I was ready to go on an adventure. Then he began to draw something. The paper started to glitter in gold writing and then he grabbed my hand and before I knew it, we were in another time and in another country. Things weren't like it is here. There, reality didn't really exist, only the reality of what we believed. It was as if imagination was the real reality. I just remember waking up in my mom and dad's car and thinking 'Did I dream it all?' I can't remember exactly what happened just bits and pieces of it."

"Yes, now I know you're crazy. So, what does this have to do with Scotty?"

"Scotty told me something similar about his time at the orphanage. It's as if what I think I experienced might have been real. I really don't know, I was so young and there's so much I don't understand. But Scotty's stories just seem to be so obvious that there's something greater at work. And when the priest mentioned The Adventure King, it reminded me of Scotty's stories and maybe the adventure and orphanage are somehow tied in together. I don't know how it all ties in together but the way the priest was talking he must have known more than what he was letting on."

"So, let me get this straight. You think maybe my nephews are on some adventure in some parallel universe?"

"Well, when you put it like that, I do sound crazy. I'm not saying that's what happened, but it just seems strange to me that's all. It could have nothing to do with it, besides, I was just a kid and kids have big imaginations."

"Well, whatever it is, I just hope my nephews are okay."

"I'm sure they are and we never know what may come out of this and how lives might change. But one thing's for sure, things happen for a reason and I just hope whoever it is making the play books for our lives and the lives of others knows what they're doing. Cause we all can use a little good in our lives, especially right now more than ever and who knows fifty years from now or a hundred years from now it might change someone's life. Heaven knows we all can use a little change from time to time,"

"Well, if destiny is at play, let's just hope our eyes are open to see it." Aunt Louise replied.

"Yes, and it's something that one should never want to miss out on. Sometimes it's staring us right in the eyes, and if we blink we might miss it."

I would like to think Aunt Louise and Mr. Owensby were talking about us when it came to destiny, but the way they looked at each other from time to time it was obvious they were talking about themselves. That ride home wasn't just a ride home, but a man and a woman connecting on a deeper level of understanding. If you ask me, destiny had its hands at the wheel and cupid was hitching a ride shooting little arrows of love in the name of adventure.

CHAPTER THIRTY-EIGHT

As Aunt Louise and Mr. Owensby bonded over the drive back to New York City, my brother Danny had been scouring the land looking for our youngest brother from the skies. He could see the sun lowering in the skies and knew he had to make his way to the village to find me and Scotty.

His worry drew near as he felt a moment of defeat from the setting sun with no light to guide him in the search of our brother. It wasn't like he could turn back the sun, so his only option was to try and make it to the village. It wasn't fully dark yet, but dark enough not to see the village from the sky. He would have to wait for night in hopes to see any windows lights from the village.

As he began to make his way back, he spotted a group of people walking with lanterns lighting their path down below him. He flew closer to investigate, hoping they could know the location of the dragon or the way to the village. As he drew near, he recognized it was none other than our adversary One-eyed Steve and his crew.

What if they are headed to the village, he thought to himself knowing that Scotty and I had already left for the village. One-eyed Steve already tried to sink our ship. There's no telling what he might do, he tough, as he hovered over them just above the trees.

"Arr.. this is the spot that marks the x," One-eyed Steve said as he gazed at the map with the lantern giving him enough light to read the map.

"Sir, what if we dig here all night too and we can't find the treasure here as well?"

"But the x means treasure. Look, what does the map say Julius?"

"It shows an x, Sir."

"And here we are at the x, Julius."

''Yes Sir, and we were at the x on our last spot and there was no treasure to be found."

"Excuses, Julius, excuses, I'm starting to think you're all not cut out for this treasure hunting. Do I sense a hint of tyranny being provoked there, Julius?"

"No Sir, it's just we are tired and it's getting late."

"I see Julius, so you just want to give up, huh, go back to the ship?"

"Yes Sir."

"Well, it's not happening. We will find this treasure even if it takes us all night."

"Sir, you need to see this!" one of the crew members yelled out.

"What is it?" One-eyed Steve asked.

As they all gathered around to a familiar sighting, looking down in the dirt that had freshly been dug up, they saw lying there the evidence of someone or something had been there already.

"It looks like there's dragon prints here as well, maybe the fierce dragon stole the treasure here as well."

"Stop calling him fierce Julius. There's only one fierce and that's me, One-eyed Steve."

"Sorry Sir, but what should we do?"

"There's only one thing we can do. We have to find this dragon and take back what's rightfully ours Julius," One-eyed Steve answered.

"How do you expect we do that Sir?"

"There's only one in these parts I hear knows the whereabouts of the dragon."

"Fierce dragon!" Julius said.

"Stop saying fierce dragon," One-eyed Steve spouted.

"I'm sorry Sir, but fierce dragon has a better ring to it, Sir."

"Arr.. I'm the fierce one and everyone knows it, Julius!" One-eyed Steve responded.

"We know you're more fierce than the dragon, but do you really want to be known to be more fierce than a dragon?"

"What are you trying to say, Julius, spit it out!"

"All I'm trying to say is if the dragon is more fierce and you defeat him it looks like you defeated an invincible adversary. But if you seem more fierce than him it will just look like you beat a weaker opponent."

"Interesting observation there Julius!" One-eyed Steve said as he tugged at his beard.

"So how do you suppose we find this fierce dragon?"

"There's only one who might know the whereabouts of the fierce dragon."

"Who is that One-eyed Steve?" Julius asked.

"The lumber jack."

"You mean the One-eyed lumber jack?" Julius asked.

"I'm the only one-eyed around here Julius!"

"Sir, I heard the lumber jack has one eye too."

"Yes, I heard he has one eye as well and he's also a great a giant," one of the crew members said.

"A giant you say, well we will have to see about that now won't we?" One-eyed Steve added.

"And where is this lumber jack you speak of?" Julius asked.

"In the village and that's where we will go."

As my brother overheard the plans of One-eyed Steve, he knew that Scotty and I were in grave danger. He knew he had to find me before One-eyed Steve found me and somehow figure out a way to use One-eyed Steve to defeat the dragon so we didn't have to, and attempt to save my brother at the same time. What he done next was something I would never think he would ever do.

"What if I can help you?"

"Arr.. who goes there," One-eyed Steve asked.

As One-eyed Steve turned around hearing a boys voice in the darkness, the crew lifted up their lanterns so the light could be shown as my brave brother walked into the mist of One-eyed Steve and his crew members. Knowing he was endangering his own life for the sake of my life and our younger brother, he knew time was running out for Timmy and this might not have been the best idea at the time but it seemed like the most logical idea. He knew he would have to face One-eyed Steve sooner or later and the sooner he could get to Timmy the better chances he had to save him and barging a deal with a treacherous pirate, well it just was something he had to do.

"My name is Danny, and I couldn't help but overhear you wanted to defeat the dragon."

"What's it to you?" One-eyed Steve spouted.

"I was thinking maybe we can cut a deal," Danny said.

"And why would I want to cut a deal with a boy?" One-eyed Steve said.

"You wanted to destroy our ship. What if I was willing to make a trade?"

"What kind of trade and who are you to bargain with the likes of me?"

"You wanted our ship did you not?"

"Sir, it's one of the boys from the ship," Julius said.

"I may have one eye Julius, but I'm not blind."

"You're looking for the dragon, so am I and I once heard someone say an enemy of my enemy is my friend."

"Well, a ship is just a ship. You're going to need more to bargain with than just a ship."

"I can help you."

"And what do you get out of it?"

"The dragon has my brother."

"And you're willing to do anything for him, I see."

"Yes, even if it cost me my life."

"Arr.. and it just might cost you your life," One-eyed Steve said.

"Did you see any treasure on your ship?" Julius asked.

"I'm quite capable of asking him for myself Julius."

"But you didn't ask him, Sir."

"Point well taken Julius. So, tell me Danny, was there any treasure on the ship?"

"I don't know if there was any treasure."

"Ha, that was a trick question. All ships have treasure," Julius said.

"Julius is right, all ships have treasure."

"If I promise to give you the treasure, will you help me?"

"I'm not interested," One-eyed Steve said as he turned his back on Danny.

"There's no way you can defeat a fierce dragon on your

own."

"Did he just say fierce dragon?" One-eyed Steve asked.

Julius began shaking his head yes as all the rest of the crew sighed in shock from Danny saying fierce dragon, expecting One-eyed Steve might lose his temper.

"Fierce dragon, fierce dragon," Danny spouted tempting a response from One-eyed Steve.

"He said it again didn't he Julius?" One-eyed Steve said as he rolled his eyes in disbelief shrugging his shoulders.

Julius looked at One-eyed Steve nervously trying to hold back his fear and shook his head saying 'yes!' hoping that One-eyed Steve wouldn't react in an irrational manner.

"Yes, I did and you need my help," Danny answered.

"And what makes you think I would want your help?"

"Sir, you should really turn back around," Julius said. As the eyes of the crew members looked upward One-eyed Steve turned back around to see my brother floating in the air.

"Cause, I can fly!"

Chapter Thirty-Nine

While Danny was conspiring a plan to save Timmy, Scotty and I were embarking on a little escapade of our own. As my mind raced with the thoughts of what Sister Milica had said about the treasure and how the giant would fit in the story. Little did we know One-eyed Steve was looking for him as well. At least I knew what had to be done in order to find the dragon but who was to say the giant would even help us at all?

"You must be Har Har?" an old woman said as we reached the giant's house.

"How do you know who I am?"

"I've been expecting you," the old lady replied.

"What do you mean you've been expecting me?"

"I got a letter."

"From The King of Adventure?"

"No, the letter was from you."

"What do you mean you got a letter from me?"

"You need help finding the dragon do you not?"

"Yes he…" I said as she cut me off in mid-sentence.

"He took your brother, and you need my son to help you find him!"

"Who's your son?"

"He's the giant you're inquiring about."

"But I didn't mention the giant."

"You didn't have to. I already knew that's why you were coming here. Please come on inside and we can discuss the matter further if you like."

As we entered the giant's house to sit down at the table, with the flickering lantern to give off its light and the smell of fresh baked bread setting at the table, I remained curious to the letter I supposedly sent.

"You said I sent you a letter, how can I have sent you a letter if I never met you?"

"All things are possible here. Time and reality isn't the same back where we are all come from. Today I can be at the village, tomorrow I could be living in France. It's up to us what we want, all we have to do is write or draw it."

"So, The King of Adventure sent you here too?"

"He sure did, and I tell you it's been quite an adventure to say the least. But your adventure has just begun has it not?"

"Yes, it has Madam."

"Well, there's things you will just have to figure out. I wouldn't worry about the letter you sent me. You will write it one day, but now is not the time to worry about it. You got bigger things to do."

"Your son the giant, is he not here?"

"No, I'm sorry he's not here. He has been out working in the forest all day long. He should be getting back shortly."

"So, he knows where the dragon is?"

"If anyone knows where the dragon is it's him. It's just well, he doesn't like talking that much, you have to pry him in other words."

Just great I thought to myself, a giant who doesn't like to talk.

How was I going to get a giant to tell me what I needed to hear or persuade him to help me? And the thought of me sending the old lady a letter darted in my mind. It was coming quite clear that time and reality didn't have its boundaries here like it did back home. It seemed as if everything here could be manipulated and be used in my favor. I think I was starting to understand some things, but still this whole new altered reality seemed quite mysterious to say the least and I was going to figure it all out no matter the cost.

CHAPTER FORTY

As me and Scotty waited for the giant in the presence of the mysterious old lady, our brother Timmy was gathering new revelations of his own in the presence of the fierce dragon.

Yes, on the outside he looked rough and scary like all dragons do but he was meek and warm hearted, a kind and generous soul under all the tough exterior. What one would think was an enemy of the people was really just a big baby wanting to do good. People feared him but they never knew that he was out to guard them.

This new altered reality had much a deeper complexity layer to it. The world of adventure had been under a ruthless attack and had been suffering the effects of an evil force that's has been trying to steal away imagination from the hearts of the youth. Draggy championed the cause to be the protector against the evil that was befalling on the land of what I would like to call imagination.

Parts of the land had been ravaged and falling prey to Vile Ones. That was the name of the evil oppressors that ruled in our world now trying to possess The Land of Imagination. They were like locusts coming in and destroying all in their path and each time they destroyed imagination from the hearts of the people a wave of destruction came and parts of The Land of Imagination would fall off into a bottomless pit of nothing. Slowly by slowly The Land of Imagination was shrinking, and Draggy and other dragons would be the fighters against The Vile Ones, but the war of good and evil was regrettably being lost.

The future of our adventure didn't just rely on us but on Draggy and all the adventurers as well. If The Vile Ones won then the imagination of the world would be lost forever. This wasn't just about me and my brothers, this was about the whole world and those who dreamed therein.

If I had known this at the time when I had started my adventure it would have been too great of a burden for me. But I guess knowledge has a way of finding wisdom and to those who learn wisdom finds a solution to any problem that lies ahead of them.

Maybe The King of Adventure knew that if Timmy received the revelation of things taking place, that his spirit of optimism would have great significance of a greater outcome and maybe him having enough wits to figure out the riddle about Draggy was the reason he was chosen to be captured.

Maybe all things do work for the greater good. Without his wits Timmy wouldn't have seen Draggy's true form and the revelation of what was taking place behind the scenes. The knowledge of The Vile Ones had not been yet revealed to Danny and I, but all things were being woven together. All our little adventures apart was playing into the greater cause and maybe we might save The Land of Imagination and ourselves in the process even when we had no clue how lost we really were.

As Timmy looked around the cave his mind pondered the treasure chest lying around in the mist of Draggy's little lair.

"You protect treasure?"

Draggy shook his head yes and smiled.

"Why do you protect it, whom does it belong to?"

Draggy pointed his fingers to Timmy and himself.

"What you mean this treasure belongs to both of us?"

Draggy shook his head yes.

"Scotty said that once the dragon is defeated you will see it's true form. What did he mean by that?"

Draggy went to the corner of the cave and grabbed a piece of paper with a pencil and lays it down at Timmy's feet and nudges the paper towards Timmy.

"What is this?"

Draggy nudged the paper again hoping Timmy would figure out what Draggy was implying.

"You want me to draw, don't you?"

Draggy shook his head yes and waged his tail.

"But what do you want me to draw?"

Draggy put his paw to his mouth and started acting like he was eating then rubbed his belly.

"I know what you want, you want that chocolate cake don't you?"

Draggy shook his head yes and wagged his tail.

"I knew it! So, do you want a big chocolate cake?"

Draggy's eyes got very big and excited and he shook his head yes.

"Then a big chocolate cake is what you will have my new friend."

As Timmy drew, the chocolate cake appeared, then Draggy took it up by his hands and began to eat it. As soon as he had taken a bite of the cake his appearance changed and the figure of a young boy stood in front of him.

"I have waited to eat cake for such a long time," the boy said as he stood before Timmy.

"You're a boy just like me!" Timmy said as he stood frozen looking upon Draggy's true form.

"Yes, I am!"

"But you're a dragon as well?"

"I'm whatever I imagine and whatever I draw just like you and your brothers."

"So, this whole time we weren't supposed to fight you but to see your true form?"

"Yes, that was the purpose of it all. There's more things taking place than you might be able to comprehend. The Land of Imagination is at risk."

"What do you mean at risk?"

"The future of mankind is at risk."

Those words shook our little brother Timmy, back home our country was off in Europe fighting tyranny and here he was in The Land of Imagination finding out that all mankind was at risk.

"What do you mean?"

"The Vile Ones are trying to destroy imagination from the hearts of adventurers. Once they do so everyone in the world is at risk. Inventors will cease to invent, artists will no longer paint, musicians will no longer create songs and anything a man dreams within his heart will be lost forever. The fight for our survival here echoes in the other worlds and what happens here effects our world and the world to come."

"What do mean other worlds?"

"There's worlds of imaginations, there's worlds of dreams, there's worlds of hope, all are always at risk of tyranny and all are at war with reality. It's up to the chosen to save it."

"So why are we chosen?"

"That I don't know, but one thing I do know is your chosen like me and whatever you're chosen for is for the greater good."

"The Vile Ones you mentioned, how can they be defeated?"

"Only by the treasures I've gathered, that's the only way."

"It's a ransom."

"No, it's what's in them that holds the power, the true wealth of life."

"What's in them, gold, rubies, diamonds?"

"I can't reveal this to you. It's not my place to tell you what is in it, but it's the one thing that defeats The Vile Ones. We must go at day light."

"But what about my brothers?"

"Don't worry about them, we will find them."

"How will we find them? We have no clue where they are. For all I know they could be back in the orphanage."

"They are still here cause you're still here, and besides, I'm a dragon. I can find them, you forget I can fly."

"But what if we meet The Vile Ones along the way."

"Then we fight them."

"But I'm just a kid, how am I to fight them?"

"I'm just a kid too, and a dragon. I fight for the people and if I can use my imagination to fight them so can you."

"You mean the letter from The King of Adventure?"

"Yes, that's our only way to withstand them until…"

As soon as Draggy said that his shape went back to a dragon and Timmy was left wondering what he was going to say. He knew whatever he was about to tell him had a huge significance on defeating The Vile Ones and somehow drawing or writing played a big part. All Timmy knew was somehow, he needed to make it back to the ship and hopefully find his brothers by day light.

That night seemed long to Timmy as he laid in the cave beside a small fire to keep warm thinking about all things that had happened and how Draggy was a boy like himself. As he looked over to Draggy fast asleep, he knew that Draggy wasn't just a dragon but a lonely boy who misunderstood and warriored for a just cause. As Timmy gazed upon the interior walls of the cave it became evident to Timmy that the dragons lair had become Draggys' prison and the only friend Draggy had was him.

As William sat and listened to his father the more, he understood his father wasn't just talking about a dragon. He was talking about his son and he was wise enough to recognize he was more like Draggy than he realized. As a lawyer he fought for the people just like Draggy. His office was his lair and some how he felt like that little boy no one understands in the body of something fierce a fierce lawyer by reputation but just a dreamer inside who had lost his way imprisoned by life itself.

CHAPTER FORTY-ONE

One-eyed Steve looked across the campfire with a suspicious eye towards Danny as if he knew Danny had alternative motives and Danny stared back at One-eyed Steve knowing he had an alternative motive. They both looked at each other as adversaries and not as someone who might help the other, but they both knew they needed the other. They had to defeat the fierce dragon and One-eyed Steve knew the only way to get the treasure was to kill the dragon and my brother knew the only way to save Timmy was to slay the dragon, but one thing that stood in the way of them defeating the dragon was the riddle that Scotty gave them and if they tried to fight the dragon there's no chance at defeating him. Little did they both know Timmy had already solved the riddle and was getting information of things taking place in The Land of Adventure.

"So, have you ever slayed a dragon?" One-eyed Steve asked.

"He's just a boy!" Julius responded.

"Right you are Julius, he is just a boy."

"So tell me, how do you plan to defeat this dragon?"

"With this!"

Danny takes his laser beam stick and points it at a tree and shoots the tree limb and it falls down to the ground. The crew members along with One-eyed Steve are stunned by the powerful weapon of Danny's. And it was clear he might have been a boy, but he had something that was of great use and it might be possible to defeat the fierce dragon. It was quite clear that One-eyed Steve needed him more than he had realized.

"We can defeat the dragon and save my brother."

"If you can fly and have such a weapon what makes me believe that you need my help unless there is something you're not telling me."

Danny knew One-eyed Steve was right and that he wasn't telling him everything. He just couldn't say he feared my safety knowing that One-eyed Steve and his crew members were headed to the village and if he could get close to One-eyed Steve and convince him we would help him maybe no harm or mischievousness might befall on us at the hands of One-eyed Steve.

"You want the treasure right? So what does it matter if there's something I'm not telling you? I'm sure you're not telling me something as well."

"Secrets, secrets, secrets, then that's what there will be. Secrets."

"I told you what I wanted and it's to defeat the dragon."

"Arr.. and I told you I wanted to defeat the dragon as well."

"But you blame me for keeping secrets, but you're a pirate and pirates can't be trusted."

"Arr.. you're right I can't be trusted."

"Then how can we defeat the dragon if we can't trust each other."

"We don't have to trust each other, we just have to defeat the dragon and what if I don't help you now? You're already looking at me like I'm your enemy. Is that what you see in my one eye, the lack of trust and honor? Well, then maybe your right, maybe

I am your enemy, but I once heard someone say an enemy of my friend is my friend. I wonder where I heard that from?"

"He said it, Sir, he was the one talking about the friends and enemies," Julius said.

"I know he said it Julius, it was another rhetorical question!"

"Oh, yes Sir, rhetorical got you," Julius turned to Danny and said, "It was a rhetorical question."

"I know!" Danny said responding to Julius.

"So, now we are at a standstill. Shall we be enemies and friends or just enemies?"

"If no harm comes upon my brothers."

"Arr.. that I can't promise you for all I know is your brother might be dragon's food."

"Sir, maybe it's not in your best interest to scare the young boy."

"And why do you say that, Julius?"

"Sir, you might want to look a little closer."

One-eyed Steve looked down as Danny had his laser beam stick pointed towards One-eyed Steve's lower abdominal region.

"Cause, if not you're gonna lose your bahoogies."

And with a lump in his throat trying to muster up his words One-eyed Steve said "Arr.. I'm thinking maybe we should be friends."

"I thought you'd see it my way," Danny replied'

"Arr.. indeed and your way might just work out."

"And for your bahoogies," Julius said snickering with a little giggle.

"Don't..... tempt him, Julius!"

"Now tell me about this lumberjack giant, how does he know where the dragon is?" Danny asked.

I got to hand it to Danny he was being fierce himself in the presence of a fierce pirate and all his crew members. Maybe Danny showed his strength or his illusion of strength to One-eyed Steve and the crew as a way of fitting in with such tough men. Little did he know, his little act of courage had won over the crew members and that of one-eyed Steve and now he was becoming one of the boys even if he didn't know it or not.

CHAPTER FORTY-TWO

As I sat at the table of the mysterious old lady with Scotty my mind had remembered the words me and my brother Danny spoke about meeting at the village by night fall. If he made it back to the village, Danny wouldn't have any clue where Scotty and I were. Not only that but would the giant be so kind to show us the way to the dragon to rescue Timmy?

"I promised Danny to go looking for him if we didn't make it to the village by night fall."

"He will be here," Scotty said.

"What if he can't find the village or what if he's lost Scotty?"

"Don't fret dear lad, I'm sure he will make it to the village before long."

"He must, cause time is running out."

As I spoke those words the ground began to shake, the door opened and the giant entered the house of the mysterious lady laying a large thick axe down beside the door.

As the giant entered, he threw down a bag of beans that he had been carrying on his back and looked down towards me and Scotty.

"Did you cut a lot of wood in the forest today my son?"

"Who be this these strange peoples?" the giant asked with

his deep voice.

"They are requiring your wisdom my son."

"My wisdom? No one has ever called me wise."

"I'm looking for the dragon."

"There are many dragons."

"I am only looking for one."

"And I'm looking for a meal," the giant responded.

"I'm sorry but he tends to get rather obnoxious when he hasn't eaten all day," the old lady responded.

"Can you help us? The life of my brother depends on it!"

The giant turned to warm himself by the fire and completely ignored me as if it did not matter what happened to Timmy. All he cared about was his meal and it was late.

"Son, you can't keep silent especially when a young boy is missing."

"I haven't ate yet, I want a meal mom."

"What if I can prepare a meal for you, would you help us then?"

"What kind of meal?"

"Any kind you would like, just let me know what you desire."

"But you're just a boy, how do you have the knowledge to make fine cuisines?"

"I got the recipes right here in my little notes I carry around with me?"

I look over to Scotty and tap my pouch revealing to Scotty I'm referring to the paper that The King of Adventure had sent me.

"Oh yes, and he makes a fabulous meal," Scotty said.

"Well, I do like fabulous," the giant said in his deep voice.

"And I'm sure a grown man such as yourself would do any-thing for a big meal?" I asked.

"Yes, a lavish meal in trade of the whereabouts of the dragon?" Scotty stated.

"There's many dragons and so little food."

"What if I could prepare a meal where you could eat until your heart's content? Would that help you to narrow down the dragons?"

"Son, you know right well there's only one dragon in these parts, and besides, I'm quite tired this evening to grind at that ole stove making dinner. Maybe you should take the boy up on his generous offer."

"Ok Mom," the giant said with a sluggish shoulder shrug.

"Now what do you say to the young boy?"

"Ham and bread with mashed potatoes and of course some beans?"

"No.... that's not what you say."

"Oh, okay I guess no beans," the giant said hanging his head and he sat down at the table.

"No, you're supposed to say thank you, and besides, you know what those beans do to you."

"But Mom, I like the beans."

"I know you do Son, but we just can't be having you eat beans tonight especially in front of guest."

"But I like the beans Momma!" the giant said as he pounded the table with his fork in his hand.

"Fine Son, but you need to promise to keep your manners at the table."

"Okay Mom."

"You promise you will tell us how to find the dragon?"

"I will help you, but can you make sweet bread with it? I always loved sweet bread?"

"Sweet bread, I sure can. I could even make you cake."

"Now you're talking! For cake I would do anything, giants get hungry!"

"I sure can do that for you."

"And you got the recipe for cake too in your pouch?"

"I sure do."

"Well, I'm a waiting for my delicious meal."

"Say no more, I will make it right now."

I pulled out the paper from my pouch and took out my pencil and began to write and as soon as I wrote the table was filled with a full course meal with ham, chicken, bread all kinds of vegetables and a large cake.

"Wow, you sure do know how to make a great meal."

"So, what about the dragon, how can I find him?"

"The fierce dragon?"

"Yes, the one who took my brother."

"People don't like him, they think he is bad."

"So, you know who he is?"

"I haven't eaten my meal and a deal is a deal, but if I tell you before I eat, you might take the food from me."

"Oh, stop with your babbling Son, there's no reason for the young boy to take away any meal from you," the old lady replied to her son.

"He is right, a deal is a deal let him eat," I replied.

"You will eat too won't you? There's plenty, we can't be looking for a dragon on an empty stomach?" the giant asked.

"We would be delighted to eat with you."

"There's nothing mightier than that which is sweet," the giant said as he took a bite of the chocolate cake.

"That's it! You just solved the riddle."

"I did, what riddle did I just solve?"

"How to defeat the dragon," I replied.

"Oh no, you can't fight the dragon. He is too fierce."

"We ain't going to fight him, we are going to feed him!"

"Well, I guess that will be okay," the giant says in his deep drawn-out voice.

"We solved it Scotty, it was chocolate cake all along wasn't it?"

"Sir, you already know!" Scotty responded.

CHAPTER FORTY-THREE

While my brothers and I made an acquaintance with Draggy, One-eyed Steve, and the giant, trouble was brewing on the outer parts of The Land of Adventure. The Vile Ones were out to erase the imaginations of the adventurers. Many times they came with their philosophy that life is not meant to dream upon. They exalted themself against those whom had visions and sought to destroy one's imagination, slowly The Land of Adventure was perishing, and the land was falling into a dark abyss and the imagination of the people was dying at their hands.

That night a great earth quake fell upon the land striking fear into the hearts of the people. Even the animals fled as The Vile Ones marched east devouring the land taking their staffs and shooting out what appeared to be lightning from their staffs, and once it touched trees or any living thing it began to turn to gray and lifeless. Black veins would appear on any life-form it touched right before its demise. Plants or any living creature were not immune to their powers and whatever it touched turned to stone. And once it had been turned to stone it crumbled to dust under their feet and once they cross passed anything they destroyed, it would fall into a bottomless pit behind them, erasing everything in their path

"What was that?", I asked startled from the shaking of the earth.

"It's The Vile Ones. I wouldn't have thought they would make it this way so soon," the older lady replied.

Hastily she stood up and peered out her window to observe the night sky light up the night. It was evident that The Vile Ones had drawn closer and by the look on her face she knew destruction drew neigh.

"Who are The Vile Ones?"

"They're the cursed ones of The Land of Adventure."

"What do you mean?" I asked as she grievously looked upon me, troubled that something bad was about to happen.

"In everything in life, there's both good and evil, and they're the evil side of adventure, they erase away all imagination."

"How is this possible?" I asked.

"Just as its possible to write or draw they erase everything. You must find the dragon tonight, only dragons can withstand them. Their power has no effect on dragons because of the dragon's strength."

"We must go now lad!" Scotty replied hastily.

"But I promised to wait for my brother."

"I will keep an eye out for your brother if someone comes asking. Besides, if you don't go now everyone is at risk, even your brother!"

I knew I had to go right at that moment. I would never risk my brother's safety and I knew they wouldn't risk mine but the one thing that weighed heavy on my mind was what could've happened to Danny. I couldn't do this without him. We were supposed to rescue Timmy together but now I would have to go on without him knowing very well that he might not be able find me. There was a great divide in my heart and it was greater than the Great Divide itself as I embarked on my new mission without Danny; all I could do was hope and pray he was okay.

Without haste Scotty, the giant, and I made our way into the forest. I could see the night's atmosphere changing above me as the night skies grew lighter then dark, it was night fall. The skies should've been dark but the lightnings from The Vile Ones lit the sky. It reminded me of the lightning from the storms back home in Reidsville but this was different. Imagine seeing hundreds of lightning strikes all at once but having no sound, lightning always has sound but this didn't. It was strange and beyond my 10 year old comprehension. It was obvious that what ever I knew of reality was not in the concept of this reality or the lack of reality. Everything was beyond my understanding.

"Have you ever seen anything like this Scotty?"

"Yes, I seen it once."

"What about you?" I asked turning to the giant as he led the way.

"Huxley my name is Huxley, you can call me giant everybody else does. I seen it once too, everyone does when they come to The Land of Adventure."

"So, what do you know about the dragon?" I asked.

"The dragon, he fights The vile Ones, and he keeps the treasure for everyone. We must take the treasure to Atlantis," the giant, Huxley, answered.

"What's in Atlantis?" I asked.

"You must go to Atlantis to fight The Vile Ones, there you will stand the greatest test in life and once you..."

"Once I what?"

Huxley became silent and refused to answer my inquiry about Atlantis, but I didn't let that deter me from pressing the matter.

"What is he talking about Scotty?"

"Sir, only you know dear lad."

"Please Scotty, just tell me for once with no riddles. How can I do all this if I don't know what it's about?"

"Only he whom sees a far off can know the answer within himself." Scotty replied.

"I'm getting nowhere with you!" I replied with frustration.

"Don't worry dear lad, you will do well. The King of Adventure knows it quite well, and once you understand the riddles and what the giant had said you will save all the land and there's no riddle in that my dear lad."

CHAPTER FORTY-FOUR

As Danny sat in the presence of One-eyed Steve and his crew members the ground beneath them began to shake.

"It's the giant, he must have found us."

"That is not the giant, Julius," One-eyed Steve said as a few animals ran by them in the dark of the night.

"Sir, the animals are running."

"What in tar-nation are they running from?" One-eyed Steve asked.

"It's The Vile Ones, it has to be."

"The Vile Ones? There's no way they made it this far yet."

As soon as he said that the earth began to violently tremble and shake.

"It has to be The Vile Ones, there's no other way to explain it, Sir," Julius spouted.

"Who are The Vile Ones?" Danny asked.

"They're the ones stealing imagination from the adventurer ones," Julius answered.

"What are you talking about?" Danny asked loudly trying to be heard over the sound of a trembling earth.

"They're taking over imagination and the land falls off into a bottomless pit each time they destroy one's imagination," Julius replied.

"I think you're right, Julius, it must be The Vile Ones. We need to get back to the ship."

"What about my brother and the dragon?"

"What about them? If we don't get back to the ship there might not be a dragon or your brother!?" One-eyed Steve answered.

"We can fight them, Sir!" Danny said as he pulled out his stick that shot laser beams.

"With what, your stick? There's too many of them and we can't beat them with that anyways. We have to defeat them with the treasures, it's the only way. We need to go!"

"You don't have to tell me twice," Julius spouted off.

"You will help me find my brother?"

"We had a deal, and we need to go now, but if you want to stay it's up to you. But the only hope you have right now is me, and you can bet your bahoogies on it!"

"I can't go with you, I got to find my brother."

"Fine, do what suits you best but me and my crew, we're going to our ship!"

"I need to go to the village," Danny said.

"The giant is the least of our worries, right now the treasure is what's important."

"Without the giant there's no dragon ,and no dragon, there's no treasure, Sir!" Danny said

"The boy's right, Sir."

"I know he's right, Julius," One-eyed Steve replied.

"Oh god, I hate being right!" Julius said as he rolled his eyes.

"Fine, have it your way. We will go to the village but if The Vile Ones get closer, me and my crew is gone.

"Sir, if we go while it's partly dark, we might get trampled on by all the beasts of the forest."

"I hate it when you're right, Julius!"

"I got an idea!" Danny said.

"I'm waiting to hear it," One-eyed Steve replied.

"What if I fly to the village?"

"What and have you betray me and find the giant all for yourself, I don't think so!"

"If I wanted to betray you I would've already!"

"No, you stay with us," One-eyed Steve insisted.

"He's right Sir, if he wanted to betray us, he would've already."

"Julius, if he leaves and the giant helps him find the dragon, he won't need us and we won't be able to get the treasure from the dragon."

"Sorry kid, One-eyed Steve is right. You're going to have to stay with us, we just can't risk it."

CHAPTER FORTY-FIVE

The violent earthquake shook the lair of Draggy, jolting him out of his sleep as my brother Timmy woke unexpectedly. "What was that?" Timmy asked.

Draggy pawed at the ground with his paws violently knowing what was happening. There was no way to communicate to Timmy that The Vile Ones were drawing near and someone's imagination was just stolen.

Draggy looked over to my brother and then back to the opening of the cave knowing he had to go fight The Vile Ones to hold them off from gaining ground.

"What, you're not going to leave me are you?"

Draggy looked to my brother then back at the opening of the lair and knew he had to make a decision.

"It's The Vile Ones, isn't it? They are getting closer, aren't they?"

Draggy shook his head yes and growled and snarled, making it known war was at hand and he had to go fight them.

"You want to go fight them, don't you?"

Draggy shook his head again, yes.

"I can't let you do it all by yourself. You're going to have to take me with you."

Draggy shook his head no, knowing he couldn't risk my brother's safety.

"You have to take me with you, I can help you fight them off."

Timmy grabbed the paper and began to draw. As soon as he was done there appeared a small cannon attached to his left arm and he was dressed in a soldier outfit just like Dad.

"Look, I can fight them too. All I need is for you to fly and I can shoot at them. You have to trust me like I trusted you."

Draggy bowed his head to the floor giving his approval to board upon his back as they both left the cave flying into the air to go fight the tyranny that haunted The Land of Imagination. Timmy gazed out into the distance and saw the night being lit up and he knew this wasn't going to be an easy fight.

Not long after the trembling the night sky that was once dark had become lighter and everything was more visible. From a distance the sound of cannon fire echoed through the night air.

"What was that?" One-eyed Steve said.

"Sir, it sounded like cannon fire."

"That's impossible Julius, there's not any cannons for miles."

"Maybe someone seized our ship and is firing the cannons from our ship?" one of the crew members suggested.

"Everyone be quiet! Do you hear that?" One-eyed Steve said.

"I don't hear anything but the guns, Sir."

"My point exactly, Julius."

"What are you saying, Sir?"

"There are no more animals running, nor the ground shaking."

"And your point is, Captain?"

"Whatever it is, someone must be firing those cannons upon The Vile Ones."

When Danny heard those words, he whispered to himself "He's still alive!" Danny didn't know how but he knew his brother was with the dragon and somehow some way he was still alive.

"You mean someone is fighting them?"

"Do you have any other explanation, Julius?"

"But the only one that can hold them off is the dragon."

"My point exactly. If the dragon is busy fighting The Vile Ones, then…"

"Awe, then the treasure isn't guarded," Julius answered cutting One-eye off in mid-sentence.

"Your right, Julius!"

"But that doesn't explain the cannons, dragons don't have cannons. But no one would dare fight The Vile Ones but a dragon. The dragon has to have someone helping him."

"You're right again, Julius. It has to be the dragon, and someone must be helping him."

"Sir, if someone's helping the dragon then it's possible to withstand The Vile Ones as well!"

"Do you want to go fight The Vile Ones?"

"No Sir,"….Julius replied.

"I didn't think so, I didn't think you'd want to risk losing your imagination."

"Sir, what if Julius is onto something here?" Danny asked.

"What are you saying?" One-eyed Steve asked.

"Yea, what am I onto?" Julius asked.

"Well, Julius just used his imagination."

"I'm not following you."

"Yeah, how did I use my imagination?"

"By saying someone is helping the dragon. Maybe it's possible to withstand The Vile Ones and maybe using your imagination is the only way to not have it stolen."

"Oh deary me... I hate being right!" Julius said.

"So, what are you suggesting?" One- eyed Steve asked.

"You have a ship don't you, what if you used it to fight The Vile Ones and held them off? You could prolong the destruction from The Vile Ones. Besides, if you helped the dragon maybe he won't fight against you. Maybe if we befriended the dragon, he won't be our enemy?"

"Sir, the kid has a point. Remember the enemy of our enemy is our friend, you said it so yourself, Sir," Julius said.

"I hate it when you're right Julius!" One-eyed Steve replied then tugged at his goatee and turned to Danny and asked, "So how do we do this young man?"

"We will need your ship."

"But our ship is on the water, how would that do us any good Danny?" One-eyed Steve asked.

"We use our imagination, remember whatever we write or draw it comes true!"

"And just how do you suppose we get our ship here?"

"We make your ship fly!"

"Arr.. good plan but there's one problem with that, there's no way we will make it there in time the ship is a half days journey."

"I can fly and bring your ship back."

"There's no way I will entrust my ship to someone else. I do believe I can come up with a better plan."

"And your plan?"

"Arr.. I will go get my ship with my trusted companions, that's my crew if you so happened to be wondering whom they were."

"You can't leave on foot, you just said it's a half a day away.

There's no way everyone can make it in time to fight off The Vile Ones."

"Well, it seems you're not using your imagination as well are you?" One-eyed Steve replied.

Danny looked at One-eyed Steve with a questionable look wondering what kind of calamities were stirring around in that mind of his as One-eyed Steve pulled out his paper and pencil and began to draw. He said, "Your right Danny, whatever we write or draw comes true! And it looks like you're not the only one who is able to fly now," as One-eyed Steve and the rest of the crew starts floating in the air a foot or two off the ground.

"I have a better idea!"

"Arr.. and what's that, Danny?" One-eyed Steve asked.

"Let me see your paper, I'll show you," Danny said.

"This better be good!" One-eyed Steve said as he handed Danny the paper and pencil.

"It will Sir, just watch."

Danny took the paper and pencil and drew and once he had drawn the picture Julius looked above him and said to One-eyed Steve, "Sir, you might want to see this."

"What's that, Julius?"

Julius pointed above their head to One-eyed Steve as their ship appeared above them floating over the trees.

"Our ship, Sir, it's floating!"

"I know that, Julius. It's a boat it supposed to float."

"Sir, it's not supposed to float in the air," Julius answered.

One-eyed Steve looked up to see the ship floating above him and turned to Danny and said, "Kid I'm starting to really like the way you think."

CHAPTER FORTY-SIX

The Vile Ones were dressed in dark hooded trench coats with staffs that they would plunge in the ground and electricity would shoot from the tops as the ground shook under them and as they walked the ground fell out from behind them. From the skies the cannons of my youngest brother filled the night air as Draggy would swoop downwards so my brother could get a good aim to shoot his cannon at The Vile Ones in hopes to prevent them from moving forward of their destruction. It was as if every time they took a piece of land it erased everything. It was up to my brother and Draggy to hold them off.

"There's too many of them Draggy!" Timmy yells.

Draggy screams in a violent manner as he swoops down and breathes his breath upon them knocking a few Vile Ones back, but no fire would come from Draggy's mouth.

"You can't shoot fire can you?" Timmy yells.

Draggy screamed at the top of his lungs trying to communicate with Timmy he can't shoot fire and the only comfort Draggy had was knowing he might be able to hold back The Vile Ones with the assistance of my brother's cannons that was attached to his arm.

"We can take them, just get me in the position."

Draggy turned in the air as my brother held on for dear life like a cowboy in an eight second rodeo. As Timmy fires his cannon with his other arm into ground missing a few of The Vile Ones but luckily sending them backwards into the bottomless pit from the force of the blast.

"Did you see that, Draggy? We got a few of them."

Draggy screamed to confirm he saw what happened.

"We got to keep pushing them back into the pit, it's the only way!"

My brothers plan to push them back was a good idea, but they were outnumbered as The Vile Ones arrogantly marched forward firing back with their staffs at my brother and Draggy.

"There's no way we can fight them, their powers are way too strong!"

Draggy screamed in anguish knowing they were too powerful and he could withstand their lightning if he got hit in the embodiment of a dragon, but my brother could not. Draggy knew he had to get my brother to safety and out of the range of fire from The Vile Ones as he nosedived in the air to retreat from the battle at hand.

"Where are we going?"

Draggy screamed and flew into the valley, nudging Timmy off his back and clawing the ground in anguish knowing he will have to leave his new friend alone and fight the battle by himself.

"What are you doing Draggy?"

Draggy turned and looked back towards The Vile Ones motioning he needs to fight them on his own and not risk Timmy's safety.

"You can't be thinking you can fight them on your own, you can't beat them without fire they are too many of them and their way too strong."

Draggy screamed and lifted up his head and pawed the ground knowing Timmy was right but feeling the pull within him to go defend the land. Then Draggy flexed his chest and arched his back and took off into the night air.

"Noooo.... you can't leave me!" Timmy screamed as Timmy is left alone in the night as The Vile Ones made their way closer marching their way towards him in the distance.

Draggy drew near to the front line of the battle to engage in war with The Vile Ones. He drew in his breath and flew swiftly through the lightnings and swooping down breathed upon The Vile Ones knocking them back forcefully into the dark abyss that followed behind them and flying past them out into the nothing that was. Cloaking himself in the darkness that swallowed up the light from their lightning.

Draggy's true form may have been a boy but he had the senses of a dragon and the instinct of war and how to fight valiantly, he was wise in the ways battle and cunning when it came to withstanding The Vile Ones and their tactics of war.

The Vile Ones were fierce themselves but not wise in battle. They used their power to overcome The Land of Adventure and when it came to battle, they would use the same tactics. From battle to battle their ways of war never deferred and was predictable which made it easy for the dragons to withstand The Vile Ones when it came to battle. All they did was walk in the straight line but the dragons moved swiftly though the skies and that gave them advantage. Sometimes they would win a battle, sometimes they would lose a battle against The Vile Ones but they still fought and they fought with the hearts of dragons.

Draggy knew he had to withstand The Vile Ones. If he didn't, imagination could be lost forever and he was willing to fight for what was rightly ours and the rights of all those who longed adventure in their souls.

Though on the outside he was a dragon on the inside he was a boy, but his spirit was a valiant warrior like all the other dragons who fought for the safety of us all. He flew with wings and under his wings was the winds of honor, and honor was his flight to war and by his heroic actions the hope for peace stirred within him. But peace never comes without a price and sometimes a price weighs heavy and sometimes we have to sacrifice our peace within us and become the warriors we were meant to be and answer the cry of war that's within us.

I would think that his anguished screams weren't just the voice of a dragon in the heat of battle but rather a voice with conviction. Either way it was his war cry, and he was answering the call within himself.

Timmy sat looking up to his friend as he left for battle, leaving him alone with only the feeling of abandonment to accompany him. He felt this before not long ago in Georgia when Dad left for the Army and the time the soldiers delivered the news of our father. My brother was only eight years old at the time but he lived more sorrows than that of a hundred men. He might have been a child but his thoughts at times exceeded the normal wits of an eight-year-old, and though he was smart at times the feeling of abandonment strove against his reasoning but deep down he knew Draggy had to fight The Vile Ones alone but he just didn't want to deal with it. He'd have gave anything to fight along Draggy's side cause Timmy was a warrior himself.

As he sat a familiar voice lingered above him and he turned upwards looking in his despair at the familiar face smiling down on him. Our older brother beckoned to Timmy from the bow of One-eyed Steve's ship.

Immediately his spirit returned back to him like a man who throws off a coat once he has come in from the winters cold. immediately Timmy discarded his despair like a raiment and took off the garment of self-pity and was in the attire of gratefulness of spirit as he beheld our brother Danny who greeted him with joy.

"Let down the clouds," One-eyed Steve shouted as a staircase formed in the shape of clouds made its way down for Timmy to board the ship.

"I knew you were alive!" Danny said as he gracefully beheld Timmy with a big embrace.

That embrace told Timmy everything he needed to hear, and Danny's arms said everything he wanted to say and there was no way they would ever be separate from each other ever again and nothing was going to stand in their way, neither rain or shine and surely not those unsavory Vile Ones.

"Where's Har Har?" Timmy asked.

"We got separated looking for you!"

"Where?"

"Don't worry he is safe. Right now we got to find the dragon."

"Draggy, I mean the dragon is fighting The Vile Ones, I was helping fight them off until he left me in the field."

"So, the dragon never tried to hurt you?"

"No, he never did and he's a good dragon!"

"Sorry to break up your reunion but I'm rather curious did you happen see any treasure?" Julius asked.

"Give the boys some time before you ask him, they just reunited Julius," One-eyed Steve said.

"Sorry boss you're right."

One-eyed Steve looked down at his watch and said, "Time

over. So this treasure, did you happen to see it?"

"I know who you are, you're One-eyed Steve."

"The one and only, so about this treasure?"

"If I tell you, will you help the dragon?" Timmy asked.

"So, you're willing to barter?"

"If it saves the dragon, then yes!"

One-eyed Steve turned to Danny and said, "Yes, he's definitely your brother!"

"So, we have deal?"

Danny knew right well where I was but unfortunately, I wasn't where he thought I would be. He really wasn't lying to Timmy but rather hiding my whereabouts from One-eyed Steve. Even though One-eyed Steve didn't trust Danny, yet Danny still didn't trust One-eyed Steve after all he did shoot at their ship earlier that day. Never the less, One-eyed Steve loved to bargain and so did my brothers.

CHAPTER FORTY-SEVEN

That night at the orphanage Sister Milica couldn't sleep. It had been storming while the lightning lit up the sky and the sound of thunder brought me to her remembrance.

"He must be in trouble!" she said as she set up from her bed gasping for air.

"Who's in trouble?" Sister Priscilla asked sitting up in her bed across the room of Sister Milica.

"No one!"

"You're not talking about Harold are you?"

Sister Milica didn't have to answer Sister Priscilla she knew exactly whom she was referring to as Sister Priscilla got up from her bed and turned on the light in their shared quarters.

"You seem to have a heavy heart tonight Sister Milica."

"You're right, the boy is troubling me."

Sister Priscilla walked barefooted on the cold tile floor in her night gown across the room and peered out the window as the night sky was lit up by lightning in the distance as she held her rosary beads in her hand searching for the right words to say to Sister Milica.

"You know we are the chosen and sometimes we have to do what's most important."

Sister Priscilla turned back given a look of approval that it was okay to go looking for me.

"It's hard to look at the storm coming and not want to seek refuge."

"What are you trying to say?" Sister Milica asked.

"I'm saying go, I will take care of things here. Go find him. There's no need to stay here with a troubled heart, I can manage until you return."

"Are you sure?" Sister Milica asked

"Yes, I'm sure we are the chosen and if we don't do what we've been called to do then who will?"

Sister Priscilla turned back and peered off to the storm brewing in the night through the window all the while knowing the real storm vexing her sister of the faith.

"But what if I'm worried about nothing and what if he's okay?"

"You see the storm coming in?"

"Yes, I see it," Sister Milica answers.

"Are we really ever okay when the storm comes?"

Sister Milica knew the nun was right and was wise in her words. She had to make sure I was alright, and she knew a great storm was brewing that she herself once had faced. and somehow, she knew Priscilla just wasn't talking about the weather but the storms in our lives.

"Its nights like these we know where we stand Sister Milica, go find the boy. I'll be waiting for your return."

The nun turned back to Sister Milica sitting on her bed and pulled out a paper from her pocket and handed it to Sister Milica and said to Sister Milica, "You know what to do!"

CHAPTER FORTY-EIGHT

The rain beat down at the front steps of Aunt Louise's apartment building as Mr. Owensby stood at the doorway with Aunt Louise to see her on her way to her apartment.

"Sorry, my umbrella it gets stuck sometimes.." Mr. Owensby said as he fidgeted with the latch trying to hold it above both of them.

"New York rain.," Aunt Louise sighed as she looked up watching the rain fall from up above.

"Yes, New York storms."

"It's quite stormy out tonight," Aunt Louise said as she turned to look at Mr. Owensby who was gazing into her eyes. She gazed back into his as she began to feel lost in his eyes.

"They have a way of making us love or hate them," Mr. Owensby answered.

"Love or hate them?" She replied in a soft tone.

"Yes, sometimes you love the storms then sometimes your wish for a day without them."

"I don't ever want to hate any storms, Mr. Owensby."

"Neither do I Louise, neither do I."

"Is that what you're wishing for right now, a sunny day, Mr. Owensby?"

"You can't wish on falling stars in the day."

"And just what would you be wishing for?" She replied hoping he would get the hint.

"This," Mr. Owensby answers as he leaned into kiss Aunt Louise on the cheek and said, "May I see you tomorrow?" in a soft mannered tone.

"Only if it's sunny," Aunt Louise responded with a soft subtle smile.

'"Well, I guess I'm going have to move the sun for you then, Louise," Mr. Owensby replied.

"You already have, you already have," Aunt Louise said as she leaned in and kissed Mr. Owensby on the lips as they stood under the umbrella and lightning lit up night skies accompanied with distant thunder.

"I will be looking forward to seeing you tomorrow," Aunt Louise whispered.

"I'll bring the stars with me if I could see you every day."

"Don't forget the stars, Mr. Owensby, a girl is always in need of a beautiful sky."

"And a guy is always in need of a beautiful lady."

"Well tomorrow is looking better already," Aunt Louise said as she turned away while their hands lingered slowly letting go from each other as she entered her apartment building.

CHAPTER FORTY-NINE

As we made it to a hill side to the lair of the fierce dragon, I felt a sudden fearfulness at the potential encounter with the dragon. I knew anything could go wrong at any given moment as I looked upon the opening of the cave that appeared more like the jaws to the gates of death. With my hands trembling I took my paper in my hand and drew chocolate cake for a peace offering for a ransom for Timmy.

"Do you want me to go with you, dear lad?"

"I got to do this on my own, Scotty," I replied.

Inside of me I knew I really wanted Scotty to enter the cave with me but I didn't need anything on my conscience if anything happened to him as I braved the lair with trembling hands.

The cave was dark and cold a shimmer of light flickered on the wall as I made my way through the lair nervously holding a chocolate cake in my hand. In my mind I imagined as if I were a knight about to go slay a dragon holding his sword with valor, but I was not holding a sword, I was holding a cake. The cake was my sword and I was going to battle and hopefully the only devouring that would be taking place would be some dragon devouring some good ole chocolate cake instead of me. Yea, it made total sense at that moment, some people and beasts have weakness and I was just hoping chocolate cake was the dragon's weakness.

As I made it to the flickering light in the opening of the cave while a small campfire burned in the middle of an opening of the cave as I studied the room, I noticed my brother and the dragon were nowhere to be found only some treasure chest that were stacked in piles in the corner of the cave. As I drew near, I saw a woman's figure in black stooping down and I suppose the crackling of my steps in the cave startled her as she stood up quickly facing me in her nun's outfit.

"Your here... I was worried about you!"

"Sister Milica, how did you know I'd be here?"

"I didn't, I drew you and it led me here, I thought you would have made it here by now and rescued your brother."

"But my brother isn't here?"

"I know."

"Do you know where he is?"

"I have my suspicions. I really think you should take a look at this."

As Sister Milica stepped forward she handed me the paper that was previously drawn upon. As I looked, I could see a drawing of a cake, a boy in form of a dragon and my brother with a cannon on his arm.

"What is this?"

"Your brother must have solved the riddle and saw the dragons true form."

"He's a boy like me?" I asked as I looked upon the paper.

"Yes, he is, just like many of us. We all were once adventurers in our youth, only now some of us stay true to the cause."

"What do you mean true to the cause?"

"The cause of always believing something good may happen," Sister Milica answered.

As I pondered her words my mind wondered at the drawing of my brother holding a cannon on his arm and his whereabouts were now more mysterious than ever.

"My brother, he has a cannon in the drawing, what does this mean?"

"Yes, I noticed, and the only thing I can think of he is helping the dragon to fight The Vile Ones. It's the only explanation I have."

"Then that's where I must go!"

"It's dangerous, you will need my help!"

"I have the giant and Scotty and I will be fine."

"You may want to listen to her dear lad, she hasn't swayed you in the wrong direction," Scotty said as he stood behind me in the cave.

"Your right Scotty, she has always tried to show me the way!"

"Then it's settled. I will go with you to help you find your brother."

"You may want to see this!" the giant yelled from outside of the dragon's lair.

As the three of us exited the cave of the dragons' lair Scotty pulled out a small telescope and looked into the goggles and focused upon the ship flying in the air in the distance as the dragon flew in the background.

"It's One-eyed Steve!" Scotty said as he handed me his telescope. I looked and sure enough, he was right, it was his ship with his emblem on his flag. I saw One-eyed Steve standing at the helm with both of my brother's accompanied by his crew members.

"He's taken my brothers captive!" I said assuming the worst

not knowing my heart was about to turn within me.

CHAPTER FIFTY

In the distance the dragon fought The Vile Ones as the ship of One-eyed Steve approached the battle ground and he pondered his plan on how he was going to defeat The Vile Ones.

"Sir we can't fire on The Vile Ones from this angle," Julius said.

"I know that, Julius!"

"What do you want to do, Sir?"

"Take down the sails!"

"Are you crazy Sir, if we take down the sails, there's no way we can sail the ship!?"

"Just do what I say, I've got a plan!"

"Oh..... something tells me I'm not going to like this!"

"Arr.. you may not like it but it's going to be one of those memorable moments Julius," One-eyed Steve replied.

"That's what I'm afraid of,"' Julius said as he cringed his shoulders thinking oh why do I work for this half-deranged pirate?

"Take down the sails!" One-eyed Steve commanded.

As the crew members took down the sails Julius stood waiting on One-eyed Steve's next command.

"Now what sir?"

"Everyone one who can fly, grab hold of a pole and those who can't fly well... you might want to hold on for dear life!" One-eyed Steve said.

"Oh god.... I know I'm not going to like this."

"Don't worry Julius you're going to love it!"

"Yes, that's what you say!" Julius said as he held onto the pole for dear life.

"Now I want half the crew to go to the back of the ship and turn the ship where we are facing The Vile Ones from a side view. And those on the left at the pole I want you to fly to the right and tip the ship so we can flip it to its side. Those under the ship I want you to go to the back of the ship and push the ship down the battle line so we can fire the cannons from a bird's eye angle."

One-eyed Steve's ship was facing The Vile One's head on. He knew he had to turn the ship to its side to get any firing position on The Vile Ones from up above. It was a tricky move but One-eyed Steve was a pirate and tricky moves came along with the territory.

As the crew members used their new powers of flying, they positioned the ship. So it was now parallel with The Vile Ones who were marching along the ledge of the dark abyss in straight line.

"Now prepare the cannons to fire at my command!"

"Sir, I hope this is going to work."

"I hope so too, Julius!"

"What do you mean, you hope?"

"Well, there's always a chance it might not work Julius"

"Oh...I was afraid you was going to say that." Julius said as he held tight to the pole and made a cross sign over his head and shoulders.

"Ready, set, fire!" One-eyed Steve yelled above the crew as

the cannons fired towards The Vile Ones.

As the ship fired on The Vile Ones it thrust through the air from the velocity of the cannons plunging the ship higher into the sky from its blast.

"Quick! Fix the sails, let it catch the air!" One-eyed Steve commanded hoping to use the sails as a parachute to slow the ship down from skyrocketing into the sky.

As the crew members quickly scrambled, flying in the air trying to fix the sails, Timmy fell from the ship towards the ground at a fast speed.

"Sir, we lost the kid!" Julius screamed out loudly.

"Fire at the sky!"

"Fire at the sky?" Julius asked.

"Yea, it will launch us back down towards the ground to get the boy," One-eyed Steve replied.

As the crew members fired the cannons towards the sky, One-eyed Steve was right, the blast from the cannons projected the ship back downwards to the ground but at a high velocity.

"Sir, the ship is falling back to the ground," Julius yelled.

As Julius yelled to One-eyed Steve, Danny jumped from the ship flying downwards to his brother Timmy, who was free falling from the sky, at fast as he could. Timmy's fate depended on if Danny could reach him before he hit the ground. As Danny flew, he watched his brother disappear from his view of sight.

"Timmy..." I screamed as I fell to my knees and I watched my little brother Timmy fall to his tragic death.

Chapter Fifty-one

As Harold sat talking, reliving the moment in his story, telling it to his son and his grandchildren, he became silent then stood up from his chair and took a small walk away from everyone and turned back to see disheartened looks on everyone's faces.

"Sometimes in life things happen to us and sometimes when we least expect it our lives are changed forever," Grandpa Harold said.

"He can't be dead Grandpa, he can't be dead!" Johnny said as he was brought to tears at the thought of Grandpa Harold's brothers' death.

Then Grandpa Harold shook his fist and looked at everyone and said, "Life changes in the blink of the eye. One moment we are here with our loved ones then in a moment they are gone. What matters the most in life is if we tell the ones we love what they mean to us. If we don't tell them, how will they know?"

"And I fell to my knees tormented in my soul. Then all of a sudden, I saw a dragon flying up out of nowhere and my brother Timmy was riding gloriously on the dragon's back. That dragon saved my brother's life, just when I thought he was dead. Sometimes things happen in life and when we least expected it our life was changed forever.

Everyone who was listening was overcome with joy knowing that Harold's brother wasn't dead but saved by the dragon. As Johnny's tears turned to happiness he clapped his hands with joy.

"And that dragon, my friends, was Draggy, the best dragon in all of the world."

I said it before, there was a lot of wisdom under that ball cap of Harold. He might look like some old guy in overalls, but he was a great storyteller. He was someone who knew how to grab hold of someone's attention and make them feel something inside and make them really think. As everyone listened to Harold's story they felt the joy when they heard his brother was alive and the sadness when they thought he had died. Timmy might have been riding gloriously upon a dragon but everyone at that party was riding on a roller coaster of emotions listening to Grandpa Harold's story.

Chapter Fifty-two

"You saved me!" Timmy said riding on Draggy's back as he flew up wards to Dannys view of sight.

Danny's heart leaped for joy when he saw Timmy riding on the dragon's back thankful he had saved our brother's life and flew to greet them both in the air.

"Look!" Sister Milica said as I was on my knees in tears, and when I had gazed out, I beheld Timmy riding on the dragon's back flying back towards the ship as Danny flew by their side.

"That's Danny and Timmy!" I said as I stood up looking from a distance seeing both my brothers flying in the air. Knowing they were both okay and together, my heart blissfully rejoiced.

"We got to get to the ship," I said.

By this time the crew members of One-eyed Steve had managed to get the sails to the ship fixed as it slowed down from its fall and set the ship upright again. It floated in the air as the dragon and my brothers flew back to the safety of One-eyed Steve's ship.

"Sir, the boy is on the dragon's back, and the dragon is staring at you!" Julius said as Draggy held onto the side looking in the eye of One-eyed Steve, and my brothers entered the ship.

"I can see that, Julius."

"Sir, I don't think He's afraid of you!"

"Yes, I can see that too, Julius."

"What do you want us to do?"

"Nothing, let's not provoke him."

"Sir, I don't think he wants to hurt us."

As Julius said that the dragon screamed as a cannon shot from the side of the ship hitting him in the side and he fell backwards into the air down towards the black abyss.

"Who shot the dragon?" One-eyed Steve said in anger.

"Sorry Sir, we didn't mean to fire the cannon it must have still been lit from one of the miss fires," one of the crew members shouted.

"Now how will we find the treasure?" One-eyed Steve shouted.

"Your worried about the treasure over his life?" Timmy yelled in disbelief.

"Sir, the kid's right!"

"I know the kid's right, Julius." One-eyed Steve replied.

"You got to go save him!" Timmy yells.

"We can't risk going into the dark abyss," One-eyed Steve replied as he looked out into the dark abyss.

"Sir, you might want to do what the young boy wants."

"Whys that, Julius?"

"Sir, it might be in your best interest to look," Julius replies.

As One-eyed Steve turned and looked Timmy had his cannon on his arm pointed down at One-eyed Steve's lower abdominal area.

"Cause, your bahoogies depend on it," Timmy says.

Then One-eyed Steve turned to Danny, who had pointed his laser stick at his lower abdominal area earlier, and said to him, "Yes, he's definitely your brother!"

CHAPTER FIFTY-THREE

While we stood looking from a distance, the dragon fell into the unknown and the ship of One-eyed Steve followed after the dragon into the dark abyss.

"The ship is going after the dragon," the giant said.

"We need to help them," I said.

"If he enters the dark abyss, he might risk the fate of imagination!" Sister Milica replied.

"How is that possible?"

"He's at the mercy of doubts, unless he overcomes it with imagination that's the only way!"

As Sister Milica said those words the ship left our sight and went downwards into the dark abyss.

While One-eyed Steve's ship entered the dark abyss, the remaining Vile Ones drew near, and the problem still remained. They were drawing closer and if we didn't do something quick The Land of Adventure would lose more ground to The Vile Ones.

"What are we going to do?"

"Sir, only you know the answer!"

"How do I know the answer, Scotty?" I asked.

"The answer is always within you, you just got to write it."

"Write what, how are we going to beat The Vile Ones? The only ones who can hold them off are the dragons."

"Like I said, only you know the answer!"

"How is that the answer?" I asked and, in that moment, I realized I just answered my own question.

"The dragons, that's the answer isn't it, Scotty?"

"Only you know the answer, dear lad."

"But there's no dragons anywhere near!"

"Again Sir, you know what was written to you, all you have to do is…"

"Draw them?" I said, as a light bulb went off in my head.

As I pulled out the paper I began to draw and when I looked up in the sky, I looked in the distance as three dragons drew near and began to fight The Vile Ones.

"How did you know, Scotty?"

Scotty looked, smiled, and tipped his hat and saying, "Answers, answers, answers will all be answered when the question is in the ears of those who may reveal to you what you seek."

"I answered my own question."

"Yes, dear lad you already know."

"So, the answers are inside of me, only I can reveal what I seek?"

"Sir, like I said you already know."

It was at that moment I started to understand Scotty's riddles, and his riddles didn't seem like riddles any longer now that I knew the true answers lied within myself' I just need to ask it and if I asked it, I could answer it. I just needed to learn to trust my own intuitions. But that didn't mean I knew it all, I was still in the dark on many things. But my understanding was growing.

CHAPTER FIFTY-FOUR

My eyes grew heavy as I watched from afar the battle taking place between The Vile Ones and the dragons, neither one of them prevailing against the other, as I fell into a deep sleep waiting for the ship's return.

I was back in New York at Aunt Louise's apartment sitting at dinner with my brothers and Aunt Louise. We heard a knock at the door and we all sat still not making a sound, knowing if we didn't answer we wouldn't get the bad news of Dad's disappearance.

The knock became louder and louder. Then the knock turned into sounds of gunfire. As we sat there trying to ignore the gunfire blazing, the walls to the apartment fell down around us and I stood in a large open field alone.

"Where am I?" I asked as the feeling of loneliness crept in. I strolled the grassy field that lead to a tree standing all alone, battered with all its leaves gone and part of its limbs broken as it stood out in the summer sun.

I knew leaves didn't fall in the summertime, only in the winter and whatever caused these leaves to fall must have been something dramatic as I looked upon it with admiration.

"It's you isn't it, Harold?"

As I turned Sister Milica stood behind me.

"What do you mean, Sister Milica?"

"You're the tree, torn and helpless!"

I knew what she meant. I was torn and helpless.

"When I was a child in Serbia, we use to plant trees out in the fields and one thing I learnt was you always have to water the young trees. If you don't, they never grow to their full potential. Sometimes it takes someone to understand us for us to reach our full potential."

"But what if it's too late for me, Sister Milica?"

"It's never too late as long as there's goodness and hope is rooted within you nothing can overcome you, not even the strongest storms of life."

I knew she was right and I had faced many storms recently. Maybe I was that tree, maybe I was seeing myself as myself, and maybe she was showing me what I needed to see.

"Can I ask you something Harold?"

"Sure Sister Milica."

"What's the one thing you want most out of life?"

"I want my family back."

"And what are you willing to do to make this happen?"

"Whatever it costs me, Sister Milica."

"Then it's never too late, is it Harold? As long as you hope, nothing is ever too late for you. As long as you have hope you have everything!"

Maybe she was right, maybe it wasn't too late for me. Just like that tree I had weathered the many storms in life but goodness and hope were still rooted in me. I don't know why she showed up in my dream that night. Maybe she knew that knock at the door was my tempest, my furious storm. Maybe she knew I just needed to see the hope still rooted within me to know everything was going to be okay. All I can say is I faced a battered tree and saw myself. I saw the tree and found hope.

"Wake up, dear lad!" scotty said as he nudged my shoulders with his hand as I woke stretching to the early morning light.

"The Vile Ones have fled the day light," the giants said.

"The ship, has it returned yet?" I asked.

"No, they're still in the dark abyss," Scotty answered.

"Then we need go to the edge!"

"But who will watch over the treasure, dear lad?"

"He can," I said pointing at the giant. "Besides, who would dare try to steal treasure from a giant?"

As we were deciding on who would guard the treasure the three dragons came and landed before us and one of them changed form. Sister Milica's roommate Priscilla stood before us.

"It's worse than we thought," Sister Priscilla said.

"Thanks for coming," Milica answered.

"You're welcome. I would've left with you if I had known The Vile Ones had prevailed this far."

"There was another dragon here last night. He got hurt and fell into the dark abyss," I said.

"We know."

"How do you know, Sister Priscilla?"

"We know what is going on with each other and communicate without words."

"Then how do you talk?"

"We use our hearts. They speak for us. It's the truest form of honesty, if a heart doesn't walk in lies."

When she said this, it was as if a light had been turned on inside of me, we as humans sometimes lie to ourselves but when we walk in the truest form of honesty, the heart is clear to hear all things.

"I think you understand, Harold, and you're right. When we walk in the truest form of honesty the heart is clear to hear all things."

"You heard what I was thinking?"

"No, I didn't hear what you were thinking."

"Then how did you know what I was saying in my mind?"

"You weren't speaking with your mind Harold, you were talking with your heart. There's a big difference in the two and only a few are lucky in this world to ever learn to the difference between the two."

"How will I ever know the difference?"

"You just have to learn to listen and when you find that one truth in life that means everything to you then you will know how to prevail against all things."

"And what is my truth?"

"Did you not listen to wisdom in your dream last night, how goodness and hope are rooted in you? If goodness and hope are rooted in you then you walk in honesty and with honesty the heart is clear to hear all things. Trust in your heart's desire, and it will come to pass."

"And how do I get there?"

"You already know the way," she said as she turned and faced the edge of the dark abyss. "What are you waiting for? Go to the edge."

I knew what she meant by the edge, its where I had to go to meet my brothers. There was no other way, and if I wanted my family back, I had to hold to what was good and I had to listen to the truth within me. But honestly, I was holding on to the edge inside of me trying my best to not fall into my own dark abyss. Sometimes I felt as if I were holding on for dear life and any moment I could just slip away. Finding my brothers was my sincere hope and that was my truth.

Chapter Fifty-five

As One-eyed Steve's ship entered the dark abyss it violently sunk into a vortex like pull, dropping into nothing at fast speed. When they had descended into the dark abyss buildings appeared, floating in the distance, mighty tall buildings lit up in the dark abyss as they fell. The buildings were luxurious and breath taking as if the buildings themselves were sent down from heaven. Lightning also lit up in the dark abyss from Vile Ones who had fallen from many battles with the dragons. There were also small houses floating, many cars, greatly designed futuristic cars, paintings, and the sounds of a thousand songs playing along with any creation mankind could think of.

"What are those?" Julius asked.

"They're stolen imaginations," One-eyed Steve said.

"Sir, the Taj Mahal?" Julius said pointing.

"They've stolen every one of the great wonders of the world!" One-eyed Steve replied.

"How can this be?"

"I don't know, Julius, maybe they're stealing away all imagination. Undoubtedly, they have stolen imagination from the King of India!"

"Oh no.... this is not good," Julius said.

"Your right Julius, this is worse than we thought."

"Oh.... I hate being right!"

"I hate you being right too, Julius!"

While they were yet speaking The Seven Wonders flew past them and many inventions and architectural buildings. The Kremlin of Russia, the Temples of Myanmar, and anything that inspired the people was falling into the abyss. Somehow, The Vile Ones have not only stolen the imagination from many adventurers but many from all over the world. It had caused a ripple effect in all the world. Not only in our world, but parallel worlds. They had even stolen visions and imagination throughout all time and space.

"Sir look the dragon." Timmy pointed as they fell holding tightly to the pole.

"Quick be prepared to save the dragon,"

"But Sir, he is further away from us. How will we catch up with him?"

"I have an idea, Julius."

"Oh, I was afraid of that," Julius responded.

"You and you go to the back of the ship, load the cannons and point them as far backwards as you can," One-eyed Steve commanded as the two crew members did what he said.

"What are you doing Sir? Last time we fired the cannons in the air it sent us flying."

"My point exactly Julius, you might want to hold on to something."

"Sir, but we are going too fast."

"Don't worry Julius, I have a plan, You're gonna love it."

"I didn't love it last time," Julius said as he hugged the pole closing his eyes waiting on the blast of the cannons.

"Ready, set, fire!"

The cannon blast propelled the ship even further. The cannons acted as rocket engines, sending the ship at a higher speed closer to the dragon.

"Sir, the dragon, he is close now," one of the crew members said.

As they made their way close to the dragon he had fallen asleep. The wound that had damaged his body, from a close encounter with a cannon where part of his wing had been ripped and torn, was bleeding.

"Sir, he's wounded badly," the crew members said as he floated several feet from the ship.

"Get him on the ship and tie him to the deck so we don't lose him in flight and hurry we need to get out of here!"

The crew members flew from the ship to where the dragon was floating and guided him safely aboard One-eyed Steve's ship.

"Yes, Sir!" one of the crew members responded and proceeded to tie him to the post as they prepared to leave the dark abyss!

"Sir, how are we going to get out of here?" Julius asked.

"Quick, mend the sails! It will stop us from the free fall and slow us down like last time.

The crew members, doubting nothing, did as One-eyed Steve had commanded, and the ship slowly came to a stop in the middle of the dark abyss.

"Sir, we have stopped."

"I noticed that, Julius."

"We are no longer falling, something is not right."

"I agree with you Julius, something don't feel right."

No longer after One-eyed Steve said that a hand grabbed hold of the deck and one of The Vile Ones pulled his body up onto the ship and stood to his feet as one after the other appeared standing on the deck of the ship dressed in their black hooded trench coats while lights swarmed from their staffs giving off light to make out their form on the ship.

"I know who you are," one of The Vile Ones said.

"Don't look at them Sir! You will turn to stone!" Julius said.

"You will not turn to stone," one of The Vile Ones said.

"Don't listen to him boss!" Julius said.

"You belong to us now and there's no way out of the abyss," one of the other Vile Ones said.

One eyed Steve looked around to see all the imagination around them floating in the air and on everyone's imaginations appeared fingerprints lit up all over them and then disappearing and reappearing as If every imagination every thought of had its own identification and the fingerprints of one's work upon it.

''You see these imaginations, they all once belonged to great minds who roamed the earth. Now, they belong to us," one of The Vile Ones spoke. As soon as he said this a familiar face appeared on the face of one of The Vile Ones.

"Why did you allow me to get hurt?" one of The Vile Ones asked.

"I couldn't find you," One-eyed Steve said as The Vile One made him began to doubt within himself.

Behind him another Vile One asked, "Why did you allow me to get hurt too?" as One-eyed Steve turned and looked the same familiar face appeared on the face of another Vile One, then the same face appeared upon faces of The Vile Ones as they all asked "Why did you allow me to get hurt?"

"I didn't allow you to get hurt," One-eyed Steve said looking around frantically at the faces that were speaking to him. "I didn't know where you were. I didn't know what you were!"

"And you see all things through your patch, and you couldn't save me, yet you allowed me to get hurt?"

"How did I allow you to get hurt?"

As soon as he said that all The Vile Ones pointed their staffs towards the dragon and the shape of the dragon turned to a boy. One-eyed Steve looked at the wounded boy on the deck of the ship and he ran down and held the boy as he lied unconscious.

"I'm sorry, I'm sorry, I didn't know where you were. I tried to find you all these years," One-eyed Steve cried allowed.

As Julius looked at the boy laying helpless, he recognized him from the pictures that hung up in One-eyed Steve's cabin in the ship.

"The dragon is his brother!" Julius said as he looked around to all the faces of The Vile Ones who wore the same face as One-eyed Steve's brother. "Sir, don't listen to them. They're trying to put doubt in your mind."

"You belong to us now and so does your brother Steve, or shall I say high priest. Your imagination has no powers here."

"Don't listen to them Sir," Julius shouted.

"We know you too, Julius." one of The Vile Ones said.

Julius closed his eyes turning not looking into the faces of The Vile Ones trying to fight back their manipulation.

"You're not going to steal my faith," Julius screamed.

"We got to do something," Timmy said to Danny as they witnessed the adults being tormented by The Vile Ones. He knew if they didn't act fast there was no way of ever escaping their grip much less the dark abyss.

"I have an I idea, it just might work!" Danny said.

"What is it?"

"Follow my lead, Timmy!" Danny answered, then he turned to one of The Vile Ones and said, "Not so fast." The Vile One looked down and Danny has his laser stick pointed at the Vile Ones lower abdominal area.

"And what are you going to do with that little stick of yours?" The Vile One asked.

"I'm going to shoot your bahoogies off."

Julius looked over to Timmy and said "Yes, he's definitely your brother!"

Then The Vile One who was reviling my brother transformed his face from a shadow into my face using his powers of familiarity to try to deceive and manipulate Danny.

"Would you hurt your own brother? What would Dad think if you hurt you brother?" The Vile One said penetrating Danny's conscience, knowing he could never hurt his brother as he lowered his stick surrendering to the thought of hurting me and breaking Dad's heart.

"But you're not my brother!" Timmy yells out loudly at the top of his lungs.

As The Vile One turned to Timmy a loud blast went off echoing through the dark abyss as Julius opened his eyes to see one of The Vile Ones flying back from the ship as the cannon hit the lower abdominal area. Yep, you guessed it, Timmy shot one of The Vile Ones right in the baghoohies.

The blast jolted Danny making him come to his senses as he began to fire at The Vile Ones as the crew members fought back as well grabbing The Vile Ones and flying through the air tossing them all off the ship, leaving one of the Vile Ones on the ship, as the blast echoed through the air bringing One-eyed Steve back to his senses as he knelt down beside his wounded brother.

"Sir, we need to go," Julius said.

"I tried to find him Julius, I really did!"

"I know Sir, he's here now and you're the only one who can

get us out of here."

Danny walked up to One-eyed Steve and put his hand on One-eyed Steve's shoulder and said "Sir, your brother will never know if we stay here."

"Why did you help me?" One-eyed Steve said to Danny.

"Cause you once said an enemy of my enemy is my friend."

"And you said that once as well," One-eyed Steve replied.

"Your right I did, and friends don't let each other down, look around you you're in the company of many friends. Sir, don't let them down they're all counting on you!"

"How can I help them?" One-eyed Steve asked still lost in his doubts from the effects of the manipulation of The Vile Ones on his mind.

"Remember, whatever you write or draw comes true."

"You're right!" One-eyed Steve said as he turned and stood up looking over to The Vile One who was standing on the ship. He said to The Vile One, "The boy is always right and whatever we draw or write comes true and you cannot and will not steal my mind cause my imagination is greater than yours." Then One-eyed Steve turned to the crew and said, "Toss him off my ship, we got a mission to complete!"

As the crew members grabbed The Vile One he screamed out loud, "But you belong to us now!"

"Do I?" One-eyed Steve said as he pulled out his paper and held it out and said, "As long as I got this, I will never belong to you!"

"But your brother, Marcus?" The Vile One responded trying to cunningly use his brother as a means to infect him with doubts.

"Don't you even say his name!" One-eyed Steve said with anger and repeated his words saying, "As long as I got this my brother will live!"

One-eyed Steve believed in the power of words and imagination so much that he could write his healing into existence, and he couldn't be defeated if he believed in his words. He held up his prize possession taunting the letter from The King of Adventure in the face of The Vile One.

"You heard the Captain, throw him off!" Julius said as the crew members threw the last Vile One from off One-eyed Steve's ship.

After the crew members had tossed off The Vile One from One-eyed Steve's ship. One-eyed Steve knew he had to get out of the dark abyss and get back to land to save his brother's life and time was precious and his brother lied frail and helpless.

"We got to hurry. Quick! Go under the bottom front of the ship and push the bow upwards so we can fly out of this dreadful pit."

"Sir, how are we going to fly out of here?" Julius asked.

"The same way we flew in. We're going to use our cannons, Julius." One-eyed Steve answered then turned to his crew members and commanded, "Quick! Turn the cannons as far south from the ship as you can and on my command fire."

Once the crew members had turned the ship up right with the cannon set in position, they embraced themselves waiting for One-eyed Steve's command.

"Fire!"

As the cannons blasted, the ship launched in the air from the force and they headed back to land out of the dark abyss.

"Sir, we are not flying fast enough," one of the crew members yelled.

"Fire as fast as you can, we need to make great speed."

As the crew members did as One-eyed Steve said the ship increased in speed as they exited dark abyss souring into the air and the ship came to land floating above the ground surface peacefully.

"There's my brother," Timmy yells out to One-eyed Steve.

CHAPTER FIFTY-SIX

As I looked up, standing near the edge with Sister Milica and Scotty, the ship drew near and a cloud of stairs came down from the ship. We stepped on the cloud and were immediately on the deck of the ship as my brothers welcomed me with an embrace.

"You should've seen it Har Har, we went into the dark abyss and saved the dragon. We were going fast, and I shot a Vile One right in the bahoogies," Timmy said.

"I shot a few in the bahoogies too," Danny said.

"I made friends with the dragon. His name is Draggy and Danny can fly just like a dragon," Timmy said with excitement.

"I know him," Sister Milica said as she looked over to One-eyed Steve.

"How do you know him?" I asked.

"He is the head priest at the orphanage."

As our attentions turned to One-eyed Steve and the new revelations of whom he was. The morale of the men was heavy when they saw the despair upon One-eyed Steve's face as he left the helm of the deck to accompany his brother who was lying helplessly from his wounds.

"I'm so sorry, I tried to find you all these years."

The boy looked up to One-eyed Steve and put his hand to

One-eyed Steve's face. As One-eyed Steve's form turned into a boy and he knelt down by his brother's side.

"I was here all along Steve."

"But how come I couldn't find you?"

"You were a pirate and I was a dragon."

"What does that matter Marcus? There's no difference between the two of us, so what if I'm a pirate or you're a dragon? We're both adventurers on a quest," One-eyed Steve cried.

Tears streamed down One-eyed Steve's face as he felt the sorrows of being split from his brother all these years trying to comprehend why it took so long for them to be reunited and why after all this time destiny brings them back together but with tragedy.

"I suppose it wasn't fit for us to meet again until now!"

"It's unfair Marcus. We should've been by each other's side this whole time!"

"It's not what we chose as the chosen but now here we are to help the chosen."

"Not... like this Marcus, not like this, not you getting hurt!"

"The curse of The Vile Ones won't last long and once I overcome their curse the strength of a dragon will heal me."

"When Marcus, how long will it take for you to be healed?"

"Soon. I must take rest or I can't change forms to heal."

"I will keep watch over him, do you have any place he might take rest," Sister Milica asked lending her hand to help Marcus to health again as One-eyed Steve turned back to his former self.

"Show her to my quarters," One-eyed Steve commanded and Sister Milica took Marcus to rest from his wounds as I stood wondering what the outcome with One-eyed Steve and his crew members might be.

CHAPTER FIFTY-SEVEN

The hope of unity laid prevalent between One-eyed Steve and I, and trust was a highly valued issue that lingered about within reasoning. I was quite suspicious of him and I was sure he was suspicious of my intentions as well. One-eyed Steve was never the kind of pirate who deferred himself away from speaking his mind nor halted himself from expressing a manner of opinion, as a matter fact sometimes he was quite bold to say the least. So bold it made the average individual shy away from engaging in words of conflict, but I was far from intimidated by his one eye or haughty words. If nothing else, I was more willing to quarrel with his wits due to the fact he had earlier risked the lives of my brothers and mine by firing upon our ship the previous day. None the less, my ten-year-old anger was present with me as we spared with words.

"You and I are one-in-the same," One-eyed Steve said as he looked at me with a suspicious eye.

"How am I like you?" I asked.

"You're protective of your brothers, are you not?"

He was right I was protective of my brothers even to the point I didn't want to trust One-eyed Steve but he let me on his ship to reunite with my brothers. I could hardly argue with him in this matter knowing how he was humbled by his brother getting hurt and I thought to myself that could've been me kneeling beside my brother hoping for a safe recovery.

"You fired upon our ship!"

"Yea, that I did!"

"Why did you fire on us? You know there's no way I could trust you if you did such a thing?"

"I only did as you asked of me."

"I never asked you."

"Arr.. indeed you did for I received a letter from you."

Was it possible that I wrote to him? The mother of the giant said the same thing. If I had written both of them surely it must have been in the future, cause up to this point I had no previous dealing with One-eyed Steve and my feelings towards him was not in his favor and there was no way I would've asked him to fire on our ship risking mine and my brothers' lives.

"And where is this letter?"

"Look into your coat pocket, all letters return to those who wrote it."

Upon his request I checked my coat pocket and pulled out the paper and sure enough I read the words:

> *fire upon our ship and say an eye for an eye cause the true deception draws nigh.*

"What does this mean?"

Scotty answered and said, "Only you know, dear lad!"

"I would never do such a thing!"

"Undoubtedly you did, or else you wouldn't be reading it," One-eyed Steve answered.

The evidence I had wrote it was in my hand. But when did I write it and why would I do that? Why would I put myself in harm's way along with my brothers? There was more going on than I could comprehend and for me to write such a thing, all I knew was something had to have inspired me or given me a reason to write it. But the question was what was it? Little did I know soon enough I would get my answers as The Vile Ones executed their plans.

"So, now I've kept my side of the bargain, it's time that your brothers keep theirs."

"And what's that?"

"The treasure of course."

"Is that why you're doing all this, for the treasure?"

"I am a pirate am I not? And no I don't do this for me, I'm doing it for you Har Har."

"What, did I write you and ask you to help me on that as well?"

"Arr.. I see you're feisty no doubt, and no you didn't write me to help you but it's my sworn duty to save The Land of the Imagination. I'm chosen just as yourself and no one who is chosen can selfishly act on their own behalf."

"But you fired on my ship!"

"To you it was yesterday but to me it was ten years ago."

"Ten years ago?"

"Arr..that is when I received the letter no doubt. If you haven't noticed time has no bounds here, your yesterday was my day a long time ago and speaking of time the full moon draws near."

"What happens at the full moon?"

"Arr.. it's the true test of one's heart and if we don't get the treasure to Atlantis by the full moon all memories of the The Land of Adventure is lost."

"So that's why you want the treasure, to save The Land of Imagination?"

"Arr.. indeed and if I'm not mistaken, I'm not the only one! One-eyed Steve said as he looked down to me with a knowing eye.

He was right, he wasn't the only one. It all made sense now. We had to get to Atlantis, we had to save The Land of Imagination or else The Vile Ones would take over. But what was so special about this treasure and how did it have the power to defeat The Vile Ones?

Maybe One-eyed Steve wasn't an enemy at all, but he was someone who had a different perspective than me. It's like a coin, just cause our view differs from another's doesn't mean we are right and they wrong or vice versa. Sometimes it takes a lot for us to believe in what someone else sees from their point of view when all we see is our perspective. I viewed One-eyed Steve as the enemy but how could he be an enemy when I was the one who sent him the letter to attack our ship and how could I hold any resentment towards him if his mission was an honorable one. He was right, we were one-in-the same but we were just looking at the same coin from our own point of view, and it was relevant we shared the same passion and his mission in life and we had to go and do what had to be done.

Then Scotty, just like in times past, stood and held his hat to his chest bowing like a circus announcer to intrigue the crowd with his words of inspiration and asked, "Tell me dear lad, are you willing to harken unto the pirate, go and gather the treasure and go on a journey across the sea and go to Atlantis and defeat the dreadful Vile One and save all of The Land of Adventure? Tell me dear lad, do you solely desire to go on a great adventure in the likeness no one's ever saw that only the greatest of men so dare to live?"

With my spirit stirred with boldness, I had only a few choice words that could be so profoundly answered. "Let's go get this treasure and go to Atlantis and kick these Vile Ones' butts once and for all!"

Then One-eyed Steve looked and smiled with a twinkle of life in his eye and filled with admiration said, "Arr.. spoken like a true adventurer!"

CHAPTER FIFTY-EIGHT

To my surprise things seemed to take a turn for the better. What I had believed to be my greatest antagonist was really my ally. We were setting sail to the dragon's lair. I stood and beheld the landscape and all its beauty and at all the different trees mingled together in the forest and how they all lived in perfect harmony. A moment of clarity struck my soul and I understood we're all are like trees of the forest. In life we all take different shapes and forms and our appearance may differ from one another but at the end of the day we all belong to the forest. I heard someone once say you can't see the forest for the trees but looking at the miscellaneous character's that stood about me it was evident, I could see the forest for the trees.

Maybe pride hit me, maybe a feeling of triumph, but all my heart could render in that moment was a sense of belonging and I was honored to say the least. Whoever gets to live like this, embarking on a great adventure to the likeliness only a few so ever dared to dream? Only books told of great adventures such as these and here I was with my brothers living it. Who can ever say they had the chance to meet an eccentric giant, or a pirate who has a comical camaraderie with his misfitted crew, or an inspiring older gentleman who changes forms and runs like lightning, or a boy who turns into a dragon, or a nun with the purest of heart? If anything I counted myself lucky, not only was I grateful for the chance to live such a great adventure but to share it with my brothers and nothing could take me down from that cloud I was flying on.

As we made it to the dragon's lair my mind was still captivated and amazed staring out as the crew members hastened not to seize the dragon's lair to gather the treasure.

My silent peaceful moment of clarity came to a haunting stop as I heard terrible screams come from inside the cave. I looked to see bodies of the crew members being slung out of the cave as the giant exited the cave with the evidence of the chocolate cake on his mouth with his axe held high above his head ready to protect the cave at all costs. And in the middle of his fierce war cry, he looked up and to see me standing on the deck of One-eyed Steve's ship.

"Sorry I was protecting the cave, they with you?" the giant says in his low drawn out tone.

"Yes, they're with me, let them in we must get the treasure to Atlantis to defeat The Vile Ones."

"Oh, why didn't you say so?" the giant responded.

One-eyed Steve turned to Julius and said, "Arr.. I told you Julius, I'm the only one with one eye around in these parts."

As we entered the cave One-eyed Steve scouted around eye bawling every treasure chest hoping to come across a one that was familiar.

"It's got to be here Julius!" One-eyed Steve said.

"Sir, there's so many of them."

"Tell the men to carry them to the ship. I will keep looking and if they come across my chest don't hesitate to tell me," One-eyed Steve responded.

"Yes Sir, you heard him boys."

As the crew members toted the treasure chests to the ship, I couldn't help but to notice how One-eyed Steve's heart was locked in on finding his own treasure chest and how he sorrowfully grieved for it.

"Sir, we found it."

"Please leave me be. Give me a moment alone with my treasure," One-eyed Steve replied.

"You heard him boys, give him some time alone," Julius commanded as he put his hand on my shoulder as gesture to accompany him as One-eyed Steve sat in front of his treasure chest and became sorrowful at heart.

As we exited the cave a great light shot out from out of the cave and we could hear One-eyed Steve weeping in tears and crying out loudly. I don't know what was in the treasure chest or what would make a man weep so heavy but whatever the riches of it was it made even the toughest of men weep like a child.

While we waited for the proper moment to reenter the cave Marcus's health was recovering at a high-speed rate inside the ship of One-eyed Steve.

"My brother, where is he?" Marcus asked as he looked up to Sister Milica as she attentively looked upon him with care.

"He entered the lair to gather the treasure. We will soon be going to Atlantis."

"And The Vile Ones?"

"They've been held off for the time being."

"My brother, he opened his chest, didn't he?"

"I'm not sure if he has or not."

"He has, I can feel it and I can hear him weeping."

Sister Milica herself couldn't hear One-eyed Steve crying in the cave due to being in one of the rooms of the ship but she knew

Marcus was telling the truth. If he could hear him his strength of a dragon was returning to him and it wouldn't be too long until he was made whole.

"Take more rest and save your strength."

Marcus closed his eyes and fell back to sleep.

As we waited outside the cave One-eyed Steve exited as all eyes were fastened on him. Whatever he had experienced left him without words. His crew stood silent with admiration and respect as One-eyed Steve walked pass them with a humbled soul and red eyes that gave evidence he had been crying,

Once we had loaded the treasure on the ship One-eyed Steve stood at the helm of the ship staring out into the distant landscape drawn away in deep thoughts.

"Sir, we need to get to the boys' ship and gather their treasure.

One-eyed Steve doesn't answer.

"Oh no, I was afraid of this," Julius said.

"Why, what's wrong with him?" I asked.

"He's looked upon the treasure, sometimes when one looks upon their own treasure it changes them."

"It's just treasure," I said.

"No, it's more than that. You will soon find out yourself but first we must get to your ship and then go Atlantis."

"I don't even know the way."

"If I may, dear lad, may I make a suggestion?" Scotty asked.

"What do you suggest?"

"Your paper, if you draw a map, it will take you to the ship."

"All I have to do is draw it?"

"You already know," Scotty said.

"What about One-eyed Steve?"

"He is not suitable to lead everyone right now, so tell me lad, will you take on responsibility as a captain and lead us all and take us on a great adventure in the likeliness not many has dared to see?''

I looked over to One-eyed Steve looking out into the horizon. Then turned to look up to Scotty and said,'' Scotty, you already know!'' I pulled out my paper and drew the map and suddenly the ship began to move flying above the trees as we made our way to the sea where our ship was docked.

Chapter Fifty-nine

The Vile Ones had changed their plans of tactics and was devising a plan to get rid of all the adventures of imagination. In times past they would only come out at night. They harnessed the night to give them a source of power and the element of surprise. After the defeat of the previous night their anger was kindled within them, and they sought revenge. No one had ever gone into the dark abyss and returned nor had anyone fought them in the dark abyss and never has anyone ever tried and if anyone had tried, surely they wouldn't have prevailed. But One-eyed Steve's ship floating in the air gave evidence that one could prevail against them. While they conjured up their plan to defeat us, we were naive to the fact we were safe by the sun's protection, and we were about to be subjected to their devious attack.

As we made our way to our ship to recover our own treasure the evening sky was accompanied with a small army of dragons flying in our direction. They drew near and the look on their faces seemed cold and bitter and very threatening.

"They're not here to be peaceful!" Timmy said.

"How do you know?"

"I'm friends with a dragon!"

While Timmy was yet speaking one of the dragons shot fire

at our ship catching the sail on fire. Our ship started to lose speed as one of the dragons landed on the ship staring at me in the eyes then looking to One-eyed Steve as if he wanted to tear us limb from limb. The crew members stood protecting the treasure with sword in hand.

"He's right, they're not peaceful," Danny said.

"But dragons are on our side," I replied.

Then out of nowhere Draggy flew to the edge of the ship and latched his jaws on the neck of the other dragon and forced the dragon off the ship fighting in the air.

"We're under attack! Load the cannons," I demanded.

As soon as the cannon fired, One-eyed Steve jolted coming out of his trance and looked and saw the dragons approaching.

"Sir, we're under attack!" Julius said.

"Where's my brother?" One-eyed Steve answered.

"Sir, he turned back into a dragon and now he's fighting one of the dragons in the air."

"They're not dragons," Sister Milica said.

"They look like dragons to me," Julius replied.

"Trust me, I would know."

"And how would you know?" One-eyed Steve asked.

"Cause I can hear them."

"Arr.. There's only one way you can hear them."

"Yes, I know!" Sister Milica said. Then she changed form and turned into a dragon and went to fight against the evil dragons approaching our ship.

It was abundantly clear Sister Milica just wasn't someone who guided others but was someone who vowed the righteous cause to defend imagination against the cruelties of Vile Ones.

"There's too many of them. There's no way we can fight them off," Julius said.

"They're here for the treasure, we can't risk any casualty."

"You're not suggesting…"

"Yes! Raise the white flag, Julius."

Surrender was not something One-eyed Steve would have so easily considered but we were outnumbered and there was no way we could withstand them, besides, it was the only assurance of our survival.

"You can't surrender, Timmy said.

"Trust me, I have a plan."

"Oh no, something tells me I'm not going to like this."

"Don't worry Julius, you're going to love it. Hand me the paper."

Julius pulled out his paper and handed it to One-eyed Steve as the evil dragons circled our ship like sharks out at sea. One-eyed Steve began to draw on the paper and suddenly, every pencil had an eraser on the end of it. Before then the pencils never had erasers because no one ever would dare to erase anyone's imagination, it was unspokenly forbidden. The only ones who would dare erase away one's imagination was The Vile Ones and now all the crew members had erasers but had no idea just what kind of tricks was floating around under that pirate's hat of One-eyed Steve.

"Everyone take out your paper and draw every dragon you see flying."

"Sir, what are you up to?"

"Trust me, Julius."

As the crew members pulled out their papers One-eyed Steve gave the order, "Hold your paper to your side and act as if we are going to surrender even our paper."

"Sir, what are you up to?"

"Don't fear Julius, it all will be okay," One-eyed Steve said as the crew members raised the white flag of surrender.

CHAPTER SIXTY

As the evil dragons swarmed the ship fear fell on the men but they trusted in One-eyed Steve's instinct and did as he said. Several of the dragons landed on the deck of the ship snarling down at us knowing at any giving moment, they could destroy us.

I stood frozen, hiding my paper and pencil in hand as one of the dragons screamed and lifted his head towards the sky and shot fire into the air signaling the other dragons to join him as two other dragons threw Sister Milica and Marcus on the deck in their human form.

"You dare to fight us with these two weak dragons? One-eyed Steve, I hear you're a fierce pirate yet your dragons are easily defeated and here you stand surrendering to us?" the leader of the dragons arrogantly asked.

Then the dragon turned looking upon Huxley the giant to ridicule him as well saying, "And you the well-known lumberjack giant is even surrendering to us. It sure does appear to be a great day of victory for us."

The giant stood silent not saying a word so he wouldn't provoke the dragons any worse by speaking and put us all in jeopardy of getting hurt.

"What, you're not going say anything Mr. Lumberjack?" the head dragon asked scoffing at him with his words.

"Maybe the lumberjack is not cut out for it, get it, cut out for it?" the other dragon said with a snarly malignant laugh.

"And your pathetic dragon thought he could fight against our great strength and prevail. It never ceases to amaze me how you adventures think you can do anything your pitiful mind dreams up."

"Leave him out of this. We all surrendered, if you want the treasure then just take it. Leave us be and we will be on our way," One-eyed Steve replied.

"Yes, leave my friend alone," Timmy said pointing his cannon at the dragon.

"And what will you do with your little gun? It's no match for a dragon," the dragon asked snarling.

"I will shoot you right in the bahoogies, and trust me no one's tough enough to get shot in the bahoogies, not even a dragon."

"No one's going to shoot anyone," One-eyed Steve said, then turning to the dragon he continued, "We surrendered, and we will do whatever you ask as long as no one get hurt!"

Sister Milica slowly took out her paper from her pocket and slowly wrote and vanished from out our sight.

"Look, even your nun won't stay to help you all. I suppose someone has even wits about them to know when it's over," the lead dragon said.

"Yea, I guess nun knew trying to help them was none of her business, get it nun of her business?" the other dragon said laughing with a malignant laugh.

"Look, we surrendered. Take the treasure, leave us be," One-eyed Steve said.

"Not only the treasure, but your paper as well!"

"I knew that was your true intentions and you can have it. We will be on our way," One-eyed Steve replied.

"We can't give up our paper!" Danny said.

"Who is this boy, talking to me as if some boy can make a decision over the captain of the ship?" the head dragon asked.

"He is my brother!" I said as I looked into the dragon's eyes.

"And who are you?"

"I'm Harold Stanfield."

"So, you're the one The King of Adventure had chosen. Looks like the drawing isn't the only thing we will be taken from here as well!"

"And what do you mean by that?"

"We will be taking you as well, Harold."

CHAPTER SIXTY-ONE

Concern fell on the faces of everyone at the party who was listening to Grandpa Harold's story. In times past he and his brothers always seemed to escape from danger but this time it didn't appear so. There were way too many dragons and defeat just seemed imminent.

"Grandpa, they can't take the paper from One-eyed Steve, and everyone, how would they get the treasure to Atlantis and defeat The Vile Ones?"

"Yea Grandpa, Johnny is right. If they don't get to Atlantis then The Land of Imagination is lost forever."

"Wait a minute Grandpa, I see what is going on."

"And what's that, Johnny?" Grandpa Harold asked.

"The dragons couldn't capture you and had taken the paper. Something had to have happened."

"Oh, I see where you're going with this. You think just because we might overcome some other obstacles that we somehow escaped the dragons."

"Well yea Grandpa, it's pretty obvious."

"And what makes you think they didn't take me?"

"Cause Grandpa, you're here aren't you?"

"Oh I see, can't pull the wool over your eyes, can I?"

"No Sir Grandpa, you sure can't, but I got a question. One-eyed Steve was going to surrender. Just how did you get out of not being taking by the dragons?"

"Yes Grandpa, and what ever happened to Sister Milica? Why did she just leave? She was always there to guide you. I don't know why she left, it don't make any since," Tomas asked.

"Well boys, sometimes in life things happen when we least expect it, and it changes our lives forever."

"So, what happened Grandpa, what happened?"

CHAPTER SIXTY-TWO

The dragons flew around the ship closing in on us as the dragon gazed upon us deviously grinning in his apparent victory. He not only had our treasure to his spoils of victory, but also the one whom The King of Adventure had chose.

I stood there thinking there's no way I'm going to go into the hands of that dragon and the mere betrayal of One-eyed Steve's surrender didn't rest easy on my soul knowing I might become the dragons most prized possession. I said it before and I'll say it again, what matters the most is family and sometimes through thick and thin its family who is there for us at the end of the day and who'll do anything for us whatever the cost. So, there I was on the greatest adventure I ever lived with my life hanging in the balance. Then I heard the greatest words I ever heard coming from an eight-year-old boy.

"Over my dead body!" Timmy shouted with a blast of the cannon echoing in the air

No one's immune to the effects of getting shot by a cannon, not even a dragon. It was evident as the dragon let out a scream of agony from my brother's cannon ball of wrath. Yea, you guessed it. Timmy shot that dragon right in the bahoogies!

The blast caught the attention of the vile dragons who

swarmed our ship from a distance, turning their predator like behavior into the likes of a hungry hunter thirsty for blood. We stood on the deck of the ship as helpless prey preparing for the worst to come, but the blast was the perfect opportunity One-eyed Steve needed to execute his plan.

"Alright boys, pull out those pencils and erase every one of those dragons' wings!"

At One-eyed Steve's command the crew members began to erase the wings of the dragons and as soon as they began erasing the dragons' wings their wings begin to disappear, evoking sudden fear on the dragons as they wailed a bellowing cry falling to their impeccable deaths.

When it came apparent to the head dragon that One-eyed Steve and us wasn't going to give up the ship and treasure without a fight terror befell him and he did what any one would do in that moment. He got the heck out of there! Who could blame him? He had been out smarted by One-eyed Steve and an eight-year-old boy who just wasn't willing to give his brother up to merciless adversary.

But my brothers Danny and Timmy just weren't having it. There was no way they were going to let the head dragon get away that easy. They both fired their weapons at the head dragon, but he miraculously escaped from their aim of sight as he swiftly flew away from the hailing cannon fire and laser beams that ripped through the morning air.

Not only did my brothers fight back but all of the crew members took to the cannons and fired upon all the dragons. As Marcus changed into a dragon form to fight the evil dragons, my brother Timmy hopped on the back of Draggy and flew into battle accompanied by my eldest brother Danny.

Then out of nowhere four new dragons emerged fighting valiantly against the evil dragons and I gazed out into the horizon and it became evident to me they just weren't just dragons. They were adventurers and Sister Milica didn't abandon us, she just left to go get help.

The evil dragons retreated once they saw that the four dragons had come to rescue us, as my brothers joined the fight shooting upon the evil dragons and wounding one of them. Once he had been hit his powers was rendered and he turned back into a Vile One. When the evil dragons saw their disguise had been compromised, they changed their forms back into The Vile Ones and lit up the sky with lightning from their staffs creating a barrier between the dragons and my brothers and escaped out of their hands.

"Look! They're not dragons."

"Arr.. I see that Julius."

"Oh, this is bad. The Vile Ones are not supposed to come out in the day," Julius cried.

"Arr..I hate it when you're right, Julius."

"Oh... I hate me being right too."

Once they had made their escape, my brothers and the dragons returned to the ship and changed forms as Sister Milica and her adventurous friends stood before us all on the ship.

"Did you see me, Har Har? I shot down a few of the dragons and I got to ride Draggy. It's so fun to fly." Timmy said with excitement.

"Yes, I see it, Timmy!" then I turned towards Sister Milica and spoke, "I thought you left us!"

"No, I went to get help. I would never leave you in harm's way."

"So, all this time you knew about The Land of Adventure?"

One-eyed Steve asked.

"And you knew about it as well," Sister Milica replied.

"Well, I guess threes no secrets among us all now!"

"We really need to get to Harold's ship and get his treasure and head towards Atlantis. We don't know what The Vile Ones have in store for us along the way."

"Arr.. indeed Milica, or shall I say Sister Milica?"

CHAPTER SIXTY-THREE

While we embarked on our quest to find the treasure Mr. Owensby and Aunt Louise were embarking on a little treasure of their own, but the treasures of the heart. Mr. Owensby patiently waited for the following day to see Aunt Louise. All he could do was envision seeing her face again and to hopefully see her smile. It might not seem like much but it's those little things in life that have the greatest impressions on one's heart. He stood nervously at her apartment door with a bouquet of flowers in hand. He had no reason to be nervous, after all he did share a moment with her, and a good night kiss the night before.

And Aunt Louise, well she wasn't too shy when it came to Mr. Owensby or nervous but his quirky demeanor made her like him more as the days went on. She found his awkwardness and charm adorable and he was definitely someone she was looking forward to seeing again. Aunt Louise was hoping Mr. Owensby would keep his promise and bring the stars with him the next day. To be honest, I have no doubt in my mind he brought the stars with him cause every time he looked at Aunt Louise, he had stars in his eyes, and he was over the moon for her.

They say you can't really see the stars under the city lights.

Well, if you seen those two falling in love you might have to really reconsider that. To be honest, I really don't think they were just seeing stars in each other's eyes but the moon and sun as well.

The day had been a long day for the both of them, but that wasn't going to stop them from seeing where this thing between them was going. Mr. Owensby had a sincere heart full of optimism. He sure knew this wasn't by chance, it was destiny and destiny did not only come walking into their lives, but it stood at the brim of the doorway as he knocked with his heart in his chest and the smell of roses in hand as Aunt Louise opened the door with a welcoming smile.

"Nice scarf you're wearing today!" Mr. Owensby said.

"Aunt Louise smiled and said, "You know I don't wear scarfs."

"But if you did it would look fabulous on you!"

It was moments like that they begin to have their own private jokes and a familiarity of each other's mannerisms. Aunt Louise's answer could've been the shuffle in the grave if it had been taken the wrong way, but to Mr. Owensby those words was just another step closer to the treasures of the heart that they were both unburying together as they both shared a smile with one another.

If you ask me, that night they met the sparks were flying and today those sparks were flying even more in the city of New York.

CHAPTER SIXTY-FOUR

As me and my brothers stood on the main deck, we looked out into the open skies that lay before us and for the first time in a while we actually got a moment to be brothers again. The last time we were together was in New York before we were sent to the orphanage, but New York wasn't what we were really thinking of at that time. For a moment we felt like pirates ourselves. Just like all the stories we heard from the fishermen down in Georgia who would tell us great tales of the sea every summer when Daddy took us to Tybee Island to get buckets of shrimp.

I was wondering how Aunt Louise was doing in New York considering she was left alone with such a heavy burden and when would've been the next time I would've seen my brothers if it had not been for The King of Adventure.

We had a bond unlike others. We lost our mother when Timmy was born, raised by a widower father, only for him to go to war and to lose him. It had been a while since the thought of Dad being alive had even crossed our minds or the thoughts of hitching on a ship and going to fight the Germans and rescue Dad, instead here we were on a big ship lost in the 1400s.

In some strange way we were fighting our own Germany and our own oppression of a dictatorship. The dictatorship of The

Vile Ones who oppressed us and any adventurer who sought out to live life to the fullest through their imaginations. Standing there it reminded me of how we soulfully wanted to go and fight Germany for Dad and how our hearts were so big in the imagination. We knew we could never go and fight them, but our play pretend hearts were full of imagination and it all was the remedy to our sorrows.

Imagination is like that sometimes it covers up a multitude of sorrows. We might be going through the worse thing imaginable or the most horrifying thing that life can throw at us. But we can imagine a better life and can daydream our lives into a faraway destination. Sometimes our hearts are like ships and we just need to sometimes climb aboard and set sail into greater waters of imagination. Sometimes we just need an escape from life and the troubles that it has for us. One day we can dream we are pirates sailing the seas searching gold, or another day we can dream we are climbing the French alps. It's up to us and who knows where our hearts might set sail as long as we let the wind in our sails. We can be anywhere at any time and if we do that, we will always be free.

Standing there with my brothers I knew one thing for sure. I was living the dream. I was living in the moment. My heart was setting sail with imaginations and there was no one in all the world that I'd rather share my adventure with than those two boys from Reidsville, Georgia.

CHAPTER SIXTY-FIVE

As we set sail on our adventure to get the treasure great things were happening back home where we came from. It was the month of April in 1945 and the allied forces had entered Germany closing to the end of WW2.

The Soviet Army broke though German defenses in Vienna, Austria. Buchenwald concentration camp was liberated further weakening the German stronghold. Soon after American forces reached Bavaria, Germany in the southeast of Germany, British soldiers liberated a concentration camp in Bergen Belsen, rescuing many holocaust survivors who had been imprisoned by the Nazi army.

Hope was finally prevailing against the dreadful horror that plagued Europe, not only Europe but the rest of the world and the malicious acts from Hitler and his brutish army.

While the world waited on the news of what was taking place in Europe as the allied forces advanced into Germany hoping the war would end soon, me and my brothers made our way to Atlantis with hope of our own to end the tyranny of The Vile Ones.

But sometimes conquering that which plagues us is not easily won. Sometimes we all fight our own wars within our hearts and in our minds and sometimes the enemy we face the most is fear. Sometimes fear is the very enemy that holds us captive in life to pursue the greater pastures. Instead of walking into the greater promises in life we often die in those fields and the grass covers our dreams and grows over us and we become a memory of whom we use to dream to be and the dream of whom we wanted to become, and those dreams are buried in the fields of yesterday's hope. Then sometimes with courage we fight against all odds and prevail. We overcome the fear of life that plagues us. We shed off the very thing that hinders us and we become free. We break loose the shackles that bind us and walk freely and enter into greater pastures in life, walking by faith, believing with the greatness of heart, and become victorious.

Sometimes I think back to the advancing armies and how they all were living in hopes for a better day. They just weren't fighting with their guns, they all were fighting with their hearts in hopes of liberation of the people. They just didn't march into Germany, no they walked by faith, they believed that freedom for all life had value and they were willing to fight for it and fight for the lives of those who could not fight for themselves. Maybe they didn't just fight a war, maybe they fought a war within themselves as well, maybe they feared for their lives but still they fought and fighting they did and they entered into the greater pastures winning back the future for all mankind.

CHAPTER SIXTY-SIX

While we stood on the deck of the ship, we couldn't help but overhear and see the conversation taking place with One-eyed Steve and his crew members. Draggy did sign language with his hand pointing at One-eyed Steve and the crew members then pointed to his mind and made a fierce face then shrugged his shoulders and wagged his tail.

"Sir, I think Draggy is asking if we thought he was a fierce dragon."

"I know what he's trying to say, Julius."

"Well yeah, we did think that, who wouldn't think you're a fierce dragon?" Julius responds.

Draggy holds his belly and burst out laughing and points his finger to himself and shakes his head no then leans in with a questionable look on his face and points at One-eyed Steve's eye, then leans back and makes a devil horn with his fingers and a mean face and then points at One-eyed Steve.

"Sir, I think he is saying you look like an evil pirate."

"I know what he's trying to say, Julius."

"He might be right, you do look kind of evil in that outfit."

"I like this outfit. All the pirates are wearing them!"

"You remember casual Saturdays and we all dressed casual,

and you still dressed like a pirate? I think Draggy is right, we have an evil pirate for a leader!" Julius replied.

"I'm not evil, I'm just a pirate!"

"Yea, I think you're right Julius, you remember when we had vegan week and needed to eat oranges to fight scurvy and what did One-eyed Steve do, he didn't even eat not one orange!" one of the crew members replied.

"Stop with all the accusations. I'll have you know I like the pirate's look and I'm never going vegan. I'm just not into salads and that don't make me an evil pirate!"

Draggy starts to uncontrollably laugh holding his belly then looks closely at One-eyed Steve again and points to One-eyed Steve's patch then shakes his head no, then points at both his own eyes then points at One-eyed Steve.

"Sir, I think he's trying to say you can see out of both eyes."

Draggy shook his head yes and wagged his tail motioning to Julius he had guessed correctly.

"Don't listen to the fierce dragon!" One-eyed Steve said.

"Sir, he's not a fierce dragon, he's your brother."

Draggy puts his hand over his mouth trying to keep from laughing then puts up two fingers as if One-eyed Steve has two eyes and really wasn't blind in one eye.

"Fine, fine, I have both eyes. Besides, all the other pirates are doing it."

One eyed Steve pulled off his patch revealing he had two eyes and the crew gushed in amazement and shock as their jaws dropped to the floor.

"Yea, but you don't have a parrot like all the other pirates."

"Fine Julius, I'll get a parrot just like all the other pirates."

One-eyed Steve pulled his paper from out of his jacket pocket and lifted it into the air. All the sailor's eyes were fixed on his paper in his hand. As he brought his hand down, he placed his patch back over his eye then began drawing. The paper lit up in light as you could see him drawing a parrot then a beautiful colorful parrot stood on One-eyed Steve's shoulder.

"Ahh, look at the cute parrot," Julius said as he went to pet the parrot.

"Eeehh eeehh, don't touch me I'm an evil parrot like my evil master Two-eyed Steve."

Draggy was like that when he and One-eyed Steve were young boys, he always played jokes on his older brother. He loved to pick on him and now that they had been reunited with each other he couldn't help but to pick up where they left off being the jokester he was. After all, he spent so much time alone as a dragon and misunderstood, he couldn't help but want to rekindle the bonding he had with his brother One-eyed Steve. Sometimes in life all we have is our cave then someone comes along and brings us out of the cave we've been hiding in and when they do, we become full of life standing in the sun and enjoying the best moments of life. For One-eyed Steve and Draggy their journey had just begun, and it was one of the best days of Draggy's life.

CHAPTER SIXTY-SEVEN

As we made it to our ship one eyed Steve ported his ship alongside ours in the water. We were greeted by my crew members who had waited all night and day for our return. But our return wasn't met with optimism but with swords of defense when they saw us accompanied with One-eyed Steve and his crew members.

"Why do you greet us with a sword?" I asked as I approached the edge of the deck revealing my presence to my crew members hoping they would understand that One-eyed Steve meant no harm and we were at peace with him, but the curiosity of why I had befriended a rival tended to provoke their questions with dispute.

"Sir, have you gone mad and took leave of your mind to be seen with the likes of One-eyed Steve?"

"We have greater things to worry about right now. Besides, he is on our side."

"On our side? He nearly destroyed our ship yesterday and you're willing to trust him?"

"Yes, I'm willing to trust any man who could go into the dark abyss and return."

"The dark abyss? No one has ever gone into the dark abyss

and returned."

"One-eyed Steve has."

"If he went into the dark abyss then that means The Vile Ones are near."

"Yes, he fought them along with my brothers and saved the dragon."

"And you're now in the company of the fierce dragon whom you were supposed to defeat?"

"Yes, and his name is Draggy and he will be accompanying us as well."

"And you're willing to trust them?"

"Yes, even to Atlantis."

When they all heard me speak Atlantis, they were all taken aback cause no one has traveled so quickly to Atlantis in all of their adventures. They knew something had to have happened for us to want to go so quickly.

"How can we go to Atlantis when last night One-eyed Steve and his crew members stole the treasure from our ship?" one of the crew members answered.

"Eeehh eeehh, evil Two-eyed Steve!" the parrot replied.

"How could he have stolen the treasure from our ship if I was with him the whole night?" Danny asked.

"We would not lie to you. He came in the middle of the night and apprehended your treasure," another crew member spoke confirming the actions of One-eyed Steve.

"Lies, lies, lies, I did no such thing. It looks as you have a crisis on your hand. It seems like your crew members are willing to provoke such a heinous act. Can we say treason lies at the deck of your ship?"

"No, we won't betray our captain, but we will withstand you!" the crew members said as they lifted their swords higher and One-eyed Steve's crew members lifted their swords in place in case an attack was made.

"There will be no fighting amongst us. There must be a solution to what is happening," I said.

"I think I know what's going on," Timmy said.

"And what's that Timmy?"

"What if One-eyed Steve did steal the treasure from our ship last night?"

"That's impossible! I was with him the whole night," Danny replied.

"Maybe so, but that still don't mean that One-eyed Steve didn't steal from our ship."

"What are you trying to say?" Danny asked.

"One-eyed Steve, you've raided a lot of ships in times past have you not?" Timmy asked.

"Arr.. plenty in my days of piracy!"

"And have you ever plundered the likes of a ship like ours on a port such as this in the past?"

"Arr.. I do suppose I have in plundered many ships in times past."

"What are you getting at Timmy?" I asked.

"Don't you see? One-eyed Steve did plunder our ship last night so our crew members can't be lying nor are they trying to provoke treason."

"I don't follow," you Danny said.

"Did not One-eyed Steve fire on our ship yesterday?"

"Yes, but he said he did it ten years ago," I replied.

"And if he fired upon us ten years ago in the past and time has no real bounds here then it's possible that he stole the treasure from us 10 years ago in his past as well."

"You know, the kid might be right," Julius said.

"I think he might be right too, Julius," One-eyed Steve said then turning to his crew members he commanded, "Put down your swords undoubtably we stole the treasure from them 10 years ago last night."

"Sir, don't you mean we borrowed the treasure?" Julius asked.

"Arr.. yes, I meant borrowed, we may be pirates but we ain't thieves!" One-eyed Steve replied.

"How would we know that our treasure is amongst the rest of the treasure? I haven't even seen our treasure chest to even know what it looks like?" I replied.

"Sir, you already know!"

"What do you mean, Scotty?" I asked.

"Scotty means you will hear it if you are willing to listen to it. Your treasure always speaks to you, you just have to listen to your heart and you will know where it is," Sister Milica indicated.

"How can I truly listen?"

"Look at your brothers."

As I looked upon my brothers, I was lost to what Sister Milica was trying to say to me. I was confused, how could looking at my brothers reveal to me where my treasure was? It was more confusing than hearing one of Scotty's riddles.

"What do you see?"

"I see my brothers."

"Have you gone this far and have lost which you wanted the most?"

Then I understood what she meant, and she wasn't talking about me seeing my brothers but being in the presence of my brothers, the very thing I longed for and what was important to me, and when I listened to what my heart was saying the treasure begin to speak to me.

"I hear it. It's here, it's been here the whole time."

"What's it saying to you?"

"It's saying it wants to free me."

"The only way for you to be free is to go Atlantis, and we must go quickly. Besides, we don't know what The Vile Ones have planned and what lies ahead of us."

"You're right. We need to go as quick as possible."

"We got two ships now, should we take both to Atlantis?"

"Your right there's no need to take both."

Captain, we have been here all night waiting on your arrival. If you think you can go to Atlantis without us you're clearly mistaken," one of my crew members replied.

"It's settled then, we will take our ship along with One-eyed Steve and his ship, besides, Sister Milica is right we don't know what The Vile Ones have in store for us and two ships are better than one.

CHAPTER SIXTY-EIGHT

As we spoke a small fisher's boat rolled up to us as we were getting ready to sail the Atlantic to Atlantis.

"Forgive me good sirs, but I have a letter for a Harold Stanfield."

"I am Harold."

"I'm sorry, I am late I had been Rollin' all night until today to get you this letter," the young man said as he stood in his boat climbing onto the ship to hand me the letter.

As I looked upon the letter it read Mr. Owensby. I was shocked and confused to why Mr. Owensby had written me and how did the young man on the small boat find me?

"It's from Mr. Owensby."

Danny snatched the letter out of my hand to confirm the name on the letter and his mouth dropped wide open, amazed at receiving a letter from him in the 14th century.

"Do you think Mr. Owensby is The King of Adventure?

"I don't know, do you?"

"I don't know. How did he send you a letter?"

"I don't know Danny," I replied.

"Well open it, there's only one way to find out!"

As I opened it the letter sparkled as gold dust floated through the air and a light shined like the other letters that we had written on or drew upon. I began to read what he wrote:

Dear boys,

You might not believe me when I tell you this, but I know where you are. Late last night I received a letter from a mail carrier who told me of your whereabouts, it just confirmed my suspicions that you had gone on an adventure, and I do believe Scotty is accompanying you three on your journey? I trust he will do his best to keep you from harm's way. He has been on many adventures himself, don't worry about your aunt she is okay and seems to be optimistic to getting you boys back.

I know you haven't been able to stay informed with what is going on in the war with the Germans, but it appears the war will soon be ending. The allied forces have penetrated parts of Germany.

I also received your letter to meet you at the orphanage along with your aunt in the next coming days. I know time and worlds don't seem to have any bounds of reality where you are, but I will do my best to greet you along with your aunt as you have requested.

I also have some terrible news. Our current president Roosevelt has passed away and President Truman has been sworn into power I will keep you informed on any pending news.

Sincerely,
Mr. Owensby

"What does this mean, Har Har? You haven't written Mr. Owensby, and how does he know where we are?"

"I don't know Danny," I answered.

"You haven't written it yet Har Har, that's why," Timmy answered.

"Your right Timmy!"

"What if Mr. Owensby told Aunt Louise our plans to go fight the Germans to save Dad?

"There's no way he told Aunt Louise. If he wanted to, he would've told her that night he met her. Besides, I wouldn't worry about that."

"You're right, there's no way he told her."

"Why are you two worried about if he told Aunt Louise? Did you not hear what he was really trying to tell us?"

"What was that Timmy?"

"That the war might be ending, and we got a new president and things are about to change."

I had to give it to Timmy he was right, we were more concerned about him telling Aunt Louise about our plans to defeat the Germans to save Dad than the fact he was mentioning we had a new president and the war on Germany was being won. Maybe I was just blind sided by the fact that I got a letter from him, and he knew our whereabouts.

"Excuse me sirs, but I do have another letter for you the young men," the mail carrier said.

"Another letter, who is it from?"

"I do not know sir, all I know is it's addressed to you. There's no name on the letter."

As he handed me the letter my curiosity was stirred within me. Whom could've sent me the letter? Maybe it was from The King of Adventure, but he always enlisted his name on the letter heading to identify who sent the letter.

Once I had opened the letter my heart leaped within me as I tried catching my breath. "It's a letter from Dad!"

When my brothers heard it was from Dad, they couldn't believe it themselves as Timmy grabbed the letter from my hand with excitement to confirm the good news.

"Read it, Har Har!" Timmy said as he handed me back the paper and we leaned in close as I began to read the letter.

Dear boys,

I hope this letter finds you well, with much regret I have not been able to write you as I have so desired. The war has been a treacherous fight. One of my fellow soldiers is from New York and has two young boys himself living in New York. We often share pictures and letters from children with each other. Maybe when the war is over, we all can get together in New York along with his wife and children. His youngest reminds me of Timmy, he is quite a smart kid as well.

I hope you're doing well and keeping your word at not giving your Aunt Louise any trouble, but I have no doubts knowing I have three good boys who keep their honorable word. A father can only be so proud.

I did receive your letter Harold it was quite an interesting letter to say the least. I like how you're using your imagination telling tall tales about how you and your brothers went on a great adventure to rescue me from the Germans and how you meet a giant and become friends with a dragon while fighting The Vile Ones along the side of a pirate. It was quit an interesting tale if I do say so.

I am sure I will hear more of your great stories in the future, you've always had a keen spirit for things of an imaginative nature. Who knows, one day that imagination might do you well as a great storyteller?

I am also rather proud of Danny as well hearing he took a job as a paper boy at the newspaper press there in New York. I suppose I raised him well and hard work never hurt anyone.

And to Timmy, well what can I say about him? I'm sure he is still passionate about Hollywood and all their movies. Your Aunt Louise told me you watch movies all the time at the theater and act like Charlie Chapman and how sometimes you make your aunt laugh when you impersonate him.

If I can say anything, I must say I have three unique children that God has blessed me with and it makes me all the more want to hurry and get back home to you boys.

There's so much I want to say to you, but right now I can't, I have to get back to the front lines. I will be praying for you boys, and if you will please keep me in your prayers until my safe return to back home.

God bless.

Your loving father

"Dads alive I knew it!" Timmy said.

"Where did you get this letter?" I asked the mail carrier.

"I got it from a concentration camp in Germany."

The words concentration camp struck through my soul with an eerie feeling. It was good news that Dad was still alive, but the fact that he was now a prisoner of war made things even more terrifying for me considering anything could happen to him. Thinking Dad was dead gave me nothing to fear and I couldn't fear him dying if I thought he was dead, but hearing he was alive in some prison camp provoked concern for his safety. If anything, it lit the fire within me and caused me to remember our

276

plan back in New York to save Dad from the Germans. I guess sometimes as kids we have our hero egos within us and that little hero ego within me wanted to kick some German butt and save Dad from prison, but for now we had to get to Atlantis and kick the butt of those Vile Ones.

CHAPTER SIXTY-NINE

As Aunt Louise and Mr. Owensby sat at dinner with candle lights in a quiet little restaurant in Manhattan, Mr. Owensby timed his words wisely to reveal the good news to Aunt Louise.

"You do know things are looking up for us in Europe fighting the Germans."

"Yes, I've heard but I haven't been reading the newspaper much. Besides, I know the owner I was hoping that maybe I could get the news from you."

"I have something I think you might be interested in."

"What's that?"

"A letter from Harold, he wrote me a letter. I got it in the mail today and I think you should really read it."

"He sent you a letter?"

"Yes, he did!"

"Why would he be sending you a letter? I haven't even received a letter from him."

"I can't answer that, but I think the letter might make a little sense."

Mr. Owensby pulled out the letter for Aunt Louise to read and as she opened it a bright light shined from the paper as scenes of our adventure appeared on the paper taking place like it was on a movie theater screen and at the end of the letter, she sees her and Mr. Owensby standing outside the orphanage along with me and my brothers.

"It's real, I just saw my nephews on an adventure!"

"Yes, it is. It's real!"

"What does all this mean?"

"It's their adventure they are on and your nephews are together. Don't you get it, The King of Adventure was bringing them together again."

"How is all this possible?"

"Who knows? All I know is they're using their imagination and imagination writes the greatest adventure a heart can dream up."

"We were standing in front of the orphanage."

"Yes, we were and if you dare to imagine Madam, it might become true."

"To have my nephews back again I'm willing to imagine anything."

"So would I Louise, so would I."

CHAPTER SEVENTY

The sea was quiet. The waves gently splashed on our two ships as we rode on the waters towards Atlantis. The sea might have been gentle on us, but inside my spirit was waves of gigantic proportions crashed into the shorelines of my soul as the ship within me was tossed and turned at the thought of Dad.

One-eyed Steve and his crew members rode aside us to provide protection in case we came into harm's way. There was comfort in knowing this, still my spirit was stirred within me.

"It must be tough on the boy."

"I do believe you're right, Julius," One-eyed Steve replied.

"You know there is only so much you can do."

"What are you saying, Julius?"

"At the orphanage, you can only do so much there."

"I do my best, Julius!"

"I know that Sir, I'm just saying not every child has had the opportunity to go on an adventure like those three!"

"Indeed, you're right, Julius."

"What I'm trying to say Sir, you have all those children you're responsible for at the orphanage but not all are lucky as them to find out their father is still alive."

"You're right, Julius, like always. I just wish I could do more for those who are without."

"You're doing your best, we all are doing our best, it's just sad the world is sometimes imperfect and full of injustice. But I know one thing for sure The King of Adventure chose him for some reason and we must honor it."

"When have we not honored The King of Adventure? We have had many great adventures and we wouldn't abandon him now."

"Indeed Sir, we've been on many adventures together, but is this not the greatest adventure of all to be in the presence of the one chosen by The King of Adventure, that's the greatest honor of all!"

"Indeed. Julius, we just need to wait and see why he was chosen out of them all."

"I don't know why Sir, but The King of Adventure knows all things. All we can do is imagine great things are yet to come."

"Indeed Julius, lets imagine great things to come!"

What people didn't know was One-eyed Steve was the head priest of the orphanage, and he had a great desire to help the less fortunate out. He himself was an orphan as a child along with his brother who was split into separate orphanages just like my brothers and I, so he had a keen interest in bringing families back together when he himself desired so greatly all these years to be back in the presence of his brother. Maybe that was part of The King of Adventure's plan to bring him and his brother back together again. I would like to hope that was part of his plan, but I know one thing is for sure, One-eyed Steve and Julius were both imagining great things to come, not only for us, but to all those who dared use the imaginations of their hearts.

CHAPTER SEVENTY-ONE

"Dad's alive. I always knew it!" Timmy said.

It wasn't that long ago when Timmy was so greatly depressed at the news of our father and me and Danny devised a plan to go to Germany to rescue Dad so Timmy might find comfort in his despair. Luckily that despair was put to ease at the news of Dad's survival. I wished I had felt the wonderous joy as Timmy did, but I knew terrible things happen in those prisons when it came to soldiers, and it horrified my soul.

I never would burden my brother with any bad news that might upset him in any matter when it came to Dad, so I kept my fears to myself and forced a smile on my face pretending to be happy while the thoughts of Dad in prison terrified me.

"Yes, he is alive Timmy," I replied.

"The war's going to be over soon, I just know it."

"I hope so."

"Me too, I want to go back home to Reidsville."

"Me too!" Danny replied.

Reidsville was the furthest thing from my mind at that present moment. I knew they had found some sort of hope in returning home, but Dad wasn't even home yet and there was no promise he would be home anytime soon or the war ending anytime soon. I know Mr. Owensby's letter was comforting to say the least, but it held no sense of reality. I didn't want to discourage them, but I had to be realistic.

"Don't you think war would be over soon, Har Har?" Timmy asked.

As soon I thought those thoughts his words shot through me like lightning catching me off guard, here I was in The Land of Imagination and I couldn't even imagine the war ending soon. I had been guilty of reality over imagination and how was our reality going to change if I didn't believe in the principal of imagination? If I could not believe it in The Land of Imagination, where had I seen marvelous things take place then how could I believe it in my own world? I had to look within myself and believe, not only believe but I had to speak it. Sometimes we birth things into life even when we don't see it and we frame the world around us by our own words.

"Yes, I do Timmy!" I said doubting within me stirred with a little hope.

Then a ray of light went off in my soul, beckoning to my hope as I recalled Mr. Owensby's letter and how the war might be ending soon. I knew there was no greater time than now to cast away my doubts and start believing in things beyond my realm of understanding.

Sometimes we go through life, and we doubt our possibilities because we look out into the storms that rage in the seas of our lives and we forget about the times when the sea was at peace and all we can see are the moments when the waves are roaring against us. It is up to us to imagine the sea will be at peace again while we wait out the storm, and before we know it life returns to its normal self and we sail into peaceful waters. Sometimes it takes those around us to remind us to believe in ourselves and to

believe in the greater tomorrow and sometimes it takes us to remind others of the same. We're all in this world together, in a
world of hope and great imaginations. Without hope and imagination greatness ceases to lift her head arrayed in the glory of a
beautiful future.

Chapter Seventy-two

As we thought on Dad and what the future might hold for us back home in our own world and time, The Vile Ones sought to destroy our very future through the wickedness of their hearts.

While we sailed into the seas towards Atlantis, The Vile Ones used their imaginations to draw their ships to take us by force on the sea and stop us from reaching our destination before the full moon. They knew if they could stop us from reaching Atlantis all imagination and memories would be lost forever giving them the victory, they so much desired.

"There's ships behind us Captain!" Huxley the giant said.

I turned to look behind me and sure enough there were many ships following us just as Huxley had said, but they were not just ordinary ships, they had lightning preceding out of them shooting into the sky above as dark clouds chaotically swarmed above in a tornadic spiral pulling our ship backwards.

"We don't have enough wind in our sails to outrun them," I said.

"I got an idea!" Timmy yelled as the thundering from the storm behind us grew louder.

"What's your idea?"

"Give me the paper, I got to draw it."

I thumbed through my coat pocket while holding the helm of the ship trying my best to guide the ship away from The Vile Ones as my brother took the paper. He began to draw on it and like the times before it glittered and shined as his drawing came to life on paper.

"You might all want to hold on for dear life!" Timmy screamed.

"Hold on for dear life, what are you talking about?" I replied.

"I believe...I know what he's talking about!" Danny said as he stood shocked with his mouth wide open looking to the ships behind us at the unfathomable danger that proceeded in the distance.

"What is it, what did you draw?" I asked. As I turned I saw a gigantic wave on the hills of The Vile One's ship headed right straight for us.

If being chased by The Vile Ones and the storm had not been scary enough, my younger brother Timmy thought it would be wise to draw a gigantic wave that could swallow us up and spit us out. In that moment, I now had my doubts my little brother was a genius. There was no way under God's green heaven we were going to survive and it was the most terrible idea I ever witnessed in all my life and it was evident I was about to become the food of the sea.

"What, a giant wave, are you out of your mind Timmy?"

While I was complaining to my brother, One-eyed Steve along with Julius, was unaware of the danger behind us as our crew members along with others pointed back behind us signaling to look at what was going on.

"Arr.. what are they saying, Julius?"

Julius turned looking back as his face become terrified at the sight of what was taking place behind him and he began to stutter.

"Si si sir ..y.....you need to see this!"

"See what, Julius?" One-eyed Steve replied.

As One-eyed Steve turned around to see The Vile One's ships riding on a gigantic wave then he turned back around and said, "Arr.. Julius, I'm going to pretend I didn't see that."

Julius squinted his eyes and tensed his shoulders and said, "Me too Sir, me too!" Then closed his eyes and said, "If you don't look at them, they will disappear." Then he opened his eyes and looked and saw The Vile Ones in the distance hoping if he closed his eyes they will disappear.

"Did it work Julius?"

Julius squinted his face in fear and said, "No, they're still there!"

One-eyed Steve turned to look back to see if there are still there and turned back to Julius and said, "I hate it when your right, Julius!"

"Oh... I hate it when I'm right too!"

"Okay men looks like we got some trouble coming up behind us get ready to hold them off!" One-eyed Steve commanded as his crew members pulled out their musket guns and stood at the back of the ship to fire at The Vile Ones as soon as they got within firing distance.

Imminent fear fell upon on us as we looked in front of us. Another gigantic wave was headed straight for us as the other wave behind us drew close ready to devour us. Now a wave stood in our path and it was obvious there was no chance for survival. We were about to get crushed between two waves.

"Did you draw another wave?"

"It must have been The Vile Ones," Timmy answered.

"They know we are close to Atlantis!" Sister Milica answered.

"How close?"

"This close!"

All of a sudden, the sea went into a swirl and our ships went in a circular motion as if the bottom of the ocean was let out under us as we went into a spiral spin.

"What you mean this close?"

"We're here," Sister Milica answered.

As our ships swirled, The Vile One's ship drew close. So close, we could see their faces if they had one as they lit up our surroundings with their lightning exposing the sink hole we were swirling around in.

I could hear cannons and gun fire coming from One-eyed Steve's ship trying to hold them off as The Vile Ones engaged in battle trying to swarm their ship to overthrow it.

"One-eyed Steve is in trouble," Danny yelled.

"Don't worry, I got this!" Huxley said as he ran towards the back of the ship jumping into the air with his axe landing on one of the ships of The Vile Ones. He took his axe and hit the deck of their ship as it broke into pieces cracking the ship nearly in half.

"He just tore that ship in half with his axe," Timmy said.

I turned back and saw one of the ships severed in half falling into the swirling sea as several Vile Ones got caught in the under tow of the waves. Huxley jumped to another ship chopping the pole of their sailboat as their sail flew into the air then smashed the deck of the floor breaking the ship in half.

"I'm glad he is on our side," I replied.

"Me too!" Danny said.

As One-eyed Steve was firing on The Vile Ones the sail that had been split from their ship flew around and hit One-eyed Steve's ship causing a great hole in the side of it as it began to sink.

"Sir, we are sinking," Julius screamed.

One-eyed Steve looked over to Julius and said, "This is the end."

Julius looked back at One-eyed Steve and said, "I wish you didn't say that."

"Me too, Julius."

"We tried, didn't we boss?"

"We sure did Julius, we sure did."

"We had some good times, didn't we boss?"

"We sure did Julius, we sure did."

Then One-eyed Steve turned to Draggy and said, "Go save yourself!" as Draggy screamed in the air with anguish and huffed in the air saddened at the tragedy at hand as water burrowed in the ship and they sunk into the sea treading water

CHAPTER SEVENTY-THREE

"No Grandpa, One-eyed Steve can't lose his ship. He just re-united with his brother," Johnny said as he sat listening at the birthday party.

"Son, even in The Land of Imagination sometimes people lose their lives."

"No Grandpa, it's not fair. One-eyed Steve and the crew can't die," Tomas said.

"Oh, they can't can they? What makes you so sure?"

"Cause, this is about brothers and imagination. All One-eyed Steve has to do is write his way out."

"Tell me Son, if it was your brother's ship sinking would you write him into safety?"

"I sure would Grandpa, I sure would," Tomas answered.

"Then tell me what you would imagine happened next?"

"If it was up to me, I would fly the ship out of the sea. After all, One-eyed Steve's ship can fly."

"That's interesting Son, but that's not what happened," Grandpa Harold replied.

"Grandpa, he can't sink, he can't sink, he has to help you get to Atlantis."

Chapter Seventy-four

Aunt Louise climbed in Mr. Owensby's car sitting in the passenger seat trying to take in the news of our adventure and how she witnessed everything unfolding on the paper Mr. Owensby received from me.

"There's something you're not telling me."

"What do you mean?"

"You sent Harold a letter."

"I never sent him a letter."

"But I saw him read a letter from you."

"I don't know how he got a letter from me, I can't explain it."

While Aunt Louise and Mr. Owensby were in conversation a mysterious young man knocked on the window motioning for Mr. Owensby to roll down the window.

"Can I help you?" Mr. Owensby said as he rolled down the window.

"Sorry to bother you so late, I've been rather busy."

"And you are?"

"Oh, sorry I'm a mere messenger. I do believe you have a letter needing to be sent to a young boy by the name of Harold Stanfield."

"I haven't written a letter to him."

"Are you sure about that, I was requested for you give me a letter?"

"Yes, I'm sure."

"Check your pocket, I'm sure the letter is there as I've been instructed to ask you."

Mr. Owensby checked his pocket and found a letter and pulled it out addressed to myself.

"But how, I haven't written him a letter?"

"You haven't written it yet but you will, time is not the same here as in The Land of Adventure. Today you may send a letter, tomorrow you may write it, and I'm the messenger who delivers the letters."

"If you're the messenger then you must have met my brother?" Aunt Louise asked.

The young man bends down to see Aunt Louise in the car holding the letter I had written.

"You must be Louise I do suppose?"

"How do you know my name?"

"I know more than you think I know and I haven't seen your brother yet but I will. I got a message that he has a letter for Harold as well."

"So, you will see my brother?"

"Yes, I will see him in Germany."

"But it's dangerous there, how can you get passed enemy lines?"

"Dear Madam, there's many of us adventurers even in Germany and to my knowledge one of us stands guard over him at the present moment and no harm will come to him."

"When will he make it home?"

"Soon, very soon. The future has already been told and written, we just need to read it."

"What about my nephews?"

"That is easy, just read what is written or drawn and you will see what is happening, but fear nothing The King of Adventure has decided to do great things for Harold and no harm shall befall him or his brothers."

"When will they come back home?"

"Soon, very soon, it is already written, and you will know when it's time for you to meet Harold but you cannot meet him until he awakes. It's the only way for him to come home."

"What do you mean he has to wake up?"

"Waking up from The Land of Adventure is the only way home, dreams and imaginations are two of the three worlds that intertwine and they all work together. When he wakes, he will be back in this present time and you will need to go meet him."

"He said for me to meet him at the orphanage," Mr. Owensby said.

"Yes, I know and you will know when it's time to meet him."

"How?"

"On the letter he sent you, all the answers you seek is on the letter my dear friend. Speaking of letters…"

"Oh, sorry," Mr. Owensby said as he handed him the paper he had written to me.

"Thanks Sir," the young man said as he went to turn away. Then he turned back and bent down and looked at Aunt Louise, "Oh, and there's answers for you as well Louise, an answer to what you've been asking within your heart. If you have pure intentions, you will see it, but only if you're pure."

The young man stands up straight, tips his hat, and disappears from Aunt Louise and Mr. Owensby's presence.

Aunt Louise looked down at the paper she was holding and realized there was more to this than she ever had thought and the only question that had been unanswered was Mr. Owensby and what the future held for both of them.

CHAPTER SEVENTY-FIVE

One-eyed Steve looked at the men as they faced their end as the ship slowly begin to sink and the sea begin to calm and stopped swirling and returned to normal as they held on to debris from the ship.

"Sir, the sea is calming."

"I see that, Julius."

"We're here."

"I know," One-eyed Steve replied.

Suddenly the sea disappeared, and all the ships sat on dry land and the beautiful city of Atlantis appeared before us, just when we thought we all was going to perish by the ruthless sea Atlantis came out to save us harkening to the fear of our hearts.

As we exited our ships and stood on the sands of the sea, we looked at the beauty of Atlantis. The skies were filled with rainbows that moved like the northern lights across the sky.

The buildings of Atlantis were made out of pure crystals that reached into the sky like skyscrapers and the walkways were laid with rubies and emeralds, it was a city built on imagination.

"Have you ever seen such beautiful place?" I asked.

"Many times, dear lad, many times," Scotty replied.

"What's so special about bringing our treasure to Atlantis?"

"Atlantis was once a place of a people who lived lavishly but became greedy in their hearts. Only when you open your treasures before Atlantis it shows what lies in your heart, if it's filled greed or pure with hope."

"Why are The Vile Ones trying to stop it?"

"They once were the inhabitants of Atlantis. They are the lost souls of greed, riches were not enough for them, they became so greedy they desired to take away imagination from men's hearts and will stop at nothing to stop those sent by The King of Adventure."

"What happens if they stop someone who was sent by The King of Adventure?"

"Then all imagination in the world will be gone forever. A man will never again dream of a better life and will be subject to never live life to his full potential."

"And what happens when I open my treasure?"

"You will see that which you treasure the most in life and your treasure is the seed of your hope and the tree of your imaginations," Sister Milica replied.

CHAPTER SEVENTY-SIX

As we stood speaking the island of Atlantis was surrounded with darkened clouds swarming outside the shorelines. As The Vile Ones approached us as I beheld the world fall into the dark abyss and the only thing that stood between us and the end of The Land of Imagination was The Land of Atlantis.

"Did you tell him that the balances must be weighed in the sessions of court?" one of The Vile One's said.

"What is he talking about, Sister Milica?"

"Your heart will be judged in the courts of Atlantis."

"And if we win, we take your prized possession," The Vile One said.

"Don't do it, Har Har, it's a trap," Timmy blurted out.

"Listen to your brother, don't go to the courts," The Vile One replied.

"I got to Timmy. They've already stolen all the imaginations from the world. If I don't try how can we save the world, what we do today will change the world forever. Our words today just might change the life of someone 50 years from now, that's worth trying Timmy!?" I replied.

"Then let the courts be in session, Har Har." The Vile One replied.

And as soon as he said that I was standing in a court room looking out into the faces of people whom I didn't know and faces I did know.

"Do you know whom these people are?" a thunderous voice asked.

"Some of them. The rest I don't know who they are."

"They are a small fragment of the souls who dare to imagine great things in the world and its upon you Harold to rescue their imaginations. If you fail here today, their imaginations are lost forever and it's their imaginations that will change the world for the greater good."

"Sir, I'm only a boy, how can I help them change the world?"

"Have you come this far and have not seen, Harold?" the voice asked.

"What do you mean?"

"A man's heart is not about how old or young he is, but what his heart has to offer, what we do in life shapes the worlds around us. It cries out in our hopes and in our doubts but it's up to us to choose which one we will live by. If a man does evil, he changes the world around him through his evil and if a man does good, he changes the world around him through his good. We heal or curse the world we live in by the choices we make."

"And how am I judged of all these things? How will I know what is right before the courts if I have yet done good or evil?"

"By overcoming, it's the only way to test one's heart and you must overcome The Vile Ones with your hope."

"It's time we make our case before the thunderous voice," The Vile One said.

"Let it be done," the thunderous voice spoke.

"You can't win, Harold," one of The Vile Ones said.

"Don't listen to him, Harold," Sister Milica said

"She has been deceiving you. She wants the treasure all for herself," one of The Vile Ones said.

"You're lying!" I replied.

"Ask her for yourself, Harold."

"Is it true, Sister Milica?" I asked her.

As soon as I asked that the room circled around me and everyone in the court spinning like a merry-go-round. I was trying to take in our surroundings, but it moved so fast I couldn't make out the faces of those who stood about and when the room came to a stop Sister Milica answered.

"He is telling the truth. I just wanted the treasure all along," Sister Milica said as she stood in the court room with her head lifted proudly.

"But I trusted you, Sister Milica."

"See the truth comes out, she wanted the treasure from the beginning."

"Don't listen to him Harold," Sister Milica said

"See her tongue is double edged, she can't keep the truth in her words, she is full of deception."

"No, you're lying, Sister Milica is good. I know her she has never lied to me."

"She and Scotty both conspired against you from the beginning. They knew if you came here, you would lead them to Atlantis, and they could consume the treasure upon their greedy hearts."

"This can't be true, it has to be lie."

"Oh no it's not a lie. Ask Scotty for yourself and see if there's any lies in his tongue."

As soon as The Vile One finished his words the room began to spin again like it did before and Scotty stood before me as I tried to focus my eyes as I became dizzy from the room that spun around me.

"Scotty, please tell me it's not true that you and Sister Milica did not conspire against me?"

"I'm sorry young man but it's true."

"But why, Scotty, why would you do this and give me hope?

The Vile One laughed and said, "Hope, these whom you trusted are deceivers of the greatest kind, they don't care for hope all they care about is their own self-indulgence."

"Don't listen to him. He's trying to put doubts in your mind," Sister Milica said.

As I stood there, I didn't know what to think. The Vile Ones whom I thought were vile were showing me that the very ones I trusted in were lying to me and the ones whom I thought were good were really evil and had evil intent for me and had been deceiving me all along.

"Tell me Harold, what have you desired the most?" The Vile One asked.

"I want to have my family back."

"And tell me Harold, when have they made this happen for you, after all you're in The Land of Imagination you can draw or write anything and when have they encouraged you to write your father back into your life, they didn't did they, but just lead you here just to take away the only thing you had left in life!?"

The Vile Ones were right at any time they could've told me to draw my dad back into my life at any moment, but they didn't they just lead me here to Atlantis.

"We tried to save you from the ship."

"You mean when you came and surrounded us as dragons?"

"Yes, we came there to save you from them."

"We were going to take you into the land of your father."

"But you didn't offer to take my brothers with me."

"They are not your brothers, Harold. They are deceivers as well, ask them and they will tell you the truth."

"How are they not my brothers?"

"Look on their faces and you can see their true form and how they sought to take your treasure from you."

As soon as he said that the room began to spin again and when it came to a stop, I looked upon the faces of my brothers and they wore two faces one for honesty another for deception. Clearly these two people I thought were my brothers the whole time were not my brothers at all but were something else.

"This whole time they were never my brothers?" I said as my heart caved within me.

"No, they're not and they are gone forever you'll never see them again, you were brought here by deception, and you can never return home."

"But what about the letter from Mr. Owensby, he said I wrote him telling him to meet me at the orphanage?"

"He never wrote you, Harold."

"But I read it, it's right here in my pouch."

"Is it really, where is this letter?"

"I have it right here." and as I went to go for my pouch to get the letter to prove to myself Mr. Owensby had written me my pouch was no longer there.

"You see, you've been deceived this whole time, Harold."

"Don't listen to him, Harold," Sister Milica said.

"Don't listen to her, she's a deceiver."

"I'm not a deceiver. Ask him to open his treasure," Sister Milica replied.

"Yes, that's just what you want is for him to open his treasure. You know as soon as he does you can take away what is truly his," The Vile One said.

"They're lying, dear lad, open your treasure," Scotty said.

"Am I really lying, has not One-eyed Steve all this time wanted the treasure for himself, let's ask him what he thinks?" The Vile One replied.

"Is this true, One-eyed Steve, have you all been out to deceive me?"

The room begin to spin but stopped as soon as it started as One-eyed Steve stepped forward not giving the room the chance to spin and spoke.

"Arr.. it is true. But I've desired to bring all treasure to Atlantis."

"See there, this whole time you've been deceived and they've wanted the treasure for themselves."

"Open the treasure," One-eyed Steve said.

"Why would One-eyed Steve tell me to open the treasure if he's wanted the treasure this whole time?"

As soon as I asked the rooms spun around like the previous times then my dad stood in the mist of all of us.

"Cause Son, they know that you could've saved me, now it's too late all they did was waste time and now I can't be saved."

"That's all I wanted Dad, was to save you!" I replied as I began to break down feeling defeated and hopeless.

"Harold do remember the dream and what I told you, it's never too late. As long as you've got hope, nothing is ever too late for you, long as you have hope you have everything."

"But how can I believe in you now, Sister Milica? You told me yourself you were only after my treasure?"

"I didn't tell you that, The Vile Ones did. They are deceiving you they know if you open the treasure then you win back imagination for everyone who ever imagined anything within their hearts."

"She's lying to you," one of The Vile Ones said.

"Be the tree with hope rooted within you Harold"

"How do I do that, Sister Milica?"

"Look at your brothers."

When she said that I looked and saw my brothers standing by seeing me in torment as I looked upon the faces of those who stood by. I saw the ones with two faces who looked like my brothers but wasn't my brothers and when I looked at my brothers, I saw my brothers.

"Do you see your brothers Harold?"

"Yes, I see them."

"And I ask you like I asked you before, have you gone this far and lost that which you wanted the most? Listen to your truth."

"How Sister Milica?"

"With your heart you will know who is lying to you and who is telling you the truth."

"Don't listen to her, she's lying to you," Sister Milica said.

"Am I really lying to him?" Sister Milica replied to Sister Milica then she turned to me and said, "Listen Harold, listen to you heart, Harold and you will know the truth."

When I heard Sister Milica talk to herself I came to my senses and looked and saw Sister Milica and The Vile One talking to each other and as I looked around, I saw Scotty but he wasn't Scotty. Then I saw Scotty and he was Scotty and likewise every one whom stood by, that I knew there was two of everyone. And as I looked I could hear the ones whom disguised themselves to be Sister Milica and the other Vile One's laughing within themselves saying we have now stolen imagination and his hope is dying.

"You must open the treasure, it's the only way to defeat them and win back the imagination," Sister Milica said.

"Don't listen to her, she's trying to steal your treasure," Sister Milica said.

"Don't listen to them, they're The Vile Ones, they are not me. Listen to what your treasure is saying," Sister Milica replied

"But it's not here, I don't see it."

"Listen and you will hear it."

As I said that I heard my treasure speak to me calling out and I knew that Sister Milica was telling the truth and I could see I was being lied to by The Vile Ones.

"I can hear it."

"What's it saying to you?"

"It's telling me to open it."

"Don't open it. Once you open it you will be faced with sorrows upon sorrows, did they not tell you this?" The Vile One said who had changed his appearance back to himself who had masqueraded himself to look like Sister Milica.

"What's in the treasure?"

"It's something of great value," Sister Milica answered.

"No, it's not. It's full of sorrows," The Vile One answered.

"It's not true and they know once you open it, they can no longer fill you with doubts cause once you do you will find the truth of your journey and why The King of Adventure sent you."

"What's in the treasure chest, Sister Milica?"

"Open it!"

"Enough of this, it's too late and the full moon is drawing near," The Vile One said.

"Listen to her, dear lad, open the treasure," Scotty said.

"But I don't know where the treasure chest is Scotty."

"It's here. It's always been here with you, dear lad, just look and you'll see it."

Sure, enough as soon as Scotty said that I saw the treasure chest was sitting right in front of me.

"But there was no key to open it."

"Sir, you already know."

"What do you mean, Scotty how do I know how to open it if I have no key?"

"The key has been given to you from the beginning, dear lad, and there's no riddle in that."

"I was never given a key, Scotty."

"Indeed, you were given the key. Tell me whom are you, Harold?"

"I am Harold Stanfield."

"Yes, but you are someone else as well are you not?"

"What do you mean, Scotty? How can I be someone else?"

"You already know, dear lad."

"What do you mean, Scotty?"

"What did The King of Adventure tell you?"

"He told me whatever I write or draw comes true and I am the author of my own adventure."

"You are the author Harold, that's the key to it all, dear lad. You don't need a key, you are the key to your own treasure. All you have to do is ask it to open and it will."

"But this whole time I thought writing or drawing is what makes everything come true."

It does but the true story doesn't just lie upon paper written in ink, but upon the canvas of your heart and as long as you imagine within you all things are open to you in this life."

When he said that I realized I'm not just the author but I am the painter to my own life and the artist to my own destiny and I hold the masterpiece of my life within me. It's just up to me to paint my future. The King of Adventure just didn't send me the paper and pencil for me to write or draw but to use imagination of my heart and all I had to do is imagine my treasure opening and it would open up to me.

"Your imagination is your words, dear lad, and your treasure is always listening."

CHAPTER SEVENTY-SEVEN

While I stood there with my heart open my treasure opened to me shining like the morning sun as I drew near to inquire what my treasure held. I looked and saw a near empty treasure chest with a small pair of shoes with mud on the sides at the bottom as sorrows filled my heart.

Immediately I was drawn away into a memory of my past, a past that I had well hidden within me, a past I had hoped I had forgotten because of the pain it caused me, but there was also joy that came into my life hiding in that old memory of those muddy shoes as my mind carried me away to that fateful day in my life.

I could smell the flowers swaying in the Georgia sun mixed with the fragrance of the Georgia pines that stood like mountains trying to cast their shadows down to shelter us from the smoldering sun of mid-July as I held my mom's hand and we made our way to the church doors to that old Baptist church that set on the outskirts of the city limits. I remembered looking down to the new pair of shoes my mom had bought me days before, I can remember the Sunday service, the music of the choir, Mom's flowered dress, her southern hat upon her head that she wore just like all the other southern women, and Dad setting at her side in the pew dressed in his Sunday suit all dressed in black while my brother Danny set next to him. I stood up wrapping my arms around my mom's neck as I looked down to her stomach to see the roundness of her belly and the life of my brother Timmy inside her.

Little did I know that wonderous day would take it's turn for the worst as we spent the afternoon at my grandmother's house and Aunt Louise and Grandma stood in the kitchen cooking fried chicken after the Sunday service like they did every Sunday. I might've only had been two years old but sometimes things happen in life that we just don't block out. Sometimes we remember the events through a song or a smell and it triggers some memory and we remember where we were and what we were doing in that time in life and it was those two ole shoes of mine that made me remember it all. Funny how life sometimes plays on the mind and the heart of yesterday and I was standing there looking and remembering my past. It was a beautiful moment to remember.

But those loving memories were met with sorrows as I heard a scream come from my mother as my dad barreled out of the front door of grandma's house as the screen door slammed behind him as he ran to that old car of ours and fired up the engine slinging gravel as he drove into the grass right beside the door and Aunt Louise and Grandma helped Mom down from the front door steps from the porch as I watched all the commotion take place from the neighbor's yard.

"Her water broke, you need to get her to Savannah!" Grandma said as Mom held her stomach in agony.

"I'm going with you," Aunt Louise said.

"Where's Danny and Harold?" Dad asked looking around frantic as he helped Mom into the car.

"Don't you worry about those boys I will take care of them," Grandma said as she took a handkerchief and wiped Mom's sweaty brow.

I don't remember much from there but Dad pulling out of the drive and driving away down that old Georgia road as I ran as fast as fast as I could trying to catch up with Dad as he faded away in the distance and I was left standing crying my eyes out standing in a mud puddle with my brand-new Sunday School shoes covered in mud.

I remember that night right before bed as Dad sat down next to me in bed and began to tell me how Mom went on a journey to be with God and he took her home and she's now in the stars looking down on us. I didn't have the knowledge at that age to comprehend what had happened to Mom all I knew is she was leaving me forever.

Mom left the world behind that night. Maybe the world might forget she ever existed. No one might not know her name a hundred years from now, but she left behind a wonderful gift to the world that night and his name was Timmy, my little brother.

I sometimes wonder what it was like for her. Did she hold onto to life as hard as she could or did her eyes fade away and she fell away peacefully into her next life greeted by a host of angels? My mind often wonders how she went and what was she thinking knowing these were her last minutes in life. If you ask me, I believe she was thinking one thing and that was she thought she was the most luckiest woman in life, she was blessed to had been loved and loved those whom loved her. Heaven knows I loved her, I'm sure she's up there dancing with the angels. I bet they even gave her a new name, a heavenly name. But as for me I'll wait until I go to that place to find out, but until then I like the name I call her, Mom. That's who she will always be as long as I'm on this earth she will always be Mom. What I thought I had hidden in me was the greatest value I could have ever had in life, and it was Mom.

I understood why One-eyed Steve acted the way he did when he opened up his treasure, he was looking at something he had lost and was searching for all that time. I don't know what he saw but I am sure it was a memory of his past and whatever it was it had value to him just as my treasure had value to me. The one thing I learnt opening up my treasure was that we're all searching for love and acceptance out of life just like how a kid draws a picture of his parents and sibling and takes it to his parents to see it, hoping to hear that it looks beautiful and that's just like us. All we want in life is to be seen like that little piece of artwork and to be noticed by the world and those whom we love. That's what life is all about to be loved. It's one of the greatest desires upon the human heart and if you ask me, it's one of the most valued treasures of all.

Sometimes I think back to that ole memory of standing there in the mud and if it wasn't for that treasure chest opening, I wouldn't have remembered the very thing I held deeply with in me. I guess it took a ship to cross the waters for me to remember the mud I was standing in for me to think of the things that meant the most out if life. Sometimes we have to walk in the mud in life to know just where we are standing and it's in that mud when we truly look out and to see what means the most in life and sometimes it just takes a ship to cross the many waters in our life to get us to that place of remembrance. Either way no matter how deep or shallow the water might be in life, we are all at the mercies of the seas within us.

CHAPTER SEVENTY-EIGHT

There I was in the balances being weighed and my heart was pure to hear all things within me and I stood the test of imagination of heart when I heard a familiar voice of a woman speak from behind me

"Harold."

As I turned, I saw her arrayed in a lovely white dress, the same one my mom had worn when we had buried her.

"Mom?"

"Yes, it's me Harold, your mother."

"But your.."

"Oh no, Harold, I am alive I have always been alive."

When she said that Danny took off running and embraced Mom with a hug as Timmy's eyes begin to water.

"Is it really you, Mom?"

"Yes, it's me Timmy. Come near and let your mother behold you."

Timmy no longer could refrain as he took off running to Mom embracing her for the first time in his life.

"I held you within my womb, now I behold you in my arms."

When she said that I could not refrain myself as well, and I took off running to Mom's embrace like my brothers. For the first time all three of us brothers were in the presence of our mom.

"Mom it's my fault you died," Timmy cried.

"Oh no, Son, don't blame yourself, things happen in life we just got to learn to overcome things, and as far as I can see, you've turned out to be everything I ever hoped for."

"Can you come back to be with us and Dad?"

"Oh, no, no Son, I can't do that."

"But Mom whatever we draw or write comes true, we can write you back into our lives."

"Son, I'm already in your lives as long as I'm in your heart and you're in mine. I will always with you, besides, I'm only an adventure away."

"But you have to come back, Dad needs you, so do I."

"It's not meant for me to come back Son, but what is meant for you is to grow in the things you experience in life. Sometimes the very thing you endure in life is the strength to those who are weaker, you must learn from the thing you experience and help the world in their pain. We all are healers to the world it's only up to us to understand how we heal it."

"How can I heal the world, Mom?" Timmy asks.

"With your character, there's no greater thing a man can possess than character. It's his character which frames the very words that he speaks and the words he speaks frames the world around him."

"Like how a man is as good as his word?" Danny replied.

Mom looked at Danny and smiled at his wisdom of heart then goes on to share her wisdom with us, "Dear sons, I have great passion to tell you that you may grow wise in your days upon earth."

"What is it Mom?" I asked.

Give hope to those whom you meet in life. What you do to-day echoes into the world and shapes the foundations of tomor-row, and if we have a tomorrow, we must live to better our to-morrow. We must always make it better for others, give hope to others, the world is hungry for it. Hope is a fountain to life and if you give it, the world shall truly drink from it."

CHAPTER SEVENTY-NINE

Aunt Louise and Mr. Owensby sat on the roof top of the newspaper factory both looking at the paper watching the scenes take place of our adventure as they sat close by each other's side. For some couples they would share a night at the theater but tonight Aunt Louise and Mr. Owensby were sharing a moment watching our adventure take place on a piece of paper.

"I hadn't seen my sister-in-law in years, my brother was devastated when she passed away. If she never would've died, he would've never joined the army."

"And you never would've met me, I'm sorry that didn't come out right, I'm not suggesting that her dying was the reason we got to meet."

"I know what you meant and you're right, if she hadn't passed, we would've never met. That's one of the reasons I just couldn't stay in Reidsville. I realized life was too short and there was something bigger out there waiting on me."

"I know the feeling. I might own a printing business but there's got to be something greater out there waiting for me to find it."

"What if we already found it?"

"Maybe we did Louise, maybe we did," Mr. Owensby replied looking at Aunt Louise with admiration as she looked down to the letter watching our adventure taking place and us three boys reunited with our mother.

"What do you think the young man meant when he said you will find the answers you are asking?"

Aunt Louise looked down to the letter I had written and, on the letter, she could see scenes of her life being played out with Mr. Owensby, and she could see a future of them two together not just a future but a life filed with many adventures.

''I think I might have an idea," Aunt Louise said turning back looking to Mr. Owensby with a smile on her face.

Chapter Eighty

While Aunt Louise and Mr. Owensby were looking with optimism to their future we were beholding our past as memories and thoughts flooded our minds standing in the presence of our mother as she held out her hand and opened it and as we looked in her hand and a swirling light appeared. As we looked at the light it was as if we were drawn into the light and the light took us to an open field where the battered tree, I saw in my dream stood.

"I've been here in my dream."

"I know my son; it is important your brothers see it as well and understand what the tree is."

As we stood in the field our dad walked in the middle of us and stood taking mom's hand and we all looked at the tree standing before us and then that battered tree in my dream started sprouting leaves, then fruits, then the birds of the air landed on them, as many animals of the land came and laid under the tree. Every creature that laid under the tree was at peace with each other, the lions laid beside the dear, and the birds sang songs as if they were songs of hope.

"Do you know what this means, my son?"

"No Mom, what does it mean?" Danny asked.

It's you my sons, your hope and kindness and how when you do good in the world your life flourishes and when your life flourishes it gives hope to others' life, and the beast of the field are those who didn't know peace but finds peace through hearing your words of hope and take part in the goodness of life from the good hope with in you."

Then Mom turned facing us and Dad and said to Dad, "Take care of my sons." Then she turned to walk towards the tree of hope standing in the middle of the field and she faded away and disappeared as a great light illuminated the field in our presence and when the great light faded, we all were standing on the beach of Atlantis then the earth began to shake violently as The Vile Ones became scared looking around them in panic.

"He prevailed to open the treasure, he has seen his heart and his imagination," one of The Vile Ones said.

Then light shot out from Atlantis and the thunderous voice from within Atlantis spoke.

"The greed of your hearts had been weighed and your deceit has been judged."

"What, you tricked us," one of The Vile Ones said.

"No, you deceived yourself with your greed and your lust to take away the imaginations of mankind."

"But it was Harold that was brought before the courts, he is the one on trial!"

"Did you not think you could enter the courts of truth and not be judged yourself? You have deceived the people and stole away their hope. Now I will allow it to be restored."

"But we were taking back what was ours from the beginning."

"You may deceive the world but you cannot deceive me, into your own dwelling you shall dwell, into your own deceit you shall walk, into your own pit shall you fall into."

"You can't do this," one of The Vile Ones cried out.

"What is done is done and so shall it be. You came here to destroy and destruction shall be your fate, you've chosen to walk in Tyranny and longed to break the hearts of the believers, your greed has led you here and your feet shall enter into the abyss."

As soon as the thunderous voice spoke, The Vile Ones began to turn to stone, then to dust as the wind blew their remains into the dark abyss and the dust of them turned into imaginations that had been stolen out of the hearts of the people. And I could hear songs upon songs, and thousands of songs full of beauty and unimaginable glory, as if the songs themselves were written by angels of heaven and I looked out into the abyss and saw buildings and ships begin to appear and anything mankind's heart had imagined was restored and the imaginations of them all were more glorious than Atlantis itself. Then I saw one of the most amazing things one could see.

Chapter Eighty-one

Grandpa Harold sat in his seat and became silent and took off his hat and placed it to his heart and was drawn away in his own imagination.

"What was it, Grandpa?" Johnny asked.

"Yes Grandpa, what was the most amazing thing you saw?" Tomas asked.

"I saw you."

"What do you mean you saw me?"

"I saw you and your brother playing football together."

Johnny's eyes began to water with tears cause all he ever wanted was to play football with his older brother.

"Did you really see me playing football with my brother?" Johnny asks.

"I sure did, as plain as day I saw the imagination of your heart and you was standing tall, taller than giants."

"What about me, Grandpa?"

"Oh, you were a giant too Tomas just like your brother Johnny and you both played your hearts out. You didn't play the fields as giants, oh no, you didn't, but you both played the fields as hero's. Heroes to one another, you taught your brother how to play and he taught you how to be a teacher."

"But he isn't tall enough to play, Grandpa."

"How can he ever learn if you never teach him? He will not always be small, you have a brother with a giant inside him just waiting to be seen just like the giant within you."

Tomas looked over to his brother crying and said, "Your right, Grandpa."

"Tell me Tomas, have you not imagined what it would be like playing in front of millions and in a big stadium?"

Tomas thinks back to all the times he's played football with his friends and he knew Grandpa Harold was right. Many times he could see himself playing in the Stadium and the crowds cheered him on.

"Tell me Tomas, would you want all the glory to yourself or would you want to share it with someone who will always be by your side?"

"Someone who's by my side of course, Grandpa."

"Close your eyes, do you see the stadium?"

"Yes, I see it."

"Are you a giant?"

"Yes, I am.."

"Run down the field to catch the ball."

Tomas imagines himself running down the field to catch the ball.

"Johnny close your eyes as well," Grandpa Harold demanded.

"Now what, Grandpa?" Johnny said with his eyes closed.

"Can you imagine the stadium?"

"Yes, I can see it Grandpa, I can see it!"

"Good now, throw the ball to your brother Tomas."

Johnny imagines throwing the football down the field as it hurls the air in a perfect spiral headed down the field to his brother as Tomas runs to catch the football.

"Do you see the ball coming your way, Tomas?"

"Yes, I see it Grandpa, I see it!"

"What happens now Tomas?" Grandpa Harold asked.

"I catch the football Grandpa!"

"What about the other team?"

"Oh, they can't catch me Grandpa, I'm too fast for them."

"Oh no Son, but there is one whose really fast and he's gaining on you, what will you do if he gets close?"

"He can throw the football back to me I will catch it," Johnny said.

"Do you see the fast player from the other team?"

"Yes, I see him over my shoulder."

"Quick, pass me back the football," Johnny says.

"If I throw it, you better catch it!"

"I will catch it Tomas, I will, I swear to you I will," Johnny said with his eyes closed imagining the scene.

"Okay, here goes."

Tomas throws the football back to Johnny and it flies through the air right at the tip of Johnny's finger tips when William their father with his eyes closed imagining seeing his two sons playing football together yells out loud, "Catch it Johnny, catch it!"

Johnny tucks the football into his chest and takes off down the field weaving his way through the other team sprinting his way to the touch down.

"You can do it Johnny, you can do it!" Tomas yells with his eyes closed imagining his brother running gloriously to the touch down goal as Johnny gets tackled at the touch down line.

"No.... ," William screamed as he saw his son tackled on the football field.

"It's okay we got a referee let him make a decision," Grandpa

Harold says.

William and his sons sat with their eyes closed imagining the football game as they wait patiently of the referees outcome.

The referee measures the ball and where it landed then a voice comes on a loud speaker says, "Well, it appears as we have touch down. The Stanfield's have won the game!"

Tomas and Johnny along with their dad shout with joy.

"Do you hear the crowd? They're cheering you both on!"

"Yes, I hear them Grandpa," Johnny said.

"I hear them too," Tomas said.

"You know what they are cheering on?"

"Us making a touchdown and winning the game," Tomas replied.

"Oh no sons, they ain't cheering the game they're cheering you on, they're cheering on your brotherhood and there's nothing in this world like brothers who stand by each other's side."

Carolyn looked to her husband with his eyes closed along with her sons and looked over to Harold with his hat on his heart with tears flowing from her eyes seeing her family taking part in a moment in life and bonding over a story from Grandpa Harold. She had longed to hear one of his stories but never would she had imagined it would have made such an impact on her husband and children as it did and she knew this story Grandpa Harold was telling was more than imagination it was a story about unity.

Johnny opens his teary eyes and looks at Grandpa Harold and says, "Grandpa, but what about your brotherhood with your brothers? It can't just end with opening your treasure."

"Your right, Johnny."

"So, what happened after you seen the imaginations of all the world?"

CHAPTER EIGHTY-TWO

I stood there beholding the imaginations of the world on the shorelines of Atlantis as the thunderous voice asked, "Harold, do you know what these things are?"

"They are imaginations of the world," I replied.

"Your right, Harold. It's imaginations of the world, and the world is lost without it. Imagination is the escape of one's reality and with hope one's imagination can become true."

"Just like the paper from The King of Adventure?"

"Yes, just like the paper, but the heart can imagine mighty things and whatever a man imagines can come true as long as he believes. You can change the world if you believe the world can change. This change is not meant for you alone but for other to believe as well, whom ever believes he can change the world can change it."

When the thunderous voice got finished speaking the land begin to form again and the oceans begin to return and all the world began to shape and form to its former state and life returned to normal as if The Vile Ones had never done any evil at all. Then Atlantis returned to the sea under us as we stood on an island out in the sea.

"So, dear lads, what do you think of your first adventure

from The King of Adventure?" Scotty asked.

"Will all adventures be like this?" I asked.

"No adventure is the same, but all adventures are the same."

"I think that's the first riddle you ever said that made sense Scotty."

"Well, then I must be losing my mysterious eloquence, dear lad."

"So, what happens now?"

"Anything you can imagine, my dear lad, the sky is the limit. Tell me what do you desire the most?"

I turned and looked at my brothers and we all looked at each other and said. "I want my dad back."

"Then you know what to do, dear lad, it's only an imagination away."

Scotty was right, it was just an imagination away and I had the very thing that could make it all happen right in my pouch. My spirit was turned within me at Scotty's words as I reached down into my pouch and took out my paper to write my next adventure.

"I can't do this," with my hand paused looking upon the faces of my brothers.

"But you have too!" Timmy says.

"No Timmy, I can't."

"Why not?"

"Cause there is no glory if I do it on my own. The adventures are not just for me, but for my brothers as well."

"What are you trying to say?" Danny asked.

"If one of you will do me the honors, I would love it if one of you wrote it instead."

Timmy perked his head up with a mischievous grin and snatched the paper from out of my hand and began to write and the letter began to shine and the lettering was in gold as in times before.

"What did you write?"

"You will see," Timmy said.

As I looked down to the paper, I saw a map of Germany. Yea, you guessed it we were about to go and fight the Germans.

"Oh....you didn't did you?"

And there we were in Mr. Owensby's printing factory standing at our war table overlooking the map of Germany with our new friends who accompanied us on our adventure, for some a table is sacred like how they broke bread in the bible or how a family sits at the end of the day saying grace or a young couple gazing into each other's eyes. Everyone has their table but ours was a war table with maps and plans to kick the Germans' butts and Germany didn't have a clue what they were about to get their self into, and there we stood at that war table and it was perfectly clear what the others was thinking. We all could see it in each other's eyes, we didn't have to say it, the truth lingered in the air, it was at the tip of our tongues we never said it, but we all was thinking it.... yea, Hitler is a prick!

Chapter Eighty-three

Little did we know Aunt Louise and Mr. Owensby had been watching our little adventure take place on the roof top of the printing factory as it all played out on the letter that I had sent him.

"They're in your office?" Aunt Louise said.

"How are they in my office?" Mr. Owensby asked as he looked down at the paper.

"I didn't believe they would really do it."

"Do what?"

"They've been gathering information on Germany from all the newspapers while they were here."

"What are you saying?"

Mr. Owensby stands up quickly and says, "They're going to try to go to Germany to rescue their father."

"You can't be serious, can you?"

"We better go stop them before it's too late."

"How do you know about this?"

Mr. Owensby put out his hand and said, "I will tell you later, we need to go now."

Aunt Louise looked down at the paper and said, "But they can't go to Germany, can they?"

"What do you think?"

Aunt Louise dusted of the doubts from her mind and said, "You're right, we need to stop them."

As they made their way down the stairs, we stood in the office planning our tactics, our plan was simple, fly in with the dragons, rescue Dad and leave. It was naive to think we could do it, but hey we were kids and naive was part being a kid besides sometimes being naive to a plan can end up being the most clever plan of all at least that's what we were banking on.

"Someone's coming," Timmy said as we heard feet running from above.

"It's the police!" Danny said.

"It can't be the police, it's not like they're on a steak out to catch a few kids and a couple of pirates," Timmy replied.

"Oh, I can't go to jail," Julius said.

"You can't go to jail, I can't go to jail," One-eyed Steve said.

"Quick! We need to get out of here, hurry draw us out of here, Harold!"

I pulled out the paper and began to draw as the footsteps got closer to us and drew a concentration camp, as I drew the letters were in gold and light shined from the page as the door slung open as Aunt Louise and Mr. Owensby stood before us and we all disappeared from their eyes as the wind from the rooms picked up strewing papers about.

"Did you see that?" Aunt Louise asked.

"Yes, if I hadn't seen it with my own eyes, I wouldn't have believed it."

CHAPTER EIGHTY-FOUR

The past few weeks Dad's jail cell had been rather cold. The last few days had not been so bad, but still it was no Hilton as he set in the corner bare footed and the lack of strength from not eating.

He passed his time entertaining himself with my letter I had sent him every day just like Aunt Louise he watched our adventure play out on the paper.

Sometimes those in prison do not have a place of escape, sometimes the only escape they have is their minds to think of places they never been or relive a memory, and the letter brought back many memories not just for us, but for Mom and Dad too.

There was a time before we came into their lives when they were young and in love themselves, he suffered a lot losing her to her pregnancy and often regretted not being able to spend more time with her. The farm took up a lot of Dad's time and from time to time he would go out to sea down at Uncle Tessie's dock and go out to catch shrimp with some of the local fishermen and would be gone out on the ocean weeks at a time. It left a heavy burden on them at times but it lifted the burden of finances, sometimes he wished he'd just stayed home a little more with her, but they just purchased their farm and he knew a little sacrifice would help better their future and the future of their children.

Those four walls were witness to his joy when he laughed at their memories and were witness to his tears when he just couldn't let go. Emotions ran wild and Mom was closer to him than she ever was since she left this earth, and he was holding onto her now more than ever, more than the times he actually got to hold her in his arms.

Love sometimes follows a man for a lifetime. He loves with all his heart and gives his all to the woman he loves and never finds love again, some might see some man and think he is the loneliest man in the world and will be alone forever but if you look inside that man's heart he is never really alone because he once loved with great admiration and nothing by any means could measure up to the depths of his passion. So, he just goes on through life knowing his best days are behind him but the best days have never left him.

It might have been years since Mom had passed, but Dad could still smell her perfume lingering like the nights they would step out and go down to the dance hall for a night out on the town and dance the night away under a Georgia moon. Or how they would sit outside listening to the crickets singing their old southern lullabies as they would gaze up to a night full of stars hoping to catch one falling so, they could make a wish. It was these precious moments he held dear not just these moments, but the thousands of moments that ran through his mind and moved his heart to joy and sorrows to tears and to laughter.

Dad might have been is some foreign jail cell, but he was free to feel the love he had lost in some old memory and those four walls that heard his tears and his joy might have been his prison, but the love he remembered with Mom was the key that freed his spirit.

The four walls to his prison were not the only company to him, Dad made a friend with one of the guards. Not just a guard, but someone who was sent by The King of Adventure who had many adventures of his own.

Many times, they would share stories about their lives and how they grew up when they were kids, Dad would tell him about growing up in Georgia and how the clay would get stuck to his feet after it rained and how sometimes the sun was so blistering hot one would have to find a swimming hole just to cool down, he painted a grand picture of Georgia to him. He told him how the pine trees seem to never stop growing and the stars over Georgia would sit like diamonds in the black velvet skies. The guard would tell Dad how he grew up in an orphanage and was split up with his brother after losing his Mom and Dad in World War One, and how they were reunited to live out great adventures.

Dad would listen intensively to his tall tales in his broken English and never judged him. Their friendship showed their commonality and how we are all the same in the world, we sometimes view ourselves different cause of the lines upon a map, but those lines on a map don't define us as human beings. We all are born into this world and we all die, we all laugh, we love, we hurt, this is the common thing we all hold in the human race and if we look closely we can see we all are the same. It's only man's hearts that learn division and by it divides the world amongst us and once we are divided we become enemies of one another.

They may have been on different sides of opposing armies, but they both saw past the lines that were drawn for them and became friends and saw the commonality they both shared. The map of the world may have had its lines drawn for them, but their friendship erased the borders between them.

CHAPTER EIGHTY-FIVE

It was April 29th and the world was about to change. Hitler confined himself to his bunker out of fear of the allied forces, he had not yet surrendered but defeat of Germany was imminent. Little did we know that destiny had greater plans for us than we had imagined. Sometimes a story writes its self even when we think we are the ones writing it.

We had flown into Germany in One-eyed Steve's ship that was newly repaired and little did we know the letter had changed course on us instead of us headed for the concentration camp we were headed straight for Hitler.

"Sir, the letter is rewriting itself!" Julius said looking down at the paper of his.

"This can't be right," One-eyed Steve said as he pulled out his paper to confirm Julius' words.

"Ours is rewriting itself as well," one of the crew members said as he confirmed the evidence.

"This has never happened before," One-eyed Steve said.

"What does this mean?" I asked.

"The letters have never rewritten themselves, someone must be behind this."

"Do you think it's The King of Adventure?" I asked.

"No, he wouldn't change the course of destiny."

"Then who would?"

"No one other than Hitler himself," One-eyed Steve replied.

"Oh man this isn't good, you're not telling me Hitler knows about us?" Julius asked.

"Who else would be a supreme ruler of The Vile Ones other than the vilest one on earth?"

"Oh god, I hate it when you're right."

"I hate it when I'm right too, Julius."

"So, what does this mean?" I asked.

"Looks like we are going into the jaws of the beast."

"Oh gosh, I wished you hadn't put it that way," Julius said.

"We will fight Hitler!" Timmy said as he held up his cannon.

"Sir, our paper just went blank," one of the crew members said as our ship jolted in the sky, slinging everyone inside.

"What's happening?" I asked frantically.

"He's erasing all of our past adventures as if they never happened!" One-eyed Steve replied.

"If he erases our past adventures, he can erase away defeating The Vile Ones in Atlantis," I replied.

"Sir, we are beginning to lose altitude," one of the crew members yelled.

"Brace yourselves fellows were headed towards land and it might be a treacherous landing," One-eyed Steve said as we plummeted towards the ground.

Julius grabbed hold of a pole and does his cross signal and said, "The odds of crashing a ship twice in one day, why do I work for this treacherous pirate?"

The ship barreled into the ground as dust flew over the bow of the ship breaking parts of the front of the ship as it turned sideways riding upon the land until it came to a complete stop. Luckily no one was hurt. There was no moment for a sigh of relief, we were met with tanks and a small platoon of German soldiers pointing their guns on us and our adventure looked like all would soon come to an end and saving Dad was no longer an option, surviving the Germans was all that mattered now.

CHAPTER EIGHTY-SIX

Dad sat in his cell watching the scene taking place and knew we were in grave danger as the guard stood at his door.

"They took my boys captive."

"Who took them?" German guard asked.

"Hitler's soldiers took them, here look and see for yourself."

Dad handed the paper to the guard through the bars as he looked down to see us captured.

"You didn't tell me they were coming to Germany."

"I didn't know myself until now, we must help them," Dad replied.

"You know what this might cost me?"

"I know but they're my sons, we have to try."

"There might be a way for me to help them, but I will need to send a letter."

"That might take too long."

While Dad was speaking the same messenger that had met with Aunt Louise and Mr. Owensby appeared out of nowhere.

"I'm sorry I am late I have been rather busy as of late. I do perceive you have a letter that needs to be sent."

The guard pulled a letter out of his pocket and handed it to the messenger.

"No one's ever attempted to write him," the messenger said looking down at the letter and whom it was addressed to.

"We must try," the guard replied.

"But he hides in the realms of thunder who knows where he might be."

"If we don't get the letter to him all might be lost forever."

"You know it's forbidden for a messenger to even go before him unless he invites someone to come near his presence."

"It's for a just cause and he will not turn anyone from a just cause."

"I will do what I can, I have heard from others that their adventures have been erased. Is this rumor true to you as well?"

"I know nothing of the sort."

"Look upon your paper and see if it's true, I fear the worst may come upon the adventurers if it's true."

"Your fears are well received. If you're correct, but I assure you this isn't possible," the guard said as he pulled out his paper and looked and saw his adventures erased from his paper.

"What does it show?"

The guard looked back up to the messenger who stood ready for an answer as the guard stood captivated in a moment of fear.

"The Vile Ones they are prevailing against us, you must go at once and deliver the message before even our letters are erased. If The Vile Ones find out our form of communications, then we will become powerless in The Land of Adventure. For now we do have hope."

The messenger looked back at the guard with fear of his future then looking over to my father who was grieved for his sons and said, "You know how dangerous this will be for me?"

"And for me as well," the guard replied.

"You must go, my sons are in grave danger," Dad said.

"For your sons' sake and for the sake of hope I will go."

"Thank you, thank you."

''Don't thank me, thank hope. It's the only treasure we have right now for our future," as the messenger said, then he disappeared.

CHAPTER EIGHTY-SEVEN

Aunt Louise and Mr. Owensby stood in his office afraid of our outcome as we disappeared from their eyes. Their fear was valid and they had every reason to fear knowing our adventure had disappeared from our papers and our powers were slowly diminishing.

"They are becoming powerless, there's no way they will be able to withstand The Vile Ones if their powers are taken from them," Mr. Owensby said.

"We can't stay here, we need to leave."

"Where can we go? No matter where we go, they will still be in danger."

"I know, but do you not remember what Harold wrote you?"

"You're not suggesting we go to the orphanage?"

"Yes, even though the adventures are being erased the letters are not. Its evident we can still see what's taking place and if can still see what's taking place then there's a chance, he will still be able to meet us at the orphanage."

"Your right Louise, that's one thing The Vile Ones haven't stolen from them yet. There's still a hope for their future."

"I only wished I knew what the messenger meant when he said, 'when Harold awakes'."

"I don't know what he meant but I do know one thing, you're right about the letter and we do have to get to the orphanage."

"Maybe there is someone there who can help us after all the letters have shown us many of the those at the orphanage are adventurers themselves."

"You're right, someone there would know what to do."

"I just hope it's not too late."

"Me too Louise, me too," Mr. Owensby said as he took Aunt Louise's hand to reassure her he was there for her and he was going to see this thing through. He knew her nephews meant the world to her and he was quite taken with us boys as well. He might have been our boss, but he was our friend as well and he was willing to do whatever it took to help us.

CHAPTER EIGHTY-EIGHT

No one said a word as we all sat awaiting our final moments in a guarded room as the guards stood watch mocking us in the other room as their faces turned to the lifeless faces of The Vile Ones. We thought we had defeated The Vile Ones, but not all of them were destroyed. It was evident they still had a strong hold on the world and we were in the middle of the jaws of the beast and there was no escaping.

The Vile Ones entered the room with their weapons drawn as they snarled with the hate that drove them to commit violence. They had no regard to human life and with any given moment they were willing to prove just how malicious they could be. They previously stripped us of our weapons, but their attentions were turned to further weaken us by taking the one thing left that could save us.

"Where are your papers?" one of The Vile Ones asked.

"You've stolen all our adventures and erased everything what need do you have of our papers?" One-eyed Steve asked.

"It's not that we need them, it's what we want," one of The Vile Ones said as they all searched us for our papers so we could not write or draw any thing leaving us completely helpless to The Vile Ones.

There we were helpless like a frail flower in the sun being scorched by the heat and our hope was falling from us like the leaves in mid-October and for a moment all I could do was think about my dream and the tree and the message Mom had given me and my brothers about hope.

While they gathered our papers from us a voice in German spoke as The Vile Ones gave a salute to their leader as he entered the room.

"So, you're the ones who have been giving us all this trouble?" Hitler spoke in English as he walked across the room with hatred towards us as he set at his desk.

"He's the one who destroyed your followers in Atlantis."

"Whom are you speaking of?"

"The boy in the captain's apparel."

"So, you're Harold Stanfield, the one whose caused all this havoc upon my empire?" Hitler asked.

"How do you know my name, and what havoc have we caused?"

"When you overcame us in Atlantis it caused a ripple in time and Germany has suffered great loss. So you think we don't know the names of our adversaries sent by The King of Adventure?"

"You won't get away with this. We will stop you."

"We've already got away with it, and it's too late for you."

"The Allied Forces will stop you."

"Not if we take away your imagination. Do you not know imagination has been the only thing holding us back our victory?"

"So that's been your plan all along, to destroy imagination and take over the world?"

"Once imagination is gone then no one will dare to imagine

to fight against us and we will rule The Land of Imagination."

"So that's your plan, to overthrow The Land of Adventure?"

"The Land of Adventure, please don't insult me, not only The Land of Adventure, but all the time and space it inhabits. I will not stop there, but I will overthrow the worlds of dreams and passions as well."

"We will stop you!" Timmy yelled out.

"And with what army, who you and your motley crew of misfits?"

"You will never take away imagination from the hearts of the people," I spouted.

"Away with them, take them to the field and send them to The Parallels of Time."

"What's The Parallels of Time?"

"Have you not told him what The Parallels of Time is?" Hitler asked as he looked around at those whom accompanied me. "The Parallels of Time is where you are suspended in time caught between worlds without the compass of hope to guide you."

"Oh no, not The Parallels of Time," Julius said in fear.

"Before you take them, burn their letters and let them see their hope perish before their eyes."

I could hear The Vile Ones laughing within themselves as they held up our papers and set them on fire as they turned to ashes falling to the floor.

"Now defeat is imminent and your Allied Forces will surrender once you're sent to The Parallel of Time, now away with them!" Hitler commanded.

The halls to the outer courts led us to the path of our destruction and darkness weighed heavy on our souls as I could feel those who accompanied losing hope. Our fate was to be The Parallels of Time. I didn't know what awaited on us in The Parallels of Time all knew was it didn't sound like a place I wanted to go and the way Julius feared it, something told me evil awaited us there. I for one didn't want to go, but we were powerless and had no way of escape from the clutches of The Vile Ones and the hope we had was taken from us and our future was obsolete.

Chapter Eighty-nine

Aunt Louise and Mr. Owensby were driving down the road to the orphanage when Aunt Louise begin to tear up.

"What is it?"

Aunt Louise hands Mr. Owensby the letter then puts her hand to her mouth trying not to cry as he pulled over to the side of the road to look at what was taking place.

"I find out my brother is still alive through the letters and now the fate of my nephews."

While the letter played out before Mr. Owensby, he became distraught as well having much doubt as we were led to be cast into The Parallels of Time.

"We can't give up on them now, Louise."

"I'm not given up on them, but there's nothing I can do."

"We still have the letter he's written us so there has to be a way for them to overcome The Vile Ones."

"But how?"

"I don't know but there's got to be a way, for now all we can do is hope and pray."

"If only we could write him out of this."

"You know what Louise?"

"What?"

"That just might work."

"What do you mean, that just might work?"

"Writing them out of this."

"But only adventurers can."

"Your right."

"But you're not an adventurer."

"But I did go on an adventure as a kid so I am a chosen one as well."

"What are you trying to say?"

"I'm saying I'm going to go to Germany and save them."

"It's too dangerous."

"I've been sitting in my office telling everyone else's story, it's time to tell mine."

"If you're going, I'm going with you."

"It's too dangerous. I'm not willing to lose you Louise."

"And I'm not willing to lose you either, so you're taking me with you."

While they sat in the parking lot, an unexpected knock got both of their attention as the younger messenger from before appeared at Mr. Owensby's window.

"Sir, I'm sorry I'm late, but I was sent to give you a letter."

"Whom is it from?"

"It's from Harold, he sent you another letter."

"He must have not written it yet."

"No Sir, he hasn't and I couldn't help but over hear your conversation and I hate to be the barer of bad news, but I've been ordered to instruct everyone to not write or draw until further notice. Until certain matters had been taken care of."

"Who would give such authority?"

"None other than The King himself, however letters can still be sent, luckily The Vile Ones have not breached our form of communication."

"If Harold still sent us a letter and he hasn't written it yet then that means he will be okay."

The messenger smiled and said "Something big is about to happen. I can't say but I would just set back and watch."

"What's going to happen?"

"Read the letter Harold sent you. It has new adventures written on it of great epic scales like I have not seen before."

Mr. Owensby opened the letter addressed to him that read:

> Dear Mr. Owensby,
> This is Harold. I am going to be okay, tell Aunt Louise we will be home soon.

CHAPTER NINETY

The messenger always brought hope to those whom needed it. Messengers belonged to a secret organization guided under the ordinance of The King of Adventure so other adventurers could stay informed with one another. The messengers were like the adventurers themselves who could travel through time and worlds. Unlike us we were only subject through time and The Land of Adventure but the messenger could travel to other worlds, world of dreams and worlds of passion where men dreamt and their dreams came true and the world of passions where the hearts of those filled with passions could inspire the world and all these worlds collided with our world forming our world into a better world.

Word had reached other worlds about how The Land of Imagination was at the brink of destruction and how many adventurers had been erased from the past. The inhabitants of both worlds, passions and dreams, were in turmoil and they knew that if we were defeated their worlds stood at the brink of destruction as well.

The Vile Ones led us out into an open field like we were lambs to the slaughter as Hitler accompanied his soldiers of vileness. The Vile Ones who once had no facial form only darkness under their hoods transformed into faces so we could see their evil appearance as they gaped on us with excitement knowing they prevailed against us as they entreated us with evil stares of despise.

I looked over to my brothers in fear for their lives as they looked at me with fear as well and I could hear the thoughts of their hearts wishing for a way of escape doubting in themselves our destiny as I remembered Mom's words echoing in my soul.

How were we to make the world a better place with our hope if our hope is dying right before our eyes and if we are sent to The Parallels of Time by The Vile Ones whose to say we will survive much less ever make it back home.

All we wanted was to come and rescue Dad from the Germans but that plan turned on a dime and we were now subject to Hitler's evil devices and his plan to take over The Land of Adventure and the other worlds. If he succeeded all hope would be lost forever. The only thing that was stopping him was our existence in the present world. Once they cast us into The Parallels of Time it was just a matter of time until the rest of the adventurers were rounded up and cast into it as well. Not only them, but The King Adventure himself. The Land of Adventure again could be swallowed up by the dark abyss taking away any form of light and hope along with the imaginations of mankind and the only imaginations that would survive is the imaginations of Hitler's evil heart.

The thought of the world under the rule of Hitler disturbed my every being. If it not been for him, we would have never been sent to the orphanage and Dad never would have gone to war and we would be back home in Reidsville playing out in the yard like kids do or climbing a tree instead of feeling the heavy burdens of the reality of war and what it does to families. It rips and tears the very fabric of family, it tears it asunder and all we have is the brokenness that it leaves.

It was not just me or my brothers who was affected by this, it was all the other children in the orphanage who had undergone the same fate as us, whom lost loved ones due to the war. Their lives were ripped apart as well, unfortunately for many of them they didn't have an opportunity to go on great adventures from The King of Adventure and were subject to the system. Who knows if they were chosen. Maybe their fate might have ended up like ours standing in an open field as captives before Hitler and his vile soldiers of malice?

"Any last words?" Hitler asked as we awaited our fate.

As I looked out I saw a familiar appearance. I don't know why I didn't notice it at first when they lead us to the open field, maybe my heart was too heavy or my mind to clouded but there was that tree in my dreams with its leaves blowing in the wind not battered as in my dream, but you could see where lightning had struck it and it was healing. All of a sudden I realized I was the tree and I was in my healing state of being and I knew something was about to happen. I didn't know what it was but the root of hope in me just wasn't about to give up.

"Sorry Sir, I am late, I have a letter for Hitler."

Hitler turned to see the messenger standing before him with a letter in hand ready to deliver.

"Who are you?"

"I was sent by The King of Adventure himself to give you a letter."

Hitler looked at the messenger studying his face as he took the paper from him that read as he read it aloud:

> Dear Hitler,
> This is The King of Adventure. I will solemnly

give surrender of myself in trade of the lives of those whom your about to send into The Parallels of Time, and I will not do so unless I receive a message back from Harold Stanfield himself confirming your compliance to my surrender.
Sincerely,
The King of Adventure

"Looks like your king is willing to give up the kingdom for the sake of all of you."

We stood in disbelief. The King of Adventure was about to trade himself for all of us. If he did that we all would still be under the rule of Hitler and subject to his rule, we might be freed from him but the world itself would not.

"Don't do it, it's a trap!" one of The Vile Ones said.

"Either way I will still rule. Their powers are defenseless against us. Besides, who can say they had a king surrender to them?"

Hitler looked over to me and said, "Now all we need to do is have Harold to confirm my compliance and surrender of The King of Adventure."

I stood there as I saw the messenger bow his head in shamefulness with a grievous face as he pulled out another letter addressed for me to sign.

"Sir, if I may, I have the letter addressed to Harold for him to sign."

"Go give him the letter," Hitler said as he stood with The Vile Ones as they gleed in the thoughts of taking The King of Adventure captive.

"Don't do it Harold, don't sign it," Timmy said.

"Yes, don't sign it," Danny said as well as I looked around the faces of the adventurers who stood round about me.

I could see the defeat on the adventurers who stood near as

they wanted freedom from Hitler, but not at the price of losing The King of Adventure.

"What should I do, Scotty?" I asked.

"Answers, answers, answers will all be answered when the question is in the ears of those who may reveal to you what you seek."

"Scotty, a riddle is the last thing I need to hear right now. I need answers on what to do."

"You already know, dear lad," Scotty said.

As the messenger came near handing me the letter for me to open with a wink and a smile then turning back towards Hitler and The Vile Ones hanging his head in a defeated manner, why did he just wink and smile at me I thought to myself. Did he know something I didn't know?

Then it all made sense as I looked down at the paper that read:

Whatever you write or draw comes true,
you're the author of your own adventure.

The King of Adventure never was about to surrender it was all a smoke screen to get me a letter to write anything I wanted on it. Little did Hitler know The King of Adventure had out-smarted him and victory was on the side of the adventurers.

But unlike any victory there comes distress and turmoil and Hitler and The Vile Ones had already begun their ritual of open-ing the hemisphere to send us all to The Parallels of Time. They had banded their lightnings together with their staffs towards the skies as a vortex begin to open above us swirling with clouds around it and inside was nothing but pure darkness.

"Send them all to The Parallels of Time," Hitler commanded.

"Are you willing to send us to The Parallels of Time before I sign the Declaration of Surrender by The King of Adventure?" I shouted as the wind became violent.

"Are you willing to sign over The King of Adventure?"

"Yes, I will sign it," I screamed loudly playing into Hitler's hand.

"Then sign it," Hitler screamed over the noise.

I looked down with my best poker face, but with a face of sadness as The Vile Ones rejoiced at my signing of the petition sent by The King of Adventure as I begin to write the letters became gold and light shined on the paper as times before then I looked up and smiled at Hitler and said, "Whatever I write or draw comes true!"

"He has deceived us," one of The Vile Ones said.

"No, your greed has deceived you, goodness always prevails over evil."

"Send them into The Parallels of Time!"

"It's too late Hitler, what I have written, I have written."

Then light shot forth not like in times past but a different light as if The King of Adventure was writing on his own paper. And when one looked into the light that shot forth and if your heart was good, one could see all the adventures that has ever taken place and began to be restored and if your heart was evil, you would see the demise that would befall you as Hitler fell to his knees seeing the Allied Forces raiding Berlin putting an end to his reign and the light shot through the sky hitting the vortex rendering it powerless.

"It's over, Hitler!"

"This won't be the last time you've heard from me," Hitler said as he pulled out his paper and wrote on it.

"Yes, it is Hitler, it is the last time anyone will ever see of you." Then Hitler and The Vile Ones disappeared from out of our sights.

"He will be back," Danny said.

"The war is over, he has nowhere to go, he saw his future."

"Now what?" Danny asks.

"We find our dad."

"Sir, if I may be an assistance to you, but I happen to know where your father is," the messenger said.

"Where is he?"

"Ask your paper and it will lead you to him."

I looked down at my paper and remembered I asked the paper to lead me to Atlantis and it led me to Atlantis and if ask it to lead me to Dad it would lead me to Dad.

"Just like Atlantis?"

"Yes, just like Atlantis. There's more to this world of imagination than one could comprehend."

"This whole time I could've drawn Dad and it would've led me to Dad?"

"Yes, but it would not lead you on the journey to face your fears and as long as your fears were present your imagination could be stolen and if it was stolen then it would've stolen your father from you again."

"You mean if I had imagined saving Dad and saved him and my fears were still there, I would've lost him again cause The Vile Ones would just steal my imagination?"

"Yes, that's why it was important to face your fears and doubts and open your treasure. If not then you wouldn't be in a place to rescue your father. Speaking of rescuing your father, you know what to do."

I looked down to my paper and then looked at my brothers and handed the paper to Danny and said, '" It would only be more honorable if the eldest brother asked."

"Are you sure about this, Har Har?" Danny asked.

"I might not know all things my brother but I do know one thing. It's your right as a brother. let's go rescue Dad."

Chapter Ninety-one

Danny looked down at the paper and took the pencil in his hand and began to write asking the letter to lead us to Dad and as it wrote golden letters appeared and we disappeared. We were standing in front of a concentration camp as we see German soldiers walk passed us not giving any thought to us as if our presence did not matter at all.

"The soldiers are not paying any attention to us?" Danny said.

"The war is over, they have no need of us," Timmy said.

"You're probably right Timmy, but where's Dad?"

The doors to the prison opened as prisoners wondered out of their cells hoping the rumor was true that the war was over and they were now free.

"Will I ever see you again?" Dad asked the guard.

"You have the letter with you. As long as you have it, I'm sure we will meet again."

"What if the Allied Forces lock you up?"

"I never harmed anyone."

"Until we meet again my friend."

"Yes, until we meet again," the guard said as he took out his paper and wrote and disappeared from Dad's sight.

"I don't see Dad, do you?" I asked as we stood outside the concentration camp.

"This is where the letter led us, he's got to be here," Danny said.

"What if he already left?"

"There's no way, the letter would've led us to where he is."

"You're right, Danny!"

Dad squinted his eyes from the glaring light that temporarily blinded him as he exited the darkened prison and once his sight came to focus, he looked out he saw his three sons standing in the light of the sun.

"Danny, Harold, Timmy?" Dad yells in a frail voice.

"Dad!" we all yelled back as we took off running to him. We threw our arms around him once we drew near.

"The war is over Dad," I said.

"I know Harold, I know," Dad said as he stood weakened from the lack of food.

"Are you okay, Dad?" Danny asked.

"Yes, sons I am okay. It looks like you boys have been on quite an adventure."

"Yes Sir, we have," I replied.

"More than you know Dad, more than you know," Danny replied.

"Sons, your father knows more than what you think he knows," Dad looked down and smiled then said, "Who would ever have imagined I'd have such great sons?"

"You Dad, you!" Danny replied.

"Yes sons, that is the greatest thing a dad could ever imagine."

Dad looked behind us and smiled as we turned to see all our friends behind us.

"When did you get here?"

"Just a few seconds ago, dear lad," Scotty replied.

"Arr.. did you think we would miss this reunion amongst father and sons?"

"Dad, meet our new friends."

Dad nodded his head to show his gesture and says, "Looks like The King of Adventure chose wisely giving you such an authentic bunch of friends."

"You know about The King of Adventure?" I asked.

"Like I said, a father knows more than you think he knows."

"But how?"

"The letter Son, it showed me everything."

"If you saw what happened, then Mr. Owensby saw everything too," Timmy said.

"Whose Mr. Owensby?" Dad asked.

"He's my boss. I will explain everything later," Danny replied.

"I just thought of something."

"What's that Timmy?" I asked.

"What if he showed Aunt Louise the paper? Man I hope she don't find out!"

"Why's that Timmy?"

"Cause, I don't want to be grounded and not get any more chocolate cake."

We all stood there and laughed at the thought Timmy worrying about getting grounded and not getting any more of Aunt Louise's chocolate cake. We went on a great journey, got split up, Timmy faced a dragon, Danny learned to fly, and made friends with a treacherous pirate. I met a giant and was taught hope by a nun, we went to Atlantis, overcame the vile ones, saw Mom and rescued Dad, and all Timmy could think about was Aunt Louise's chocolate cake. I guess after any long adventure one does have a great appetite, and chocolate cake and home didn't sound so bad to me.

"Will you be coming home with us now?" I asked.

"Son, I can't right now. But it's time for you boys to go back home. I will see you soon enough."

"But why can't you come home now, Dad?" Timmy asked.

Dad looked out and saw his fellow soldiers and said, "Because of them. I can't leave my brothers."

We knew what Dad meant. He couldn't leave his fellow soldiers, just like us brothers, we just couldn't leave each other as well. Dad wasn't just saying he couldn't leave them, what he was really saying is a man must wear his honor and we were listening. Dad had a way with words that inspired us. We traveled all that way to rescue Dad, but maybe Dad traveled all that way to rescue us. We set out to be Dads' heroes but, in the end, it was always Dad who was our hero.

"Sons, I know you want to stay, but you have an aunt who must be worried to death over you."

"What are you saying, Dad?"

"It's time for you boys to go home."

"But we just got here."

"I know sons, but your aunt needs you. Besides, I will be home soon and the last thing she needs is to be worried about you boys."

"Dad is right," Danny said.

"But how do we go back home?"

"Son, you're the author of your own adventure, just write it."

I looked up to Dad and smiled knowing he understood and pulled out my paper and looked down at it and Dad gave us all a hug goodbye. Then I turned to see the fellow soldiers as they stood by frail and hungry, whose lives were torn apart from the war and I couldn't help to think of the kids at the orphanage whose lives were torn apart by the war too. Who knows, one of these men here could've been the father of one of those kids at the orphanage and my heart went out to them. As I began to write on my paper the lettering turned gold and light shined up the letter as a table of food set before the soldiers filled with meats and all deliciousness and sweet tea as me and my brothers disappeared being portalled back home.

Chapter Ninety-two

I woke up out in a field with the grass as my pillow to an early morning dressed in the clothes that I had worn the day I left the orphanage. Am I still in The Land of Adventure I thought to myself as I made my way through a small patch of trees to a winding road.

There was no houses or cars in sight for miles as I walked hoping to make my way back to civilization and the car pulled alongside me coming to a stop. The car door opened and a familiar voice called out my name, "Harold."

As I turned to see who spoke to me, Aunt Louise stood outside the car and I ran to embrace her with a hug as Mr. Owensby stepped out of his car with a proud look on his face.

"You did it!" Mr. Owensby said as he took off his hat putting it to his chest as a gesture of respect.

"I did, didn't I?" I replied.

"You sure did, young man, you sure did."

"You got my letters?"

"Yes, I got them," Mr. Owensby answered.

"Dad will be home soon."

"We know," Aunt Louise replied.

"So, you know all about the adventure?"

"Yes, all of it, even your mother," Aunt Louise said as she took Mr. Owensby's hand.

"I knew it!"

"Knew what?" Aunt Louise asked.

"You and Mr. Owensby."

They both looked at each other knowing what I meant by, you and Mr. Owensby. It was rather obvious this whole journey brought them closer and we turned out to be matchmakers after all.

CHAPTER NINETY-THREE

Moments later we pulled up to the orphanage and we were greeted by Sister Milica, Priscilla and head priest Steve, better known as One-eyed Steve who waited for my arrival.

As we parked my feet were heavy and didn't want to budge. My heart wanted to stay in that car forever, I didn't want to go back to the orphanage, I just wanted to go home.

"I see your heart is heavy," Sister Milica said as I exited the car.

"I want to go back on an adventure with my brothers."

"You can but right now is not the time. There are more important things we must address at the present moment."

What is more important than going on an adventure with my brothers, I thought to myself.

"You forget we can hear what your heart is thinking, Harold," Sister Milica said with a smile.

"We had some unexpected guests show up while you were away," Steve the head priest said.

"Who?" I asked.

One-eyed Steve turned towards the door of the orphanage as Timmy and Danny both exit the front door running, throwing their arms around Aunt Louise.

"Excuse me, but I hate to intrude in the sanctity of this reunion, but my name is Julius and I have a letter of a great importance that you might want to read," Julius said as he walked up handing Aunt Louise an envelope.

"Is it from The King of Adventure?" Timmy asked.

"Sorry, it isn't Timmy, but just as important," Julius answered.

Aunt Louise opened the letter and began to read. She began to tear up and said, "it's signed Julius Santiago."

"At your service, dear Madam," Julius replied.

"What does it say Aunt Louise?" Timmy asked.

"The State has just rewarded me temporary custody of you boys."

"I'm quite sorry, I would've signed the letter sooner, but I was on an adventure," Julius said.

"You work for The State Department and you're an adventurer as well?" I asked.

"Guilty as charged," Julius replied.

"So, we are going home?" I asked grievously.

"Why are you sad, this is what we wanted?" Danny asked.

"I know, but I can't be so selfish Danny," I replied.

"What are you getting at?" Danny asked.

"Whatever we write or draw comes true," I replied.

I looked towards the orphanage and pulled out my paper and began to draw and the letters turned to gold and it began to shine like in times past.

That day was like any other day to the children at the orphanage, little did they know their lives were about to change. My heart felt compassion for them all because I had been where they were in life and it was my firm conviction we should always give back to others.

The sound of a thump sounded all throughout the corridors and hallways of the orphanage. It got their attention as the thumping sounds increased, one by one the kids filled the hallways leaving behind what they all were doing as they made their way to the foyer then out into the courtyard. They all were filled with amazement as hundreds of ships sat as far as the eye could see and the sail beat the pole making a thumping sound.

"I've been lucky. I got to see my Mom and my Dad, and Dad's coming back home. But they have no one," I said as I held my paper in hand.

Just like before a cloud lowered down in the shape of stairs awaiting to be boarded as a voice called out from the ship.

"Dexter!"

When Dexter looked up he saw his Mom and Dad together and he began to cry saying "Is it really you?"

"Yes, it's us Son, come aboard."

Dexter doubted me when I had first heard the thumping noises when I went on my adventure and now here he was hearing it as well. Not only hearing, but he was looking up to see his family that he lost and with tears he boarded the ship and the ship sailed away.

Child after child was reunited with their mother and father until all the ships had left, while One-eyed Steve looked down to the ground saddened as he saw the whole orphanage leave with their parents.

"Can I ask you something?"

"What is it, Harold?" One-eyed Steve replied.

"Did you really think I would forget about you as well?"

One-eyed Steve looked at me with a surprised look and jittery hands and said, "You're not saying what I think your saying are you?"

"I just smiled as the last ship sailed into the courtyard and One-eyed Steve's brother Marcus stood on the deck waving with his mother and father.

"It's your time to be reunited with your family, Steve, or shall I say One-eyed Steve?"

"That was the one thing I treasured the most, my family," One-eyed Steve said as tears ran down his eyes.

"Don't we all treasure that the most?" I replied.

"Yes, don't we all, don't we all?" One-eyed Steve said right before he entered, looking down and saluting me.

"Until we meet again, my friend," I said.

"Arr.. until we meet again!" One-eyed Steve replied as he sailed away with his family into a new adventure.

Timmy turned to Aunt Louise and asked, "You know all about our adventure?"

"Yes, I sure do Timmy."

"You're not going to ground us for going to Germany, are you?"

"No, Timmy I'm not," Aunt Louise answered.

"Good, because I didn't want to get grounded from your chocolate cake," Timmy replied as we all laughed at Timmy with his comedic timing.

Months later life went back to normal We went back to work for Mr. Owensby right before Dad came home. Then a little time passed and Mr. Owensby married our aunt and we moved back home to Rincon, Georgia, with Dad and lived on the family farm. We had many more adventures not only in The Land of Adventure, but many out on those back dirt roads of Rincon, where the pines touched the skies and the night sky looked like diamonds clothed with black velvet skies, a place where we called home.

Chapter Ninety-four

It was the summer of 1985 when everything seemed mysterious, and the world was innocent through the eyes of a child. I was only ten years old that summer, the day I got to sit with Mr. Harold Stanfield, as he told his story to his grandchildren. It wasn't just a story about hope, imagination, or family but it was a story about change and how a story can inspire and change someone for the rest of their life.

That day I saw two brothers change towards each other and become best friends. I saw a husband change and give more of his life to his family and I saw a son reconcile his relationship with his father.

I said it before and I say it again, there was a lot of wisdom under that ball cap of Mr. Harold Steinfield. He wasn't just wise in words, but wise in heart and loved his family.

Many times through the years I've traveled back home to that little town of Rincon, Georgia and often times drove down Ebenezer Road and parked my car and walked the grounds where I first heard Mr. Harold Stanfield tell his tall tales and thought of how it inspired me as a kid.

Many days in my youth I would watch the mail arrive and run across the street hoping just maybe I might receive a letter from The King of Adventure himself. The letter never came but I hoped anyways.

Who knows if Mr. Stanfield's stories were true or not, or if The King of Adventure was really real. All that matters is the imagination was real and as long as we have imagination in our hearts, we have the passions in life to do extraordinary things. If we dare to use what we imagine, who knows, we might just change the world.

I've come to learn that the imagination is within us. Just like how Harold and his brothers used the imagination of their hearts and minds and it came true for them, and it might come true for us as well.

The truth is we all are the authors to our own adventures and our own lives. Our future is within our hands it's just up to us how we live our lives. As long as we live life with hope rooted in us and keep the treasures of our hearts close to us, we will always live like Harold and his brothers, who faced their doubts and conquered their demons, who won a war by peace, who lived tall tales and lived the adventures of brotherhood.

We don't have to wait for The King of Adventure to tell us we are the author to our own adventure. Great adventures await us and the world is hungry to hear it. The time is here and now to live it. You are the king of your own adventure!

The end!

Made in United States
North Haven, CT
23 October 2021